MARIE FLANIGAN

HIDDEN FURY

For Colin

Hidden Fury
Annie Fitch Mysteries™

Red Adept Publishing, LLC
104 Bugenfield Court
Garner, NC 27529
https://RedAdeptPublishing.com/

---

1. http://StreetlightGraphics.com

Chapter 1
Sunday Afternoon, April 21

They say when you're dying, you see a light at the end of a long, dark tunnel, but when I was dying, I didn't see that. I saw nothing. Instead, I felt a complete collapse of self, like all my molecules were suddenly connected to all the other molecules. I was indistinguishable from the grass, the trees, the fence, the air, the bullet.

"Annie," Celia said. "What are you thinking? You look a million miles away."

"Nothing." Annie smiled. "I'm just enjoying the weather." She wasn't interested in upsetting Celia with the truth, that spring always reminded her of getting shot—the first time. Of course, she'd been shot in the shoulder in the middle of winter just a few months ago, so perhaps next winter would bring up that fun experience. She wondered what percentage of cops were shot on duty, and what percentage of private investigators. The numbers had to be pretty low, yet she'd managed to fall into both groups. She was in the middle of an improbable Venn diagram.

Annie looked up and saw Celia tugging a fifty-pound bag of soil from the back of Annie's old Jeep Wrangler. "Sorry," Annie said, stepping over the low brick wall that separated her patio from the driveway of her small apartment complex. She reached for the other end of the bag.

"Don't strain your shoulder," Celia said.

"I'm fine. Why did you have to get such big bags?"

"It's more cost-effective. Besides, that brick planter needs to be completely refilled."

Annie sighed. Celia cared more about the aesthetics of her patio than she did. Every year after Tax Day, like clockwork, Celia began to pester her about sprucing up her patio. It'd taken a week, but they were finally getting around to it. Long ago, Annie had decided it was easier to go along with Celia than argue. Celia was a good friend. The least Annie could do was let her help.

They dragged three more bags of soil over to the planter and began dumping them in. Celia pushed an errant sable curl off her forehead and redid her thick ponytail before going back to the Jeep and pulling a tray of plants out of the back seat.

As she was assessing which plants should go where, Celia said, "I might have thrown some work your way last night."

"Oh?" Annie asked, surprised.

"Yeah, Ted and I were having dinner with a friend of his, Preston Farr. Do you know him?"

Annie shook her head. "Should I?"

"He owns Farr Reach Farm."

"The pick-your-own place on the edge of town? I love that property."

Celia smiled. "I know, which is why, when Preston said he was having some issues with vandalism and was thinking about installing some security cameras, I thought of you."

"Because I just took that class."

"Exactly," Celia said, her smile widening. "You might be getting a call."

Annie had recently expanded her private investigation business to include security installations. "That would be great." She paused, remembering days spent picking apples and berries with her grandparents. "Talk about the best of both worlds. Can you imagine having all that property right in town?"

"Actually, no. I can't imagine how it hasn't been subdivided. Developers have put so much pressure on property owners, and it's hard to turn down that kind of payout. You'd be shocked how many calls I get from developers every year," Celia said, "and I'm out in Purcelllville. I can only imagine the number of calls he must have to field with a property that large in Leesburg."

"Well, I hope he calls me. I could use the work," Annie said.

"I hear you." Celia arranged another bunch of flowers in the planter.

"So," Annie said as she picked up another plant. "You and Ted seem to be seeing a lot of each other. How is that going?"

"It's going," Celia said.

"You always say that." Annie handed her another tray of flowers. "What does that mean?"

Celia shrugged. "It means everything is fine."

"Just fine."

"Fine is good."

Annie raised her eyebrows.

"All I want is fine. There's no drama. No one is expressing their undying love. We get together, we have fun, and that's that."

"And you're okay with that?"

"I'm thrilled with that," Celia said as she pressed another plant into the dirt. "Besides, since when are you the poster child for planning the future?"

"Oh, I'm not, clearly. But you and Ted sound like you've got something good. I'm happy for you."

Celia turned around and looked at her with her I-can-read-your-thoughts expression, but all she said was "Thanks."

After they finished planting flowers and cleaned up, they walked into town for lunch. The day was warm but not hot, and Annie lived right downtown, so the walk to Delirium was quick. Delirium was Celia's latest restaurant obsession. She couldn't get enough of the Belgian restaurant's mussels and french fries. After each consuming a pot of *moules frites*, they walked back to Annie's apartment. Celia headed for home, and Annie took Chester for a walk. The little white bull terrier mix was all wiggles with excitement, as if they didn't take two walks a day every day. She wished she could muster that kind of enthusiasm for their routine. After the walk, she settled down to review a report she was sending to a company that she did background investigations for. Her phone rang.

"Fitch Investigations. Annie Fitch speaking."

"Hi," a man said. "My name is Preston Farr. I was told you might be able to help me with a security issue."

"Sure," Annie said, silently thanking Celia for the referral. "What do you need?"

"I own Farr Reach Farm in Leesburg, and we've had some problems with vandalism. The police suggested I install a security system."

"I can certainly help you with that."

"Fantastic. How soon are you available?"

Annie put him on speaker and opened the calendar on her phone. "I have an appointment tomorrow afternoon with another client, but my morning is free. Would that work for you?"

"Morning is great. Is seven o'clock too early?" he asked.

"Not for me," she lied cheerfully.

"Perfect. I'll see you then. The farm is—"

"I know where it is," Annie said. "I live in Leesburg."

"Great. Come up the back drive to the house, then. I'll see you tomorrow."

When Annie hung up, she looked at Chester. "It looks like taking that class is going to pay off, buddy."

Chester rolled onto his back for her to rub his belly.

Annie let out a soft snort and complied. "I can see you're really worried about it. But that's how I pay for kibble, so you should pay more attention."

He remained unconcerned.

Chapter 2
Monday Morning

Farr Reach Farm was the last undeveloped farm within the town limits. It sat right on the edge of the town and county line and was clearly a vestige of Leesburg's agrarian roots. As Annie drove up the long gravel drive to the house, she thought of herself and Ford, then the best of friends, running up and down the long rows of trees, playing hide-and-seek, while her grandparents picked fruit. She sighed, thinking about Ford. Things had been so simple between them when they were kids. She wished it were still like that and wondered what he was doing at the moment and where in the world he was doing it.

Annie shook her head to stop herself from going down that path. She had work to do.

The stone farmhouse was large but not sprawling like one of the modern mansions that peppered the suburbs around Leesburg. Annie parked her car next to a dusty Polaris UTV in front of a four-car garage and walked up to the front porch, where a thirtysomething white man sat drinking a cup of coffee. Wearing an old ball cap from Tractor Supply, a gray T-shirt, jeans, and dusty work boots, he had the rugged, tanned look of a man who worked outside.

"Hi," he said, standing. "Are you Annie?"

"Yes. Preston?"

"That's me." Preston Farr shook her hand. His hand was big and calloused. He had a firm handshake but not too firm, which Annie appreciated, since she hadn't yet regained full grip strength in her right hand after the shooting. He smiled and offered her a seat at a bistro table with a thermal carafe and two cups. As he held out the chair for her, she noted he was only a few inches taller than she was, putting him around five-nine or ten. He was shaved bald but had a nicely trimmed brown beard and a pleasant smile. He seemed pretty fit, too, not that she cared—because she didn't. Clients were off limits, and anyway, she still hadn't sorted out the current situation with Ford, who either was or was not her ex.

"Coffee?" Preston asked, taking the chair opposite her.

"That would be great." The coffee was much appreciated. She took a sip and looked around at the farm. The early-morning light filtered through the trees of the orchard and reflected off the rooster-shaped weathervane on top of the garage. She took note of the layout of the buildings and considered where cameras might be placed to view the house and garage.

While she drank her coffee, Preston opened a tri-fold map that was on the table. It was a colorful, cartoonish rendition of the farm, clearly drawn for the pick-your-own crowd. "I thought it might help if I showed you a map of the property and where we keep the equipment."

"Perfect," Annie said.

Preston pointed to various buildings on the map, many of which he'd clearly added with a Sharpie. "As you can see, in addition to the drive you came in on, we have one gravel road that bisects the farm, and we've got several narrower dirt roads off that. They damaged equipment in several open sheds and lean-tos on the property, but I can't secure all of it in locked buildings. That's just not practical. We've also had some graffiti on some of the public buildings."

"I understand," Annie said. "Cameras set up with Wi-Fi, backup power, and SD cards are probably your best bet for coverage. There are a wide range of options. Some can be triggered at the same time as a photosensitive or motion-sensitive light, and some have night vision. Which you choose depends on whether you want the light, how much money you want to spend, and what kind of resolution you're looking for."

"What do you recommend?" Preston asked.

"It depends on what you want. Sometimes the light can be a deterrent, like if you think the vandalism is being done by kids. But I think the night-vision cameras are better and more reliable than the cameras that rely on a motion sensor or a photo cell. They're also usually HD and have a longer range, but I can take a look and give you quotes for different setups."

Preston nodded. "That sounds good."

"Are you just interested in cameras on the outbuildings, or do you want the house and garage covered as well?"

Preston raised his eyebrows as he sipped his coffee. "I hadn't really thought about putting cameras up here. I haven't had any problems at the house. It's mostly been around the apple barn. The majority of the equipment is kept in sheds around there."

"How about an alarm system to go with the security cameras?" Annie asked.

"I'm not looking to pay a monthly fee for monitoring," Preston said.

"It doesn't have to be that kind. Stand-alone systems will go off if someone breaks a window or tries to come through a door when the alarm is armed."

Preston made a face. "I kind of hate those things. They seem to go off of their own accord and make so much noise. People come out here for the peace and quiet."

"Okay." Annie understood his point as she looked at the parklike farm around her. She found it hard to believe they were right in town. "We can start with cameras and add an alarm system later, if you think you need it. Did the police make any suggestions?"

"Nothing specific. They just recommended I take security measures."

"Do you have a sense of who might be vandalizing your equipment?"

"Not really, although I doubt it's kids." Preston frowned. "It's too... I don't know... specific. If it were kids, I'd expect things to be knocked over, broken, or tagged with spray paint—that kind of crap. This is equipment disabled. Spark plugs or distributor caps removed. Tires slashed and profanity painted but only in public areas, like the side of the apple barn."

"You're right. That doesn't sound like kids. I'm sure the police already asked you this, but do you have any enemies?"

Preston laughed. "No. At least none that I know of. I'm not really an 'enemies' kind of guy."

Annie had to admit he'd seemed pretty affable so far. "Fair enough. Do you mind if I ask you how you got this place?"

"My brother and sister and I inherited it from our grandmother."

"Anyone contest the will?"

He made a face, like he was surprised by the question. "No."

"Was it split evenly?"

"Not exactly. The way the will was written, if one of us wanted to run the farm, we got a controlling share. If that person later decided to sell, the proceeds of the sale would be split evenly three ways."

Annie raised her eyebrows. "So, selling would be a big windfall for them."

"I know what you're thinking, but I'll tell you what I told the cops. My siblings don't need the money. They were both fine with me taking this on. None of us wanted to see it sold off and developed. We all grew up here, in the foreman's cottage, just over there." He pointed at a small white clapboard house, which stood a couple hundred yards away, just visible through the apple trees.

"Who do you think is vandalizing your equipment, then?"

"I haven't the slightest idea."

"Well, I think you should cover the house and garage, too, but I can structure proposals with and without that."

"Okay," Preston said.

"So, now I just need to look around."

"I thought we'd take the UTV. It's the easiest way to get around the farm."

"Do you mind if I make notes on this?" Annie asked, holding up the map.

"Nope, that's your copy."

"Great. That'll make it a lot easier."

"Let's go, then," Preston said.

Annie followed him to the dusty green utility vehicle she'd parked next to. She grabbed a pen and a tape measure from her car and stepped into the passenger side of the old Polaris four-seater, and Preston drove down the central lane of the farm. On either side were the apple and pear trees in long rows that she remembered from her childhood, and the sight filled her with a sad nostalgia. Her grandparents were both gone, and at least for the time being, Ford wasn't in her life anymore either. "Are you still doing the pick-your-own stuff?" she asked to break away from that line of thought.

Preston nodded. "Yeah, that's our primary revenue stream this time of year. It's too early for any of our apples, but we'll start having people out here, picking strawberries, in a few weeks."

"I used to love to do that with my grandparents when I was a kid," Annie said.

"Here?"

"Yeah."

"You grew up in Leesburg?"

"No, I grew up in Arlington, but my grandparents lived here. I spent all my summers and a lot of weekends with them."

"I wonder if they knew my grandparents," Preston said.

"Probably. It seemed like they knew everyone."

He smiled at her. "Small world."

She smiled back but mostly just to be polite. Aspects of the world were small, but since Ford had been gone, the world had felt vast, and he felt very far away. To confuse matters further, he'd been cryptic about their relationship before he left. He'd said he liked things the way they were, but she didn't know what "way" that was. Last year, she'd thought she knew, but she wasn't so sure anymore. Annie hadn't even heard from him in months. She rarely knew where he was when he wasn't home. When asked, he always said he was working for the State Department. In a technical sense, that was probably true, but a lot of agencies of a secret nature were under the State Department's umbrella, and she was certain he worked for one of those. She just didn't know which one.

Annie snapped back to the present as Preston stopped the Polaris in front of a large shed. "This is where we keep our mowers and the small tractor."

"Was this one of the sheds that was vandalized?"

"Yeah, the bastards made a real mess in here. Sorry. Excuse my French."

Annie chuckled and got out of the vehicle. "You don't need to worry about me. My ears aren't that delicate."

He smiled again.

She walked around the shed, taking some measurements and making notes. When she was done, he took her to another shed, and she repeated the process. After that, they drove up a small hill to the apple barn, which was red and had a big green apple painted on one side.

"They didn't break into this building. All they did was paint 'Fuck you' on the side facing the picnic area and the bouncy house."

"Classy," Annie said.

"Oh yeah, this was definitely done by a group with discerning taste."

"You think it was more than one person, then?"

Preston shrugged. "If it was one person, they did a ton of work in a few hours in the middle of the night. I think it was at least two people, maybe three."

Annie nodded. "You're probably right. What do you have here? A hundred acres?"

"Just about. Not all of it's planted, but yeah, the property is ninety-nine acres. The orchard accounts for fifty acres, and we have a little over ten acres in berries, which is double what we used to have. Then we've got about twenty acres in hay, but I'm thinking about expanding the orchard to plant some varieties good for hard cider."

"Sounds like you have a lot of plans." She got out of the Polaris, and he followed her.

"I do. Currently, we use this building for selling jelly and apple butter and baked goods, but I'm looking into converting part of it into a cidery."

Annie let the tape measure snap back into its housing. "Cider seems pretty big these days."

Preston nodded. "It is. It seems like an opportunity to do something different with all of this, but I'm worried it might be a fad. I don't know. It's a lot to think about."

From where they were standing, they could look out over the entire property. The main house, garage, and foreman's cottage were off to their right. Another tree-lined driveway led to the front of the main house. Beyond the houses were the orchards, which ran down to a creek and along the length of the property. Directly in front of them were the hay fields, and to the right were all the berry fields and play areas for the children.

"It's a beautiful place," she said.

He smiled at her. "I think so too."

It took another hour to get the rest of the measurements, then he drove her back to her car. "I'll get the estimate to you tonight or to-morrow. I'm doing background checks this afternoon, so what I find might impact how long it takes to get you your estimate."

"Background checks?" Preston said.

"I contract with a couple of local companies. I've completed the online searches, but today I've got to go conduct interviews," Annie said, opening her car door.

"That sounds interesting," Preston said.

"It can be, but usually, it's pretty standard stuff. As it turns out, most people live pretty normal lives."

"Fair enough," Preston said, smiling. "I'll look for your email, then."

"Great," Annie said.

"Listen, before you go, I don't suppose you'd want to grab dinner sometime?"

She smiled at him. "As policy, I don't go out with clients."

"Right," Preston said. "Of course."

"Thanks, though." She got into her Jeep.

He nodded, and as she pulled away, he gave a little wave.

Well, that was flattering, she thought. Even if she were comfort-able dating clients, she didn't know how she felt about dating at all at the moment.

Chapter 3

Monday Afternoon through Friday Afternoon

Annie's interviews of a tech company's potential employees' friends and neighbors proved fairly uneventful. Of the three people she'd been asked to check out, only one had any red flags—a gambling problem. The other two were model citizens, which made for a pretty boring afternoon.

On the other hand, she was done with her reports to the employer quickly, so she had time to work on Preston's estimates. The price of security cameras had dropped so much since they were first available that she didn't bother with the lowest-end models. Annie broke the estimate down into as much detail as she could and gave Preston three options and hoped she was at least in the ballpark if he got other estimates. She thought that the job could be effectively done for the best price using long-range professional cameras with night vision and a Wi-Fi connection. Not all of Preston's sheds had power available, but with the long-range cameras, not every shed would have to have one. Several of them were in sight of each other. Some options for add-on alarm systems rounded out her research. She wrote an email that outlined her thinking then attached the estimate and sent it.

"Well, Chester," she said to her little white dog, who was quietly ripping the stuffing out of a toy bear at her feet, "that's a good day's work. Want to go for a walk?"

The terrier expressed his agreement by jumping in circles while she got his leash.

WHEN ANNIE AND CHESTER arrived home from their walk, Preston had already answered her email and accepted the best and most expensive option, although he'd decided to wait on an alarm system. Annie was a little surprised he hadn't gone with the moderate choice, given that he'd only had one incident of vandalism. On the other hand, she certainly wasn't going to tell him that. She emailed him back, suggesting a few options for days that she could come set up the equipment, and told him she would need half the total up front. Sweaty and hot from the walk, she went to take a shower.

By the time she was out, Preston had emailed her back and sent the money to her PayPal account. She sat down and ordered the equipment on the spot then called Celia.

"You are my favorite person ever," Annie said when Celia answered.

"Naturally," Celia said. "But why am I your favorite today?"

"Preston Farr just accepted my estimate, has already sent me a payment, and scheduled an appointment. How awesome is that?"

"Pretty awesome," Celia said. "When are you going out there?"

"End of the week. I just ordered the equipment. Everything was in stock. I should have it by Thursday, and I'll be out there on Friday morning."

"Perfect," Celia said.

"I know, right? I'm hoping he has lots of friends who also need security systems, and he'll talk me up."

"Given that he grew up around here, I think the odds are in your favor," Celia said.

"Me too. Thanks again. I owe you."

"Noted. I'll talk to you later."

"Right."

Annie was so pleased about that security-system class paying off that she decided to put on some music and clean her apartment, which had been neglected of late. As she folded clothes and enjoyed the mix of pop tunes her phone shuffled to the Bluetooth speaker in her bedroom, an old Macy Gray song came on. She reached for her phone to skip it, but the phone was in the kitchen. As Macy sang about dreaming of someone, Chester came in from the living room.

Annie looked down at him and sighed. "Do you think Ford ever dreams about us?" Chester stared back at her intently, and she rubbed his head. The problem was that Annie had no confidence that she ever crossed Ford's mind while he was away, and that seemed like an untenable position.

THE REMAINDER OF ANNIE'S week was filled with more background checks and some physical therapy. Her shoulder was taking its time recovering from the shotgun wound from just before Christmas. Although she hadn't needed surgery, the pellets that hit her had done enough damage that she needed a lot of physical therapy to get the muscles moving again. At least she was down to once a week, and the physical therapist thought she would be done soon.

On Thursday afternoon, the cameras for Farr Reach Farm arrived, but the box was damaged, and two of the cameras were broken. Annie called the distributor, and they assured her she would have replacements Saturday morning. Frustrated, she emailed Preston to explain, and he agreed to having her install what she had Friday then finish on Saturday.

Once she had Friday confirmed, she called Matt to see if he was available to help her. Matt had been one of her first collars back when she was a cop. At the time, he'd been ten years old and had just lost his mother to pancreatic cancer. He'd stolen his aunt's car to look for his absentee father, in hopes of going to live with him instead of his aunt. He and Annie had bonded over dead mothers. She'd lost hers at age seven to a car accident. Annie had kept up with Matt over the years. He was still living with his aunt, who had compassionately forgiven him for stealing her car, and was finishing an associate degree in electrical engineering at Northern Virginia Community College. He'd been doing odd jobs for Annie since she became a private investigator, and he'd always done excellent work.

On Friday morning, Matt arrived early and helped Annie pack the working cameras along with a ladder and a drill, and they headed to Farr Reach Farm in her old Jeep Wrangler.

"Are you ready for a day of climbing ladders and pulling wire?" she asked Matt.

"I'm always ready. The question is, Are you, old lady?" Matt asked, playfully arching an eyebrow at her.

"Who're you calling old, buddy? I happen to be in the prime of life."

Matt snorted.

She mock frowned at him. "You're an impertinent kid. You know that?"

He laughed.

She shook her head. "I figure we'll get the cameras in place, then I'll get the software set up while you finish the wiring."

"That sounds good to me."

Annie couldn't help remembering the scrawny black kid with the big red Afro, who'd driven his aunt's car into a ditch just outside of their neighborhood. He'd turned into a thoughtful, soft-spoken young man with broad shoulders, and his red hair and beard were trimmed to the same short length. *Where does the time go?*

Preston waved from the porch when she pulled into the driveway and parked in front of the garage. He walked over to her Jeep. "Good morning."

Annie smiled. "Hi. Preston, this is Matt. He's going to help me get your cameras set up."

The two men shook hands.

"I was just having some coffee on the porch. Care for a cup before you two start?"

"Thanks, but we should get to it. This is going to take a while," Annie said. She would have liked a cup of coffee, but she was paying Matt by the hour, and besides, she was trying not to encourage Preston's interest.

"Suit yourself," Preston said. "Call me if you need anything."

"Will do," Annie said.

She and Matt headed for the apple barn. The entire building smelled of baked apples. The kitchen in the back of the building was where the jellies, pies, and sauces were made, and it smelled like someone was cooking.

Annie ignored the desire to see what was going on in the kitchen and focused on the task at hand. The plan was for the hard-wired cameras to go around the apple barn and be tied into the computer that was already in Preston's office off the kitchen. She would set up four cameras that effectively covered the entrance and egress to the property and the parking lot at the apple barn. Because the cameras were to be wired into the router, the whole morning would be spent climbing and drilling and running cable, but the system was the key to security on the property. The other four cameras were wireless and would be set up in two of the outbuildings where equipment was stored, as well as at the house. Unfortunately, the two cameras that were damaged in shipping were wired cameras, but she and Matt ran the wire and positioned the brackets so that on Saturday, all Annie would have to do was come back and install them. Matt did all the ladder work, while Annie set up the software and occasionally handed him tools or pulled wire.

As they worked, Annie thought about the vandalism and how odd it was. The farm was in a nice part of town—not that there were really any bad parts—but more importantly, it was a beloved local institution. She looked up at Matt, who was on the ladder. "Hey, did you hear about the vandalism they had here?"

Matt looked down at her. "No. What happened?"

"Somebody spray-painted obscenities and damaged some of the equipment."

"Kids?" Matt asked.

"I don't think so. Seemed pretty targeted."

"Weird. Who attacks a farm?"

"Right?"

He stepped off the ladder. "That's the last one in here."

Annie looked at her watch. It was noon. "Do you want to break for lunch or keep going and be done for the day?"

"I've got a bottle of water and a granola bar in my backpack. I'm good with that."

"Perfect," Annie said, and they went outside. It was starting to get hot, and bugs swirled around them. Most of the trees where they were working were in full bloom, and the sweet fragrance of apple blossoms was strong.

While Matt ate his snack, Annie unpacked the first of the wireless cameras and drank a bottle of water. Preston already had two Wi-Fi repeaters in the orchard to make it easier for guests to post pictures to social media—urged on by flyers prompting people to share the fun. Installing the cameras and networking them with the software would make for a simple afternoon. She swatted the gnats that were gathering around her head as she put backup batteries into each of the cameras.

When she was done, Matt was ready to get started again. They headed to the sheds, installed two of the cameras, then went to the main house.

As they pulled in front of the garage, Preston was talking to a man on the porch. Annie lingered at the Jeep so they could finish talking. The man looked like he worked on the farm. He had on jeans, a long-sleeved shirt, a cowboy hat, and work boots. When their conversation ended, Preston saw her and walked toward the Jeep while the man went toward the apple barn.

"Hey, how's it going?"

"Good. We're ready to do the house." Annie was pleased that the setup was going so well and appreciated Matt's electrical skills.

They headed to the porch to continue the installation.

PRESTON WALKED UP AS they were putting their tools back into the Jeep. "You two done for the day?"

"Not quite," Annie said. "I need to go back to the apple-barn computer and make sure it's picking up these cameras, and I need to install the app on your phone and make sure it's connecting. Although I can do your phone tomorrow when I come with the other two cameras, if that's more convenient."

Preston nodded. "Yeah, let's take care of the app later. I've got a meeting to get to."

"Sounds good. We'll just finish up here, and I'll see you tomorrow."

Chapter 4

Friday Night through Saturday Afternoon

The Loudoun Board of Supervisors was having its monthly meeting, and one of the items on the agenda was the county's historic cemeteries. Loudoun was growing rapidly, and issues with developers not respecting the cemeteries in their construction projects had come up. Several dust-ups had already occurred between developers and local groups wanting to protect graves. Celia had come to town to attend the meeting because of some questions about the graves on her property. Annie was there for moral support.

"I understand the desire to protect the graves and to provide access for living relatives," Celia said as they walked from Annie's apartment in the historic district to the county building in the center of town. "But I'm concerned about the horses and liability. I can't afford to fence off a path to those graves. If someone gets hurt trying to gain access, isn't that going to be my responsibility as a landowner? What's that going to do to my insurance rates?"

"That's a good question. I don't know," Annie said. "Do you know who's buried there?"

"No. The graves were there when my grandparents bought the place at auction ages ago, not long after they were married. The three grave markers are too eroded to read."

"So, it's just three?" Annie asked, wondering if the county would even care about three graves.

"It's at least three, but I was over there the other day with Marc and Gary, and it looked like there were other depressions that could've been graves."

It always surprised Annie that Celia and her ex-husband, Gary, and his current husband, Marc, got along so well. Celia had often said that Marc was the nicest thing about Gary. "We counted twelve in total, and some of them had what looked like fieldstone markers."

"Oh." Annie knew from recent articles about places like Belmont and Compass Creek that slave burials were often marked with fieldstones.

"I know, and if slaves are buried on my property, then their ancestors have every right to know about it. I just don't know what that means for me."

"How are they going to know who's buried there if they aren't marked?" Annie asked.

"Some families record that sort of information in Bibles."

"Oh," Annie said again, fairly certain that no such records existed in her family. "Well, I'm sure a lot of people have those exact same questions. I bet you get answers tonight."

"I hope so," Celia said as they reached the five-story brick-and-glass Loudoun County Government Center. "You know, my dad always said he thought slaves were buried back there. Given what I've read recently, I think he was right. I wish I'd paid more attention when he talked about this stuff."

"Meh, kids never pay that much attention to all the stuff their parents are into."

"I know. But now, I want to know all that history, and he's in Florida and has moved on to other interests. That's not to say he won't tell me anything I ask. I just wish I'd asked when they lived here and he was really into it."

They made their way to the boardroom on the first floor. The room was arranged with the board of supervisors sitting up front in a long panel facing tiered seating for the audience. Annie and Celia took seats on the top tier and waited for their item to be called. Even though the cemeteries were an early agenda item, it took nearly an hour to get to them. Annie started to regret not insisting that they stop at King Street Coffee before going to the meeting. She was tired from setting up the cameras earlier in the day, and the leg she'd been shot in a couple of years ago was starting to get stiff from sitting. She shifted in her seat to ease the pressure on her leg and try to wake up some. Annie caught herself starting to doze off again and shook her head and sat up straighter.

Celia leaned over and whispered, "I'm sorry this is so boring."

"No. It's fine," Annie whispered back. "I should pay more attention to local politics, anyway." Like many people, she only actually paid attention around election time. She shifted again and was surprised to notice Preston sitting four rows down on the other side of the aisle. She nudged Celia. "Isn't that Preston?"

Celia looked and nodded. "He probably has a family cemetery on his land too."

Since Preston was in front of them, he hadn't noticed her. He looked nice in a light-blue button-down shirt and khaki pants. He had something very appealing about him, but she resolved not to explore that—which was a challenge, since her mind would rather wander to Preston than attend to what had been an incredibly boring meeting.

When the board finally reached the cemetery item, a woman from the planning department stood and explained the process. Her presentation answered all of Celia's questions, so they left at the first break. Preston stayed in his seat, talking to some people in the rows in front of him.

LATE THE NEXT MORNING, the replacement cameras arrived, and Annie texted Preston to see if she could bring them over. He said yes, so she headed to the farm.

As she pulled in front of the garage, Preston came out of the house in jeans and a plain white T-shirt, carrying two paper to-go cups. He handed one to Annie. "I felt coffee was in order."

"You felt right," Annie said and took a sip. He'd remembered that she took it black, which made her smile at him. "Any problems last night?"

"No. It's been quiet. I don't know whether that's because whoever did it saw the cameras and left, or they've just lost interest. Either way, I'm happy."

"Good," she said. "Getting the rest of the cameras up shouldn't take too long. Oh, and I need to get the app set up on your phone."

"Right," Preston said. "We can take the Polaris."

"That's okay," Annie said. "I don't want to hijack your morning. I can drive the Jeep."

"I don't mind, and it'll be faster in the Polaris. You can't cut through the orchard with the Jeep." He put the ladder on the UTV while Annie transferred the tool bag and cameras. "Where's your assistant today?"

"He has a group project for one of his college classes."

Preston shook his head. "Those are the worst."

"Right? I'm so glad to be out of school."

Preston started the UTV. As they drove toward the apple barn, he said, "So, how was your week?"

"Pretty good," Annie said. "The usual stuff. How about you?"

"I spent most of my week checking to see if the grafts are taking."

"Grafts?" Annie asked. The only thing she could think of that got grafted was skin, and that didn't seem to apply to a farm.

"Yeah, apples don't grow true to seed, so if you want a specific variety, you have to graft that variety onto an existing tree."

"Seriously? You can't just plant an apple seed and get an apple tree?"

"Oh, you can. It just won't be the same apple as the one you got the seed from."

"Huh."

"Yeah, it's a pain, but that's how their genetics work. I have some new varieties I'm trying to start and others I'm looking to do away with, so I'm grafting new stock onto existing trees. It's fiddly, so you have to check and make sure it's taking. It's always something around here," Preston said as he pulled the UTV in front of the apple barn. Annie got out and went to grab the ladder, but Preston reached it first. "I've got it. Where do you want it?"

Annie pointed at where he should set up the ladder and sighed. Though she felt bad that he was helping, she was also grateful. She pulled on a pair of fingerless work gloves, tucked a screwdriver into the back pocket of her jeans, and climbed the ladder. Preston stood there watching, which made Annie uncomfortable. She couldn't help wondering if he would notice that she only climbed the ladder with her left leg. Because the bullet had torn a chunk out of her thigh muscle, her right leg wasn't as strong as her left one. She shook off the thought. It didn't matter how she climbed the ladder, only that she got up there.

Once she had the camera hooked up, she had to concentrate to use the screwdriver left-handed. The grip in her right hand wasn't strong enough to get it tight, because the same bullet that messed up her leg had also injured her hand. Preston moved the ladder around to the other side of the building for her, and she climbed slowly up to perform the same procedure. By the time she climbed down, her right leg was aching and tensing up.

Annie walked back to the UTV, self-conscious that she was limping. Preston followed her with the ladder. She dropped the screwdriver back into her tool bag then went to make sure the cameras were on the network.

As she walked into the apple barn, Preston asked, "Are you okay?"

"I'm fine. Old injury. It acts up sometimes."

Preston shook his head. "Sports, right? I used to play football. Messed up my elbow pretty good, and it took forever before I could straighten my left arm out all the way. What did you play?"

Annie sat down at the computer and pulled up the security cameras. "I didn't. It was a work injury. So, here are your cameras."

Preston stood next to her and leaned in for a better look. He smelled faintly of sandalwood.

"It looks like everything is online." She explained how the software worked, how it recorded, and how to access it from his phone. "If you give me your phone, I'll get the app set up for you."

"Great." Preston handed her his phone.

A dark-haired man with a cowboy hat walked into the barn.

"Oh, hey, Alejandro, come look at the new security system."

The app had already finished downloading, so Annie handed Preston back his phone. He introduced her to Alejandro Flores, the farm manager.

Annie explained how the app worked while both men listened.

"That's surprisingly simple," Preston said.

"These systems have come a long way from when they were first available."

"Hopefully, this will take care of the problem," Alejandro said. "The berry baskets came in, so I need to put them in the shed, but you have the key."

"Oh, sorry, I forgot to put it back." Preston fished a set of keys out of his pocket.

"Nice to meet you," Alejandro said to Annie then went back outside.

"Are we all set?" Preston asked Annie.

"All that's left is the remainder of your account balance, and we're all done. Do you need me to send you a second invoice?"

"Not unless there was a change," Preston said.

"Nope. Same price."

Preston tapped his phone.

Annie's phone chimed with a message from PayPal, telling her she had money.

"So that concludes our business, yes?" Preston said.

"Yes."

He smiled at her. "Great."

Annie stuck out her hand, and Preston shook it. "It was great working with you," she said. "Let me know if you need anything else."

"Will do. I'll see you around."

She nodded and got in her car to head home. The little thrill of Preston's warm, calloused hand in hers left her with an uneasy sense of guilt. Preston seemed like a nice guy, but she barely knew him. Still, it felt good to be the focus of someone's attention, no matter how mild. Ford was gone, and almost in spite of her, something deep inside her was looking to move on.

Chapter 5
Monday

Annie didn't hear from Preston for the rest of the weekend, so she assumed all was going well with the cameras. On Monday, she had more background work to do for another company. After conducting an interview, she stopped by the post office to check the PO box she kept for business correspondence. As she was sorting her mail over the recycling bin, Preston walked in.

His face lit up when he saw her. "Hey," he said, walking over to her.

"Hi."

He looked down at the mail in her hands. "This is how you sort your mail?"

"It's the most expedient method I've found."

He ducked his head and put his hands into the back pockets of his jeans. "Smart. Probably prevents huge piles of paper from forming on your kitchen table."

Annie smiled at his shy stance. "It does."

Preston raised his eyebrows. "Would you have dinner with me now that I'm no longer a client?"

Annie was surprised by his directness. So much for shyness. "Uh, but you're a former client."

"Surely that can't count," he said in feigned disbelief. "What if we just meet for drinks? Super casual, like drinks in jeans."

"Drinks in jeans? Is that a thing now?" Annie asked, amused by his tenacity.

"If it's not, it should be. Besides, meeting for drinks hardly counts as a date." He gave her a hopeful look and rubbed a hand over his shaved head. She wondered if he always did that when he was nervous. He was cute in a completely earnest way.

"You know what? Sure."

"Fantastic," Preston said, grinning. "How about tonight? Seven thirty at Tuskies?"

"Okay."

"Good, I'll see you then." He winked at her before walking into the main part of the building, away from the mailboxes. Annie couldn't help noticing the way his jeans fit. *Nice.*

WHEN SHE LEFT THE POST office, Annie drove home, second-guessing her decision the whole way. She took Chester out for a walk and called Celia.

"Hey," Celia answered. "What's up?"

"Are you busy?"

"Not really. Are you okay? You sound weird."

"Thanks," Annie said, stopping on the sidewalk so that Chester could sniff around. "I just did something potentially crazy."

"Oh?"

"Preston asked me out, and I said yes."

"And this is crazy because he's your client?" Celia asked.

"No. I mean maybe, but it's not like I was doing PI work for him—following his wife or something."

"So, you haven't done anything unethical," Celia said.

"No."

"I'm lost now. Why is this crazy?"

"Because... because I don't know. Ford and I left things so vague before he went overseas." Annie sighed. "Is it weird that I can't tell if this is cheating?"

"Yes," Celia said firmly.

"Why?" Annie said.

"Cheating is pretty obvious when you're doing it. There's no gray area there."

"Are you sure?" Annie said. "I feel like this is a gray area."

"I thought Ford said he wanted things to be like they always were." Celia was clearly irritated. "And weren't you guys always free to date other people? Didn't you date other guys in high school and college and while he was in the military? Wasn't he dating other women then too?"

"Yes, but—"

"Has he Skyped you or emailed you or even sent you a text since he left?"

Annie sighed sadly. "No."

"Has he contacted you at all?"

"No." She hated how much it hurt to admit that. She'd known Ford her whole life, and he'd ghosted her. Any breakup was painful, but Ford wasn't just some guy. He was her best friend. He'd turned his life upside down for a year to help her after she was shot. She couldn't believe he'd ended things between them the way he had.

"Explain to me how this is cheating, then," Celia said.

Annie shook her head but didn't answer. She ran the toe of her shoe along a seam in the sidewalk.

Celia sighed. "Sugar, if you're not ready to date yet, then don't. But that should be about you, not about Ford."

"How do I know if I'm ready?" Annie asked, her voice cracking.

"Well, you said yes, so that makes me think you're ready."

"Yeah," Annie said, covering her eyes with her hand. "Why did I do that?"

"I don't know. Why did you?"

"He tricked me."

"Really? He tricked you? Preston? He doesn't seem like the tricky type."

"Yes, well, he tricked me with his pleasant conversation and his politeness and his hands."

"Oh?" Celia said. "Ooh."

"Not like that," Annie said, frowning. "But he has really nice hands. Kind of big and calloused. And I like the shape of his head. Bald looks great on him. And he smells good."

Celia laughed. "Oh my. You just want to get laid."

Annie pressed her hands over her face. "I so do. It's terrible."

"Why is it terrible?" Celia asked. "It's normal. Ford's been gone for months without a word. If you were a man, you wouldn't give it a second thought."

"Yeah, but I don't even know this guy. Not that I'm planning on sleeping with him, anyway."

"Did he ask you over to his place for dinner, or did he ask you out?"

"Out. We're meeting at Tuskies for a drink in a few hours."

"He's not even picking you up? That's not a sex date."

"No," Annie said. "But still. I don't know what I'm doing."

"It sounds like you're just meeting for drinks. I doubt he's planning more than that for your first date, which makes him seem like a gentleman. When Ted and I had dinner with him, he struck me as a really nice guy."

"Yeah, he strikes me that way too," Annie said. She thought a nice guy might be a welcome change. Not that Ford hadn't been nice. In some ways, he'd been incredibly kind. But Ford had a switch in him, and when he flipped it, Annie and their life in Leesburg seemed to disappear. Ford was two people: Leesburg Ford and Work Ford. And Work Ford apparently didn't think about Annie at all.

"So, go out with him and find out. What's the harm?" Celia asked.

Annie realized she'd stopped paying attention. "I don't know. What if Ford comes back?"

"What if he does?"

Chester tugged on his leash, and they continued down the sidewalk. "I don't know. I mean, in the past, if we were with someone else, sometimes we stayed with them, and sometimes we didn't." The whole truth was rather more complicated than that, but she didn't feel like explaining the complex dance she and Ford had been doing since their teens.

"So how is this different, then?" Celia asked.

"I guess it isn't," Annie said.

"Then why not see where things go with Preston?"

Annie nodded. "Right. No reason not to." She was sick of being by herself, and Ford had made his choices. She should start making choices of her own, and Preston did seem nice.

"Exactly," Celia said.

TWO HOURS LATER, WHEN she'd tried on every pair of jeans she owned in combination with ten different shirts, Annie was starting to see a lot of reasons not to go on the date. But she'd already said yes, so at seven fifteen, she started walking the three blocks to Tuscarora Mill. As she walked, she wished she'd gone with looser jeans, but the ones she wore were lighter weight, and the evening was warm. Annie had chosen a red V-neck T-shirt and sandals, and she started to wonder if red wasn't sending the wrong message, but she stopped herself. She was having drinks with a nice man and didn't need to worry. She'd gone on first dates before. Of course, she hadn't been on one since before she got shot—the first time. But that shouldn't matter. A date was a date. No big deal.

Daffodils and tulips were in full bloom in people's yards as she walked to the restaurant, and the evening air was heavy with the threat of rain. She crossed the parking lot and went up the wooden stairs to the restaurant. Clearing her throat, she stood up straighter and opened the heavy wooden door. The lights were low, and it took her a minute to spot Preston waiting at one of the small tables in the bar area. The restaurant was a converted grain mill, and the heavy timbers and some of the large gears of the mill were visible in the rafters over the bar. Annie had hoped she would beat Preston there, but no such luck. He waved when he saw her, and she joined him at the table.

"Hi," he said.

"Hi. I hope you haven't been waiting long."

"No, I just got here."

A waitress came over and got their drink order. Local Port City beers were on special, so Annie ordered an Optimal Wit, and Preston ordered an Integral IPA.

"You like wheat beers?" he asked.

"Yeah," Annie said, trying to quell the nerves in her stomach. "Not a fan?"

"I like the hoppy beers, so I usually go with IPAs."

Ford did too, Annie thought but said, "IPAs are usually too bitter for me. How are the cameras working out? Any problems?"

"Nope. So far, so good." He smiled at her.

"Great."

She felt awkward. Preston usually had an easygoing way about him, but he kept fidgeting with the stack of cardboard coasters on the table. She wondered if he was nervous too.

The waitress returned with their beers, and they each took a sip.

"I have to confess," Preston said, "I don't go on a lot of dates."

Annie chuckled. "Me either."

"Good. We can bumble through this together, then," he said, smiling.

"Perfect. I like to set low expectations right from the start."

Preston chuckled and took another sip of his beer. "To be honest, I don't go out much at all."

Annie shook her head. A large group in the corner erupted into laughter. She leaned forward to be heard. "Me either. Small-business owner."

"I hear that." He turned his beer in his hands. "I guess since you're a PI, you probably looked me up."

She arched an eyebrow. "Actually, no. Should I have?" She had intended to do that *after* the date, if it went well.

He quirked his lips. "Not really. If you do, you'll mostly see stuff about the farm then a few articles on the incident that led to my divorce."

Alarm bells began to ring in Annie's head. *Great. What did you do to your wife that was so horrible that not only did she leave you, but it also ended up in the news?* The thought must have registered on her face.

Preston held up his hands. "It's nothing awful. It was just this freak thing."

"So..." Annie said slowly. "You want to tell me, or should I just get out my phone and look it up now?"

He shook his head, smiling ruefully. "I've already freaked you out, and we aren't even ten minutes in. I'm really out of practice." He sighed. "I know you're not supposed to talk about your ex on a first date, but you're going to find out, anyway, so here's what happened. Um... to start with, my ex-wife's mother's people are from Blacksburg. They own several hundred acres of farmland in that area, and that's where she and I lived. We ran one of the farms. Her dad's family, though, is from Alaska. They live in a town called Bethel, and basically the only way to get there is to fly or take a boat. A few years ago, her dad had shoulder replacement surgery, and Dana, my ex, went up there to help her mom take care of him during his recovery." He stopped talking and took a sip of beer.

The corner group started laughing again and called for another round of beer. They were all in business suits and seemed to be celebrating something.

Preston took another sip of beer. "Right, so the short of it is she never made it."

"What?"

"She took a charter flight from Juneau and never arrived."

"I don't understand. What—?"

"They crashed. She and the pilot were presumed dead. They searched for them, but it's almost a thousand miles from Juneau to Bethel. They couldn't find them."

"But you said you were divorced, not widowed."

Preston nodded. "That would be the weird part. I flew up there to be with her parents and to... I don't know... just be closer when they found her. But they didn't. Six weeks went by, and I'd started doing the paperwork to have her declared dead. Then she and the pilot limped into a little village in the middle of nowhere." He shook his head. "It was crazy."

"Wow," Annie said. "That *is* crazy."

He cleared his throat and had a long drink of his beer. The corner group asked the waiter to take a picture of them and shifted around so that they would fit in the photo.

"She came home with me, but..." He sighed. "Her heart just wasn't in it anymore. She missed Bob, the pilot. And after she'd been home a couple of weeks... well... she was pregnant."

Annie put her left hand over her mouth.

Preston nodded. "To make a long story slightly shorter, they live outside of Juneau now and have a lovely little girl. She has blue eyes and curly red hair, like her father."

Annie nodded and looked into Preston's warm brown eyes. "Wow," she said again.

"Yeah, it was kind of a thing. Her family felt terrible about it, and so did she, and so did I. I think even Bob felt bad. But what can you do? She had a life-altering experience."

"I should say so." Annie certainly understood about life-altering experiences. She tucked her right hand under her thigh. She was being silly and just delaying the inevitable by keeping her bullet-scarred hand out of sight. For all she knew, he'd noticed the other day and just hadn't mentioned it. Nonetheless, she kept her right hand under the table.

Preston took another long drink of beer.

"On the whole, I have to say that's the best divorce story I've ever heard," Annie said. "And I've heard a lot of them."

"I guess so, in your line of work." He smiled at her. "So, that's my story. What's yours?"

Annie shrugged. "Not so interesting. Grew up in Arlington, went to college at George Mason, became a cop, left that, and became a private investigator."

"Why be a PI?" Preston asked.

"I like being my own boss," Annie said and took a sip of her beer. The corner group had resettled themselves around the table and were all looking at their phones.

Preston nodded. "Me too."

"It took some getting used to, though. At first, it was odd, investigating for clients as opposed to for the town. It's a very different job, but I like it. I'm good at it."

Preston smiled. "I can attest to that."

"And I hope you will to anyone who asks," she said with a wink.

She knew she should probably mention the shooting, but it felt like an attempt to one-up the tragedy of his situation. Besides, he was likely to go home and look her up, anyway, and the internet would tell him more than he ever wanted to know. She decided to just let that happen. The shootings were too hard to talk about, anyway.

They ordered a couple of appetizers to share and sat for the next hour, talking about his property. He talked about the complexities of owning it in a limited liability corporation with his brother and sister. Annie recalled her days there as a child with her grandparents, leaving out all the times she went with Ford and his parents.

When the waiter came to ask if they wanted a third beer or anything else to eat, Annie declined, and Preston asked for the check.

After he paid the bill, Preston said, "I should probably get going. It's past my bedtime."

Annie glanced at her phone, which was sitting on the table. "Nine o'clock?"

"I'm a farmer. Early to bed, early to rise, and all that."

She chuckled. "Fair enough."

"This has been fun, though," he said, standing.

Annie rose too. "Yes, it has."

As they were walking to the door, Ford's parents walked in.

"Baby girl!" Boo, Ford's father, said, holding his arms out to her.

Annie hugged him.

"You look great," he said, holding her at arm's length.

"You too," Annie said. He looked like he'd lost some weight since she'd seen him last.

"Ollie's got me out walking every morning," Boo said, patting his still-expansive belly.

"I'll slim him down yet," Ollie said in her throaty voice, which was still laced with a Russian accent. She said it lightly, but her eyes shifted between Annie and Preston.

"Well, I won't hold you up," Annie said. "Enjoy your dinner."

Boo and Ollie wished her a good night, and Annie went outside.

Preston followed. "How do you know Boo Otley and his wife?" Preston asked.

"I've known them my whole life," she said. "And he's my landlord."

Preston nodded. "Wow."

"How do you know him?"

"I don't, not personally. He's in the chamber of commerce, and he's farm-friendly. Quite a character."

Annie chuckled. "That, he is."

They were standing on the sidewalk outside the restaurant. "Where did you park?" Preston asked.

"I didn't," she said. "I walked over."

"You live downtown?" he asked, raising his eyebrows.

"Yeah."

He looked around. "I'll walk you home."

Annie shook her head. She wasn't ready for him to do that or for what allowing him to do that might imply or to feel like she wanted what that might imply.

"But it's dark out," he said, clearly concerned.

"It's Leesburg." She laughed. "And there are streetlights."

"Hey, a guy was murdered here during the winter," he said seriously.

"Yeah. I know, but that's not something that happens every day." She knew a lot about that murder, given that the dead guy's wife had been her client at the time. "Relax. We have a very low crime rate."

"You say that, yet I just had to have security cameras installed."

She chuckled again.

"Look." His earnestness was endearing. "I'm not trying to invite myself to your place. Please, at least let me drop you off."

She sighed. "Fine."

They walked to the parking lot and got into Preston's old green Ford F-150. A fine layer of pollen covered the entire truck and a dented, well-used truck box in the bed, so she was surprised to find the interior fairly tidy.

"This might be the cleanest work truck I've ever been in," Annie commented.

Preston's cheeks reddened. "I might have cleaned it up before I came over here tonight."

She arched an eyebrow at him.

"I didn't know if you might want to go to a movie or something afterward," he said awkwardly. "I didn't know how it was going to go."

She pursed her lips. "Uh-huh."

He started the truck. The drive to her apartment took less than two minutes, so at least the silence that settled between them didn't last long. When she told him where to turn, he said, "That really was quick."

"Told you," Annie said.

He stopped the truck in front of her door, put it in park, and turned to face her. "So, I'll call you."

"Sounds good," she said, holding eye contact. "I should go."

"Good night," he said.

His tongue ever so slightly touched his lips, so she knew he was thinking what she was thinking, but a good night kiss seemed premature. Plus, he was still behind the wheel, and the truck was running, which meant she would have to be the one to lean in. She wasn't ready for that either, so she opened the truck door instead and stepped over the low brick wall and down to her patio, closing the truck door. Feeling a bit like an awkward teenager, she turned, and he was still looking, so she gave a little wave, unlocked her front door, and slipped inside.

Chester was lying on the sofa when she came in, and he perked up his ears and cocked his head.

"Oh, shut up," she said.

He put his head back down but continued to watch her. Annie considered calling Celia but decided that, too, was premature. She sat on the sofa next to Chester and pulled her laptop toward her. She'd had a nice time. Not an amazing time—the earth didn't move—but she'd enjoyed her evening enough to accept another date if he called. She typed his name into the search box. Fact-checking his story wasn't a bad idea, although it was so bizarre that it was probably true. He would likely go home and look her up online too. Once he read about the shootings, he might decide she was too broken to call for another date, anyway. She shrugged at the thought and realized she was fine either way.

An hour later, after she'd read several newspaper articles about the crash and the search-and-rescue efforts, she was forced to admit that Preston was exactly as he had presented himself. She found it weirdly refreshing.

Chapter 6
Tuesday

The next morning, Annie was up early to start doing background-check interviews. She'd already taken Chester for his walk and had her thermal cup full of coffee in her hand when a knock came at the door. She opened it to find Ford's mother standing on the patio with a pained expression. She was one of those women who aged slowly and looked at least a decade younger than they were, and she kept her dark hair expensively dyed to hide the gray, which masked her age further. As always, she was impeccably dressed, in black slacks and a blue top that set off her eyes perfectly. Her only pieces of jewelry were her wedding band and diamond stud earrings that Annie suspected cost more than she made in a month.

"Good morning," Ollie said. "I'm sorry to bother you so early."

"Um." Annie stepped back from the door. "It's no bother. Come in." She was trying for casual, but an icy chill ran down her spine. *Has something happened to Ford?*

"You are clearly on your way out," Ollie said but stepped inside anyway. "I won't be long."

Ollie wouldn't be so casual about bad news, so Annie relaxed some. She closed the door and set down her coffee. "Have a seat. You want a cup of coffee? Or I could make you some tea."

"No, no." Ollie remained standing. "I just wanted... What's happened, Annie?"

Annie raised her eyebrows, confused. She was so scared just a moment ago that she'd lost the plot. "I'm not sure—"

42

"With you and Ford? You were on a date with that man last night. Were you not?"

"Ah." Annie cleared her throat, a new sinking sensation coming over her. There was no point in lying. "Yes."

Ollie seemed to lose energy and sat down on the sofa. Annie took the armchair, and Chester jumped into her lap. Annie ran her fingers over his short white coat.

"I thought so," Ollie said quietly. She shook her head. "I knew something was wrong."

Her eyes held volumes of concern, but they were the same clear blue as Ford's, so Annie found it difficult to look at her and didn't know what to say. She should have known Ford wouldn't have said anything to his parents about their relationship.

"What happened?" Ollie asked again.

Annie shook her head, sad and irritated with Ford for putting her in this position. "Nothing. He went back to work and—" She teared up, and she hated that.

"And what?"

Shrugging, Annie said, "He wanted to go back to the way things were before."

Ollie sighed. "Oh, Ford. I told him not to go back overseas."

Annie gave her a weak smile. "He loves his work. He doesn't—" She shook her head again. "We just want different things."

"He loves you."

"I know that. I love him too. But he's not in love with me. Honestly, I'm not sure he's ever been in love with me. We were best friends that let things get complicated, and that was probably a mistake. Even if it wasn't, we let it go on way too long."

Ollie sighed again. "I'm so sorry."

"Don't be," Annie said, trying not to cry. "You and Boo mean the world to me. I have no hard feelings, but he's definitely done. He hasn't spoken one word to me since he left—not a phone call, not an email, not even a text. Nothing. But I'm guessing you've heard from him."

"He Skypes when he can," Ollie admitted.

"Right," Annie said, blinking back tears. She had guessed he was probably contacting them, but found it surprisingly painful to have that confirmed. "I've got to move on. I can't spend the rest of my life waiting for Ford. Life's too short."

Ollie nodded. "I understand."

She stood, and Annie got up too.

"I'm very sorry," Ollie said.

"Me too. But it is what it is. All I can do is let go."

Ollie nodded and hugged her. "Don't be a stranger."

Annie hugged her back. Ollie was the closest thing she'd had to a mother since she was seven years old. "I won't," she said, but that wasn't entirely true. Seeing Boo and Ollie just made letting go of Ford harder, which was why, since he'd left, she'd been putting her rent in the mail instead of dropping it by their house like she used to.

Ollie gave her one last fretful look and left.

Annie blew out a slow, calming breath. She wished she could crawl back into bed and curl up with Chester for the rest of the day, but that wasn't going to accomplish anything, and she had bills to pay, so she picked up her coffee and keys and went to work.

BRAMBLETON WAS A RELATIVELY new development in Loudoun that was planned around the Metro expansion past Dulles Airport. As Annie navigated through a labyrinth of townhouses and garden apartments in search of the home of her first interview, her phone rang through the car's Bluetooth connection. The screen on her dashboard showed that it was Preston. Surprised that he was calling so soon, she pulled into a parking space in front of what she hoped was the right building and took the call.

"Annie, hey. Listen, I know it's a little soon to call, but I need you in your professional capacity."

"I'm on a job right now," Annie said. "Can I call you later?"

"Sure. I've got a meeting tonight that I really need you to attend if possible."

"Can I call you back in an hour?"

"That works. Thanks."

Curious but unwilling to be late for the interview, Annie got out of the car and headed for apartment B6 in the brick complex in front of her. A woman with two nose rings and an asymmetric haircut answered the door.

Annie introduced herself and handed the woman her card.

"You're here about the background check?" the woman asked.

"Yes."

"Great. Well, let me tell you, Mitch is a dick, but I never saw him do anything illegal."

"Okay," Annie said, amused. Most of the people she interviewed weren't nearly that direct. "I do have a few questions, though."

"Yeah, sure. Come on in."

TWENTY MINUTES LATER, Annie had everything she needed. She couldn't recall a more enjoyable interview. Generally, the interviews for background checks were pretty dull, so it felt nice to get someone with a snarky sense of humor and a willingness to talk. As she got back in the car, Annie remembered Preston's phone call and tried to think of what he would need from her in a professional capacity. She hoped the farm hadn't been vandalized again. Maybe he'd decided to do the alarm system after all. That would be good money for her but awkward too. She regretted agreeing to go for drinks with him. On the other hand, it really had just been drinks, so she decided it wasn't that big of a deal as she called his number and put the location of the next interview into her car's navigation system.

Preston answered on the fourth ring. "Annie, hey."

"Hi. So, what's up?"

"My brother and sister want to meet and talk about the new security measures, and I'd like to have you there to answer any questions they might have."

"When do you want to meet?"

"Does six o'clock work for you? My sister is picking up a saddle she had repaired in Middleburg and wants to come out after. My brother will just Skype in."

"I can do that," Annie said. She'd never dealt with a limited partnership before, but it made sense that Preston's siblings would want to understand how the farm was being protected.

"Great. Having you there will really help. I need to get going, but I'll see you later," Preston said with undisguised cheer.

Annie couldn't help but like the guy. He completely lacked guile. Either that, or he was the best actor in the world.

After conducting five more interviews, Annie went home, her head swimming from all the conversations and information. She would write up her notes in a report for her client the next day. For the time being, she wanted to walk Chester and take a break before going to Preston's.

WHILE DRIVING UP THE long drive to the farmhouse, Annie couldn't help wondering how the meeting was going to go and whether it meant anything that Preston had taken her out for drinks the previous night. He'd been so cheery on the phone that it seemed unlikely that the meeting was a way for him to put things back on a professional level. On the other hand, maybe he was just a generally happy guy, and after looking her up, he'd decided he couldn't cope with her baggage. He did, after all, have a considerable amount of his own baggage to lug around. She reminded herself that she wasn't bothered either way and that the meeting was just part of the deal, although she wondered if she should be charging him for the visit. She hadn't done enough security installations to know whether it was just something people asked for or Preston's situation was unique. As she parked in front of the barn, Preston walked toward the farmhouse with a slender blond woman in jeans and a summer top that, despite being casual, still managed to project authority. *This must be the sister,* Annie thought and got out of the car. Preston waved to her, and the two walked over.

"Annie, hey, this is my sister, Ruby Myers. Ruby, this is Annie Fitch. She installed the security system."

Ruby gave Preston a look that indicated she didn't know Annie was going to be there, but she stuck out her hand. "Nice to meet you."

Annie shook her hand then followed them into the house, where he'd set up a laptop on a large oak dining table. Annie looked at the house as Preston went to get everyone a glass of iced tea. Most of the furniture was old but well-made. The décor didn't really look like the taste of a man in his thirties, so she assumed that they were his grandmother's furnishings and had come with the house. Although the idea that Preston really liked lace and porcelain knickknacks tickled her.

She bit back her amusement as Preston came out of the kitchen, carrying a tray with three glasses of iced tea and an open package of chocolate chip cookies. "I'm starved," he said. "I haven't had dinner yet."

"Me either," Ruby said and reached for a cookie.

"Have a seat," Preston said to Annie and set the tray on the table.

Ruby opened the laptop and clicked on the Skype icon. "Emory should be calling any minute."

Despite the fact that Preston ran the farm, Ruby clearly ran the show. A phone call came through within moments of Ruby starting the program, and she clicked on it to answer. A man's face filled the screen. He looked a lot like Preston, but instead of shaving his head, he kept his remaining gray hair cut short.

"Hey, you two," he said heartily. "Oh, wait—you three. Who's this?"

Ruby made the introduction and explained that Annie had installed a security system at the farm.

"Security system? When was that decided?" Emory asked.

Preston cleared his throat. "I decided. The berries are going to be coming in soon. I can't have people spray-painting obscenities in places where the public will see."

"I completely understand," Emory said. "But are you sure that wasn't jumping the gun a bit? I mean, you've just had the one incident, right? It was probably just kids."

"That's what I said," Ruby chimed in. "Why spend the money, if it's just a one-off?"

"It wasn't that much money. And we've had other smaller incidents but nothing that rose to the level of calling the police until this last time." Preston told him what the system cost, and his brother let out a long whistle.

"We have a difference of opinion on what qualifies as a lot of money."

"Oh, come on," Ruby said. "It wasn't that much. Besides, if it gives him peace of mind—"

"Hey." Emory held up his hands. "Look, I know this was upsetting, but I wish you'd run this stuff by me first. I mean, how much of the farm is even covered?"

"I'm going to let Annie explain all that," Preston said.

Annie spent the next ten minutes explaining the security system, what it covered, and how it could be expanded if necessary. "Any questions?" she asked when she was done.

When no one asked anything, Emory said, "I appreciate you explaining all that, Annie. I'm sure it makes Preston feel much better to have the cameras up, and hopefully, that'll solve the problem."

"I'm sure it will," Preston said.

"Absolutely," Ruby said, patting his arm. "Listen, I've been gone all day, and I'd like to get home to Ari. Are we done here?"

"Fine by me," Emory said. "You good, buddy?"

"Yep," Preston said. "Oh, wait. One more thing. A local reverend contacted me. She wants to talk about the slaves that used to work the farm. She was looking for a church, too, but she said it was on the other side of the creek, down at the bend, so I told her that belonged to Mr. Nichols."

"That's right," Ruby said.

"But she still wanted to talk about the slaves—possible graveyards, where they lived, and all that, so—"

"That's not a good idea," Emory said. "You don't want to bring all that back up. It's bad for the farm's image."

Ruby scoffed. "You know what's bad for business? If we don't talk to her, and she goes to the press. That would be terrible."

Emory rubbed a hand down his face. "All right. Talk to her, but let's discuss it as a group before you move forward with anything beyond that. That's not too much to ask, is it?"

"I can do that," Preston said.

"Good. Then I'll sign off. Y'all have a good night," Emory said, and the screen went dark.

"I'm going to go too," Ruby said, standing. "Nice to meet you, Annie."

Annie rose and shook Ruby's hand. "I should go too. I'll walk out with you."

Preston followed them out. He hugged Ruby goodbye then turned to Annie. "Actually, before you go, do you think you could take a look at the app? I'm having problems seeing camera four."

"That's weird," Annie said. "Let me see your phone."

Ruby got into her car and started backing out as Preston handed Annie his phone. He waved to his sister, and she waved back before starting down the driveway.

"I don't really have a problem with the camera," he said, taking his phone back. "I just wanted her to go away so that we could talk."

"Oh."

"Do you see why I wanted you here?"

Annie thought it was pretty clear, but she didn't want to be the one to say it. "Well, I was happy to explain the system."

"They act like I'm a child instead of grown man. It's not so bad when I'm one-on-one with either of them, but get us all together, and I might as well be ten years old." He shook his head in frustration. "I know what I'm doing. This place is earning a better profit than it has in the last decade, and that's down to me, but do you think they see that? No. They talk to me like I'm an idiot. What do you want to bet that she's calling him from the car right now?"

"I wouldn't take that bet," Annie said with a sympathetic smile.

"Smart. I really *am* hungry. Do you want a sandwich?"

"Sure. That sounds good." She followed him back inside. The kitchen was large and bright with white cabinets and appliances. At some point, it had been renovated, since it didn't look nearly as old as the outside of the house would imply. Preston put four slices of bread in the toaster and rooted around in the refrigerator. "Mayo or mustard?" he asked.

"Mustard," Annie said.

He turned around and leaned against the counter. "It occurred to me that I probably should have said something besides asking you to come out for the meeting when I called you earlier."

Annie raised her eyebrows. Clearly, he wanted to clarify their position, but she wasn't sure which direction he meant for that to be.

"What I mean is..." He put his hands into his back pockets. "I had a really good time last night, and if you're interested, I'd like to get to know you better."

She smiled at him. "I'd like that."

The toaster popped, and she caught his grin as he turned around to get the bread. "Great."

While he quickly put together two ham-and-cheese sandwiches, he asked Annie to pour drinks. "I've only got iced tea, water, and beer."

"Iced tea it is, then," Annie said. She had a slightly giddy feeling, which she decided was ridiculous but couldn't help it.

"Glasses are in the cabinet above you. Chips?"

"Yes." She got a pitcher of tea out of the refrigerator and poured the drinks, but as she followed him to the table, she couldn't help wondering if he'd looked her up online. Uncomfortable with that line of thought, she decided to stick with work for conversation. "How was your day? Any more vandalism?"

"Nope," Preston said around a mouthful of sandwich. He swallowed. "Just typical headaches. Dealing with deer, checking the grafts in the high-yield section—that kind of stuff."

"What's a high-yield section?" Annie asked.

"Those are the trees that produce the most fruit, but we don't let the pick-your-own people into that area. Not that they would want to pick over there, anyway. It lacks the nostalgic feel of the bigger trees."

"Oh. I didn't realize there was another section." She didn't recall seeing anything like that as a kid.

"Yeah, it's on the other side of the farm, away from the public areas. The pick-your-own stuff is good for quick cash from the mature trees, but it's not the best way to harvest and sell apples. The orchard is in transition right now, and it's hard to know which way to take it," he said.

"Sounds complicated."

"It is," Preston agreed. "And since it's not just my money, there's a lot of pressure to get it right."

"I thought your brother and sister weren't involved in the farm," Annie said. "But then on the call, it seemed like they were."

"They aren't, really, at least not in the day-to-day operations. But they're just as interested in turning a profit as I am, so they're also interested in expenses and marketing."

"That makes sense."

"I'm sorry," Preston said. "I'm sure this is all pretty boring."

"Not at all. It's actually nice to talk to someone else with their own business, even if it's really different from mine. I totally understand the pressure."

He nodded. "I can imagine, especially after going from the security of a regular income."

Annie chuckled. "Tell me about it."

They finished eating dinner, and Preston asked Annie if she'd like to go for a walk. The sun was starting to go down as they walked through the orchard, and the air was heavy with the scent of apple blossoms.

"This really is a beautiful place," Annie commented.

Preston nodded. "It's worth saving, which is why I'm looking into working out something with a land trust for the development rights."

"What would that do?" Annie asked.

"For one, it would lower the taxes considerably. My brother and sister aren't quite ready to commit, though."

"Why is that?"

"Because depending on how we do it, it could be permanent, so that's a big commitment we'd be making for future generations."

"I get that," Annie said.

They walked in silence for a while, enjoying the evening.

"I saw you at the board meeting the other night. Celia and I were sitting a few rows back from you. She has a cemetery on her property and wanted to know what the ramifications of that are now that the county is mapping them."

"We have a cemetery on our land too. That's one of the reasons I went." He took her hand. "Come this way. I'll show you."

They came out of the orchard and went up a small rise to an area that overlooked the orchard and a stream that ran through the farm. A graveyard was marked off with a black wrought-iron fence. The stones varied from so worn as to be almost unreadable to laser-cut granite that looked new. As they stood looking at the old cemetery, Preston continued holding her hand. She was relieved he'd taken her left hand so that he wouldn't feel the big scar on the palm of her right one.

"Pretty much my whole family is buried here."

"Wow," Annie said. "I have no idea where most of my family is buried."

"It's probably easier to keep track when you've owned the same property since the 1700s. The land was a grant to the first Emory Farr from Lord Fairfax himself."

Annie was sure she'd never met anyone with such deep roots in one place. "That's impressive."

"I guess, although parts of it have been sold off over time. It used to be five hundred acres, and it's getting harder and harder to hold on to what's left, with taxes being what they are with the land values around here." He shook his head.

"That sounds stressful," Annie said.

He shrugged. "Some days. But I really love the land. I can't imagine letting it be developed."

Annie looked around at the view. She marveled that they were inside the town limits. Preston pointed toward the other side of the cemetery. "That's the high-yield section."

Rows and rows of narrow trees stood on frames. "It looks like some kind of freakish vineyard."

"Kind of, yeah."

"Nothing warm and fuzzy about it."

"No, but it's the most effective way to grow apples."

"Fair enough. I'd rather walk through the pretty trees, though."

"Yeah, me too. Can I tempt you with a nightcap or a cup of coffee with a leftover cookie?"

"I can't do coffee this late, unless you have decaf."

"I do."

"Then I'm in," Annie said.

"Great."

They held hands all the way back to the house. Annie tried not to analyze it, just enjoy it and ignore thoughts of Ford and his mother's concerned face from earlier that morning. She liked Preston. He was solid and rooted in the community in a way that Ford would never be. Not for the first time, she wished she had a more normal dating history. She'd had boyfriends other than Ford, but it had been a long time. Dating wasn't that easy as a female cop, and she really hadn't been that interested. Her on-again, off-again relationship with Ford had been easy to manage while she focused on her career. Then when he'd spent a year taking care of her after she was shot the first time, she'd misinterpreted his actions as a readiness to settle down, but that had not been the case. For Annie, her whole life had changed. Gone was the career and all the ambition that went with it. Her goals as a private investigator were much more modest. She just wanted to do a good job and earn a decent living. Although it hurt to think about, she couldn't really blame Ford for leaving. She wasn't who she used to be. She'd changed, but he hadn't, and that wasn't his fault or hers.

Meanwhile, Preston's hand was warm and calloused and felt good holding hers. He was sweet and handsome, and she was lonely.

At the house, Preston told her to have a seat in the living room while he put the coffee on. Annie looked around the room. Bookshelves lined one wall. She read the titles, wondering whether the books, like the furnishings, were inherited or were Preston's. The nonfiction books on agriculture and vehicle maintenance didn't look very old, but the craft books and shelves of novels, mostly mystery and some romance, were dusty and didn't appear to have been touched for a long time. Her mind drifted back to the vandalism. She couldn't understand the motivation behind it. Then she remembered Preston telling his brother about other incidents that hadn't warranted a call to the police.

"Hey," Preston said as he walked in carrying the same bag of cookies he'd served earlier. "Coffee will be ready in a minute."

"Great," Annie said. "I was just looking at your books."

"Most of those aren't mine," Preston said. "Nannie was a big one for novels. I should probably clear them out—donate them or something—but I haven't taken the time."

Annie glanced around the room. "I'm guessing a lot of this stuff was your grandmother's."

"Why do you say that?" Preston asked with a blank expression. He plucked a crocheted doily off an arm of the sofa. "I love a good doily." He couldn't maintain the ruse, though, and grinned.

Annie laughed. "I had you pegged as a doily guy from the start."

"It's the crochet. I just love it. Can't get enough."

"Do you do it yourself, or are you just a collector?"

"Oh, myself, of course," he said, laughing, then set the cookies on the coffee table and took a seat on the sofa.

"You and Celia could be besties. She might actually prefer you to me. I'm hopeless with crafts."

"Celia, yeah, Ted's girlfriend. See, I knew she and I got along well. Now I know why."

Annie laughed again.

The coffee machine beeped, and Preston got back up. Annie followed him into the kitchen. "Listen, I meant to ask you earlier—you told your brother about other vandalism incidents before you called the police. What else was vandalized?"

Preston got a couple of mugs out of the cabinet. "Nothing serious. Someone let all the air out of the tires on one of the tractors."

"Let the air out how?"

"They weren't slashed, if that's what you're getting at," Preston said as he poured the coffee.

"So, someone stood there and held the valve open? How long does that take?"

"A while. That's why I didn't call the police. Alejandro let one of the farm hands go, and I assumed he did it as a parting shot, but then a few days later, someone removed the spark plugs from all the ATVs."

"But you don't think it was the same guy?"

"No, because right after the first incident, he called Alejandro and asked if he'd take him to the airport, because he'd found a cheap ticket back to Bolivia."

"I assume Alejandro took him."

"Yep." Preston handed her a mug. "Let's go sit down. I'd hate for those cookies to go to waste."

"That would be tragic." Annie followed him back to the living room. When they'd taken their seats on the sofa, she reached for a cookie. "This is nice."

"They're just store-bought," Preston said.

"They're still good, but what I meant was how nice it is that you can leave a plate of cookies lying around, and no one comes along and eats them all."

Preston raised his eyebrows. "You've got kids?"

"No, a dog, and I could never leave cookies out with him around."

"I like dogs. I've been thinking about getting one. What kind is yours?"

"West Highland white terrier and miniature bull terrier mix."

Preston cocked his head. "What does that look like?"

"Small with short but unruly white hair. He's pretty cute and mostly good but not with food. He's a little thief."

Preston chuckled. "Sounds like a handful."

"Not so much. He's my pal. I take him with me whenever I can."

"You should bring him out here. There's so much space for him to run."

"He'd love that, I'm sure."

"I like small dogs, but I was thinking of something bigger that could help with the deer situation. My grandmother always had a pair of Great Pyrenees when we were kids, and she never had a problem with deer. She also had a little terrier that was a house dog but killed rodents in the barn, kind of like his day job. Between him and the feral cats, we never had an issue with rats or mice."

"I think I would have liked your grandmother," Annie said.

"She was a pistol." He sighed. "She really loved this place."

"I can see why."

Quiet settled between them as they drank their coffee. Annie's thoughts drifted back to the vandalism. The idea of a disgruntled farmworker made the most sense. "So, have you let any other workers go that could have a grudge against you?"

Preston smiled and shook his head. "Wow, you're like a dog with a bone."

Annie shrugged. "Once a cop, always a cop."

"To answer your question, no. Stop worrying about it. This really cool chick installed a security system for me. I've got it covered."

"Cool chick?" she asked, raising an eyebrow at him.

"Hot babe?"

She gave him a stern look.

"Amazing woman?"

"Better," she said, smiling.

"See? I'm teachable."

She chuckled. "On that note, I should go. I need to let Chester out."

He nodded. "Yeah, it's past my bedtime, and I have a full day tomorrow." They both stood, and Preston stretched, yawning. "Sorry."

"Don't be. It's late."

Preston walked her out to the car. "How would you like to come over for dinner Monday night? I'll make something. It'll be better than sandwiches. I promise."

"You cook?"

"I'm not going to be on the next season of *Top Chef* or anything, but I know my way around a kitchen. Six o'clock?"

"All right, then," she said and reached to open the door.

"I'd like to kiss you," he said quietly.

Her breath caught, and her pulse raced as she turned back to him. "I think I'd like that too."

He leaned in and brushed his lips softly against hers. *In for a penny,* she thought and opened her lips slightly. He took the hint and deepened the kiss, drawing his right hand up to cup her neck. She leaned into him and let herself enjoy the moment until his left hand lightly squeezed her right shoulder, and she winced.

Preston stepped back, holding up his hands. "What happened?"

The change in mood was so sudden that she was thrown off for a moment. "Nothing." She cleared her throat. "That shoulder is still a little tender. That's all."

He cocked his head at her. "A little tender from what?"

"What?" Annie suddenly realized he hadn't done what she assumed everyone did in the Internet age. She shook her head. "No big deal, just an injury a few months ago." She wasn't sure why she didn't just tell him. If they were going to keep dating, he was going to find out eventually. If only he'd just spent a little time online, she wouldn't have to explain. Still, the idea of getting into it left her cold. "I should go. I'll see you Monday."

"Yeah."

He stepped back so that she could open the car door. When she closed it, he tapped on the window. She pressed the button to lower it, and he leaned in and gave her a soft kiss on the lips.

"I'll see you at six, then," he said. "Bring your dog. He'll love the farm."

She nodded. "I will. Good night."

"Night." He waved as she drove down the lane, wondering what she'd gotten herself into.

Chapter 7
Saturday through Monday

Saturday morning, Annie talked to Celia on the phone.

"Dinner at his house sounds like it might be a sex date," Celia said. "I mean, he said to bring the dog, so there's no need to go home, right?"

"That's what I thought. Why did I agree? It's too soon, isn't it?"

"I don't know about that. You're ready when you're ready. You could always just go home or cancel if you're not ready."

"I'm definitely ready."

"Really?"

"Okay, maybe not definitely," Annie admitted. "I mean I am physically. I'm just not sure my heart is. Besides, I don't think he's googled me."

"What difference does that make?" Celia asked.

Annie could hear her washing dishes. "Because if he's looked me up, he knows I've been shot, and he's fine with it. But if he hasn't, then he might not be."

Celia turned off the water. "Wait a minute. You haven't talked to him about being shot?"

"No."

"Annie, why?" Celia asked, concern evident in her voice.

"It just didn't come up." That was a lie. Annie had had several opportunities to discuss it, but she had sidestepped all of them.

"Because you avoided it?"

Annie sighed. "Possibly." Celia was clairvoyant sometimes.

"Why?"

"I don't know. If the scars weren't so obvious, I'd put it off. But they *are* obvious, and the ones on my shoulder are still really red."

"You should tell him and not just because of the scars," Celia said. "And you should do it before the sex date."

"Maybe I don't have to tell him. Maybe he already knows, and if he hasn't looked me up by now, surely he'll do that before Monday. He has all weekend."

"You're just going to assume that?" Celia asked.

"I don't know."

"Okay," Celia said with a tone that made clear what she thought Annie should do.

ANNIE SPENT THE REST of the weekend doing chores and running errands, all while trying to decide how to approach Preston about the shooting—or shootings. Intermingled with that concern were anger and disappointment with Ford for putting her in such a position in the first place. That probably wasn't entirely rational, but she couldn't help it. She felt how she felt. In the meantime, Preston texted her about an upcoming concert at a small local venue, and they went back and forth about music they liked. She enjoyed the exchange. His taste in music was broader than she'd expected, and it was fun getting to know someone new. Most of the people in her life, she'd known for at least a decade, and many of them a lot longer.

MONDAY MORNING, ANNIE went to Sterling and tried to figure out how to get photographic evidence of a guy faking an injury for workers' compensation. He'd been ratted out by a coworker, but the company needed evidence before proceeding.

The guy had hung big tarps from tall oaks to conceal what he was doing in his backyard. According to his coworker, he was enclosing a porch back there. She looked at the other houses on the street. He had two neighbors with second-floor windows facing his yard. One driveway had no cars in it, but the other driveway had an aging Oldsmobile Cutlass parked in it. She walked over to that house and knocked on the door.

An elderly man opened it. He was unshaven and wearing a threadbare but clean bathrobe over flannel pajamas.

"Hi," Annie said. "I'm so sorry to bother you, but I'm a private investigator looking into allegations that your neighbor is faking a workers' comp claim." She handed the old man her card. She'd found, since she started working as a private investigator, that the direct approach was often best, especially when asking people for help.

He pulled a pair of thick glasses out of his robe pocket and put them on to read her card. "Do you have any other ID?" he asked.

She showed him her private investigator's license, which had her photograph on it.

"Come in," he said. "It doesn't surprise me at all that he's faking. He's been nothing but a thorn in the side of this neighborhood since he moved in."

"I'm sorry to hear that." Annie looked around at the house, which was clean but cluttered. "What kind of trouble has he caused?"

The man went on for a while about what a jerk his neighbor was. He didn't cut his grass often enough, left his trash cans by the curb for weeks at a time, and never cleared the snow off his part of the sidewalk.

When he paused to take a breath, Annie said, "I was hoping to use one of your upstairs windows to take some photos. Would that be all right?"

"Yes, it would," the old man said.

She followed him upstairs.

"I don't think he even has a permit for that work he's doing. Seems shady to me. Can you do anything about that?"

"I'm sorry. That's not in my purview, but you can call the county permitting office. They can tell you if there's a permit for that property."

"I might just do that," the old man said as he led her up a narrow stairway. He had to move some boxes out of the way for her to reach the window in a spare bedroom that was obviously used primarily for storage.

"There you go," he said when the path was clear.

"I really appreciate this." The view was perfect, and she could clearly see the man lifting and hammering and doing all manner of work he shouldn't be capable of with the injuries he'd claimed. "Perfect," she said. With some effort, she managed to open the window, then she started shooting video and snapping stills. After twenty minutes, she had everything she needed.

"Thank you so much," she told the old man.

"Would you like a cup of coffee?" he asked.

"I wish I could," she said. "But I really need to go." He shook her hand warmly before she left.

She went home to write up a report and attached the photos and videos to an email she sent to her client. Those kinds of assignments were her bread and butter. The murder case that had gotten her shot the previous year had turned out to be good for business. All the newspaper articles were like free advertising, and business had steadily picked up.

After she'd taken care of the report, she looked through her email, answered some inquiries, sent out an invoice, and returned some calls. When she was done, it was after three o'clock.

Annie closed her laptop and thought about calling Preston and canceling their plans. She wanted to see him, and she wasn't even worried that it might be a sex date, because frankly, that sounded good too. Mostly, she didn't want to talk about the shooting. She really hoped he'd checked her out online and decided it didn't matter, but she had no way of knowing unless one of them brought it up in conversation. On the other hand, if he saw her naked, he would definitely notice. And if she stayed the night, he would see how stiff and sluggish she was in the morning and how long it took her to get sorted enough to get on with her day. She wasn't sure she was ready for that.

Sighing, she let her head fall back against the sofa. Chester nudged her hand with his muzzle, and she petted him. Preston had said to bring Chester. That would help. Chester always helped when she was stressed. Besides, he'd invited her dog to dinner. She couldn't cancel on a guy who would do that. On the other hand, having Chester with her prevented her from using him as an excuse to leave. But maybe she wouldn't want to leave. Maybe it would be a great night.

She sighed again and got up to take Chester for a long walk. If he was going to be a houseguest, she wanted him to be a tired houseguest. If the evening didn't turn out well, and she wanted to leave, she would leave. It didn't matter whether she had Chester or not.

DRIVING TO FARR REACH Farm didn't take long enough for Annie to have second thoughts. She'd settled on a khaki skirt and a light-blue silk-blend T-shirt as her outfit for the evening. Chester was wearing a clean collar, and she'd bathed him. Changing the dog's collar was probably overkill, but the other one had been pretty grubby.

She parked her black Prius next to Preston's old farm truck and got Chester out of the back and put him on his leash. As they were walking up the slate path, Preston came out onto the porch, wearing jeans and an untucked madras shirt.

"Hey," he said, setting a bottle of wine and two glasses on the porch table.

"Hi. This is Chester."

Preston knelt and held out his hand to the little terrier, who gave him a sniff then let Preston pet him.

Looking up at her, Preston said, "He's missing an eye."

"Oh god!" Annie replied in mock panic. "He had both of them this morning!"

For a second, confusion crossed Preston's face, then he laughed. "I guess you hear that a lot."

She shrugged and smiled. "He was like that when we found him."

"Where was that?"

"At the Fairfax recycling center. My brother, Joey, works there," Annie explained.

"Oh." Preston stood. "What does he do?"

"To be honest, I'm not sure. He works part-time in the sorting facility."

"So, he found the dog."

"Not exactly. My dad and I went to pick up my brother from work, and we saw Chester wandering around the parking lot."

"You rescued him," Preston said. "That's great."

"Yeah, although sometimes it feels like the other way around."

"I get that." He gave her a once-over. "You look nice."

"Thanks." It had taken her an embarrassing amount of time to settle on her simple outfit.

"Glass of wine?" he asked, holding up the bottle. "I thought we'd start out here, since it's a nice night." He set the wine on a table in front of a white rattan loveseat on the far end of the porch.

"That sounds good." She felt annoyed by how nervous she was.

"I got a couple of rib eye steaks to throw on the grill."

"I love rib eye," she said with a smile.

"Me too." Preston poured a glass of wine and handed it to her. "How was your day?"

Annie had a sip of wine. "Pretty good. I got a lot done. How about yours?" she asked.

"I spent it deer hunting in the orchard."

"How'd you do?"

"I got four, but honestly, I could have killed forty and not made a dent in the deer population."

"Four deer still sounds like a lot. No more problems with vandalism, then?"

"Not unless you count the deer," Preston said, smiling. "Any cool cases this week?"

Annie told him about her morning, but even as she talked, she thought about telling him about the shootings. She hadn't wanted to bring it up while he talked about deer hunting, though, because that seemed like too grim of a segue. Besides, she didn't want him to think she was anti-hunting or anything, because she wasn't. As long as he didn't shoot her, they were golden.

"Earth to Annie," Preston said.

She tuned back in. "I'm sorry. What?"

"I asked if I should start the steaks."

"Oh." She cleared her throat. "Maybe in a minute. Can we talk for sec? There's something I haven't brought up, and I need to."

"Sure."

She poured herself some more wine. Ever conscious of her emotional state, Chester came over and sat next to her leg, leaning into her. She rubbed the top of his head.

"I should probably have mentioned this before," she started.

His face fell. "Please don't tell me you're married."

"What? No. Of course not."

"Whew," he said, obviously relieved.

Annie opened her mouth to say something, but nothing came out. She couldn't think how to start.

He cocked his head at her, waiting. When she didn't say anything, he said, teasing, "There's no way you used to be a guy."

"What? No. Stop guessing." She arched an eyebrow at him playfully. "Are you saying that would be a deal breaker?"

"I didn't say that," he replied, smiling.

She laughed.

"Seriously, I'm hungry. Tell me your deep, dark secret so that we can eat."

"This could all have been avoided if you'd just googled me," she said, frowning.

He reached for his phone. "I could do it now."

"Don't. You can do that when I leave, if you want more details."

He left his phone in his pocket but looked concerned. "More details about what?"

She sighed. "I'm sorry. I'm making this worse. It's just really hard to talk about, but if we're going to get closer, you need to know."

He leaned toward her. "Are we going to get closer?"

"I hope so."

As he leaned in farther, he put his hand on her knee, and she clamped hers over it before he could slide it up and find the scar on her thigh. He backed out of the kiss and looked at her hand over his.

"I need to say this," she said.

He ran his other hand over his head. "Oh man."

Realizing that he might be thinking something very different from the truth gave her the courage to proceed. "That second day at the farm, when you thought I was limping from an old sports injury, I told you I'd hurt it at work."

"Yeah," he said, clearly worried.

"That was true, but the way I hurt it..." She slowly blew out a breath. "Was someone shot me."

His eyes widened. "Seriously?"

"It happened a while ago. Basically, I was in the wrong place at the wrong time. Total fluke. Anyway, the guy shot me through a window, and the bullet went through my hand." She held out her right hand so that he could see the tiny entrance-wound scar. "And lodged in my right thigh." She turned her hand over so that he could see the large star-shaped scar on her palm. "The muscles have a tendency to tighten up around the scar, so I limp sometimes."

Preston reached for her hand and ran his thumb along the outside of the scar on her palm. "That's crazy," he said in a kind of awed voice.

She cleared her throat. He was right. It was crazy but not nearly as crazy as that not being all of the story. "Yeah, um, then Friday night, when you kissed me, and you put your hand on my shoulder..."

"Yeah?"

"It's tender because last year, I was on a case and got hit in the shoulder with bird shot."

His jaw dropped.

"Not a lot," she added hastily. "The doorjamb took most of the blast."

"Wait," Preston said, clearly trying to wrap his head around that. "The wound on your hand was from bird shot?"

"No. That was a nine-millimeter."

"Someone shot you with a pistol and a shotgun? How does that happen?"

"It was two different occasions," Annie said, closing her eyes. "I'm sorry. I'm making this confusing. I've been shot three times. Twice on the first occasion and once in the shoulder at a different time."

"I thought the bullet went through your hand into your thigh," Preston said.

"The first bullet did," she said.

"But there was a second bullet?"

She nodded.

"Where did that go?" he asked.

They'd been talking very softly, barely above a whisper. He was still holding her hand, so she lifted it and, using her hand to guide his, ran his fingers over the thick scar on the right side of her head.

Preston gasped. "Holy shit!"

"It's kind of hard to talk about," she said, embarrassed to find tears threatening.

He surprised her by moving his hand around to the back of her neck and gently pulling her into a hug. She rested her head on his shoulder.

"Christ, you could have died," he said softly. The sincerity with which he said it and the warmth of his arms around her touched her in a way she hadn't expected.

She blinked back tears. "Yeah," she said, her voice cracking. "But I didn't."

He leaned back and kissed her again.

They never got around to dinner.

Chapter 8
Tuesday Morning

Annie awoke the next morning disoriented. The sun was in her face in a way that was impossible in her apartment. She opened her eyes to a large white room with dark hardwood floors and remembered she'd spent the night with Preston. She smiled. Preston had been a revelation—a nice man and a good lover.

Chester lay curled up asleep at the foot of the bed, but he lifted his head when she sat up. Ford had never let him sleep on the bed. She felt a stab of guilt about Ford but shook it off. He'd chosen to go. He was the one who wanted things back to the way they were.

She yawned and got out of bed. Her panties were on the floor, so she pulled them on, looking around for the rest of her clothes. Then she remembered that the previous night's escapades had started on the porch and proceeded through the house. She was fairly certain her clothes were strewn about downstairs, and she looked around for a robe but didn't see one. A wingback chair sat in one corner of the room with some clothes draped over it. She picked up one of Preston's T-shirts and sniffed it. It smelled clean, so she pulled it on. Her leg was always stiff in the morning, so she stretched, trying to loosen the muscles, before slowly and carefully going downstairs. Chester followed her.

Annie was distracted by the smell of coffee. She always found it difficult to wake up without caffeine. Her brain had been sluggish in the mornings since the shooting, and her speech could be a bit thick and slow until she'd had a cup or two. Preston wasn't downstairs, which was a relief. She would rather not see him until she felt more like herself.

A note was propped against the coffee maker.

Annie,

Had to get some work done. Have coffee. I'll be back by 7:00.

We can have breakfast.

Preston

He'd left a coffee mug out for her. She smiled and filled it. The clock on the microwave told her it was just after six, so she had plenty of time to get sorted before Preston returned. So far, he knew she'd been shot, but he wasn't aware of what exactly that meant for her day-to-day routine, and she wasn't entirely ready to share it.

Chester started his I-need-to-go-out dance. A stone wall wrapped around the front yard, so she let him out that way.

"Go quick, quick," she told the little terrier.

Annie sipped her coffee and stretched her leg again while she waited for him to come back to the door. The little guy hadn't had any dinner, and she felt bad. She opened the fridge and found some lunch meat, so she took a slice of roast beef for each of them. She was ravenous. Chester came back to the door, and she gave him his snack. She yawned and went to refill her coffee cup.

The back door burst open, causing her to jump. She turned around to see Alejandro helping Preston inside and holding a blood-stained rag to his head. Blood covered Preston's face and shirt.

"Oh my god!" Annie hurried toward them. "What happened?"

Alejandro got Preston seated on one of the kitchen chairs. "I found him wandering around in front of the apple barn like this."

Annie took over holding pressure on the wound and leaned down to look at Preston. "What happened?" she asked again.

"Someone hit me," he said thickly.

"I already called the cops," Alejandro said.

"Did you ask for an ambulance too?" Annie asked. Preston was losing a lot of blood, and he didn't seem fully aware of what was going on.

"I told them someone hit him. I figured they'd send one."

Someone knocked on the front door. Chester started barking.

Annie held out a palm to him. "No!"

The little dog quieted but remained alert.

"I'll get it," Alejandro said.

Annie turned to see her former partner, Detective Gunnar Janssen, coming through the door with Mike Hartt in uniform behind him. Gunnar's jaw dropped when he saw her, and she blushed as she realized she was standing there in nothing but one of Preston's T-shirts and her panties.

"What are you doing here?" Gunnar asked.

Annie refused to give in to embarrassment. She was a grown woman. "What does it look like I'm doing here?"

Gunnar actually blushed a bit, but he had sense enough not to say anything.

"Is an ambulance coming?" Annie asked.

"I don't know," Gunnar said.

"He needs to go to the hospital."

"No," Preston said. "I'm fine."

"You are not fine," Annie insisted. Because of her own experiences, head wounds made her feel panicky.

Gunnar turned to Mike. "Call in and tell them I'm going to take him to the hospital. Then go with..." He turned to Alejandro.

"Alejandro Flores."

"Go with Mr. Flores and see where this happened."

"On it," Mike said. Pulling the microphone from his shoulder strap, he stepped outside to contact Dispatch.

"We should get him to the car," Annie said.

"Annie?" Gunnar asked.

"What?"

"Don't you think you should put on some clothes first?"

Her face heated. "Right. I'll only be a minute. Go ahead and get him into the car."

She grabbed her silk T-shirt from the back of the sofa, her skirt from the floor, and her bra from the stair rail then stepped into the powder room in the front hall. It only took a minute to get dressed. The adrenaline coursing through her had woken her more completely than coffee ever could. She ran her fingers through her hair to try to control it, grabbed a hand towel from the rack, and went back out. Her shoes were on the porch, so she slipped them on before heading for the car. Her leg was still stiff, but she moved as quickly as she could.

Annie got into the back seat next to Preston, where he sat holding the rag to his head. "Let's go." She turned to Preston. "Here, let me." She kept the blood-soaked rag against the wound and covered it with the towel. She really hoped that rag was clean.

Preston seemed grateful that she was holding pressure, and he sagged some.

Gunnar put on the lights but not the siren and headed to the hospital. He glanced at Annie through the rearview mirror. "Did you see the guy who hit you?" he asked Preston.

"No," Preston said. He looked pale and clammy. Annie worried he might be in shock.

The hospital wasn't far, but morning traffic made the trip longer than it should have been. She felt weird about being in a police car again, especially in the back. None of it felt right. After what seemed like an hour but was probably less than fifteen minutes, Gunnar pulled in front of the hospital emergency room.

"Come on, Preston," Annie said then helped him out of the car and put her shoulder under his arm to stabilize him.

"Let's go, buddy," Gunnar said, getting on the other side of him. Gunnar was such a big man at six-eight that he just put his hand under Preston's other arm and helped get him inside.

Whether it was because he'd come in covered in blood, he'd come in with a police officer, or the ER didn't seem that busy, they took Preston right back to a room. Annie and Gunnar followed. She pushed back the waves of nausea and panic that always threatened whenever she went into a hospital. Something about the smell and the sounds of the equipment sent her right back to the time after the first shooting, when she'd been in the neuro ICU for weeks.

"Does he have a wallet with him?" Gunnar asked. "That'll help with getting him registered."

"I don't know," Annie said and started looking for it.

His wallet was in the back pocket of his jeans. Preston jumped then giggled when she reached for it.

She smiled at him. "Calm down there, cowboy," she said.

The moment of amusement made her feel better, although Preston wasn't exactly the giggling sort, so she put that down to the blow to the head. He seemed drunk. A tech showed up to take him for assessment. Someone else directed Annie and Gunnar to Registration.

As Annie sat down with someone at Registration, Gunnar said, "I'll be right back."

By the time she was done with the clerk and had taken a seat in the waiting area, Gunnar was back and handed her a cup of coffee and a breakfast sandwich.

"I thought you might be hungry." He sat next to her and unwrapped his own sandwich. "I know this isn't your favorite place."

"I *am* hungry," Annie said. "Thanks. I'm fine. At least we're not at Fairfax Hospital. That would really freak me out."

He smiled sympathetically as she unwrapped the sandwich. He'd gotten her bacon, egg, and cheese on an English muffin, remember-

ing her breakfast order despite almost two years of not working together. He'd also remembered she took her coffee black.

Annie smiled at him. She missed the big guy. "They said it
shouldn't take long. They're having a slow morning."

"Lucky." Gunnar took a sip of his coffee. "So, you and Farmer
Boy—how long has that been going on?"

"Not long."

"What happened to Ford?"

"Nothing. He went back to work overseas." She sipped her coffee.

"Oh. I thought that was pretty serious." He took another bite of
his sandwich.

"Me too, but I've been wrong before." She glanced away from his
scrutiny and drank her coffee while watching people move in and
out of Registration and through the door that led back to the ER.
"How are things going with you?" she asked, desperate to focus on
something besides where she was and what had happened to Preston.

Gunnar ran his fingers through his thick blond hair and blew out
a frustrated breath. "Ellen and I are separated."

"I'm sorry to hear that," Annie said, but she wasn't surprised.
She'd never felt like they were a particularly good match.

"Yeah," Gunnar said, shaking his head. "But you don't need to listen to me whine."

"It's not whining. Besides, I could use the distraction after the
morning I've had."

Gunnar nodded. "I just don't want to be one of those three-
strikes guys, you know?"

"This is only number two," Annie said.

"Yeah, but two is awfully close to three." Gunnar sighed.

"It'll be all right. You're a good guy."

"If I'm so good, then why do my wives keep leaving?"

"I don't know," Annie said, smiling sympathetically. "Why do they?"

Gunnar cleared his throat. "Well, Mel left because she said we got married too young and she didn't know who she was anymore. Ellen says we've grown apart."

"Do you agree with them?" Annie asked.

Gunnar shrugged. "I guess. Mel and I were probably too young to get married. I'd just turned nineteen, and she was only eighteen. I have no idea why we did it. It's not like she was pregnant or anything. We just wanted to get married. We went to college married. Who does that?"

Annie shrugged. "And Ellen?"

"I don't know. I'm not sure we were ever together enough to qualify as having grown apart. I kind of think we were always apart. Looking back, I don't even know why I married her."

"I always assumed it was because she was smokin' hot," Annie said and grinned at him.

Gunnar shook his head and blew out a long, slow breath. "Yeah. That probably had something to do with it. But you know, she also had her own life, her own career, and family she was close to. I thought she'd be fine married to a cop who worked weird hours because she was so independent."

Annie grimaced. "I'm really sorry."

Someone called her name.

She stood and glanced at Gunnar. "It'll be okay."

As Annie followed a woman in blue scrubs back to the room where Preston was waiting, anxiety bubbled in her. The antiseptic smell of the emergency room was more intense, and the equipment's beeps were constant. Preston was sitting up on the side of a bed. He opened his eyes when Annie came into the room. A doctor was applying Steri-Strips to close the wound on his head.

Annie winced and averted her eyes. "Hey," she said. "How are you feeling?"

"Pretty good," Preston said slowly.

Annie looked at the doctor. "Is he really?"

"He's got a concussion, but there's no indication of a skull fracture or bleeding in the brain, so he should be fine. Someone needs to be with him for the next twenty-four hours. Are you able to do that?"

"Yes," Annie said, nodding. She started going through the exercises to control panic, listing things she could see, hear, smell, and touch. But many of the things in her immediate surroundings were what was causing her anxiety, so the exercise was only so helpful.

"I'm so sorry," Preston said, taking her hand.

"For what?" Annie asked, concentrating on his hand in hers. "You didn't do anything."

"This isn't how I wanted our morning to go," he said thickly.

She squeezed his hand and smiled at him, grateful for the contact. It helped ground her. "Me either, but it's fine."

"He's just about ready to go," the doctor said as she placed a bandage over the wound. "I'll get his discharge notes ready, and a nurse will bring them back to you."

"Great. Thanks," Annie said.

"Take it easy for the next few days, and really rest the first twenty-four. You don't have to stay in bed but nothing vigorous," the doctor told Preston. "Obviously, if your symptoms get worse or you start vomiting, please come back immediately."

"Okay," Preston said. "Thanks."

Annie sat with him while they waited for the discharge paperwork, which was awkward, because they didn't really know each other that well. He was alert enough to be embarrassed but not clearheaded enough to really express it.

"Sorry," he muttered.

"Don't be," Annie said.

He didn't pull his hand away, and she didn't either. Maybe he needed some grounding too.

Several minutes later, a nurse returned with the paperwork. She went over the instructions again. "In a few minutes, someone from transport will bring a wheelchair to take him to the curb at the main entrance. Go ahead if you want to get your car and pull around."

"Thanks." Annie touched Preston's hand. "I'll see you in a few."

"Yep."

She hurried back to the lobby, reminding herself to walk calmly. Gunnar was pacing and talking on the phone, but when he caught sight of her, he hung up.

"We're all set," she said. "We can get the car. They'll bring him to the main entrance."

"Sure."

Annie followed him out to the parking lot. Once they left the building, Annie took a deep breath of fresh air and let it out slowly.

"What'd they say?" Gunnar asked.

Annie repeated what the doctor had said, concluding with someone needing to stay with Preston for the next twenty-four hours.

"And that's you?" Gunnar asked.

"Looks like."

He wrinkled his brow at her like he was going to say something.

"Thanks for staying," she said to preempt his comment.

"I don't mind," Gunnar said. "I know hospitals aren't your thing. Besides, it didn't take that long, and I've got to go back to the farm, anyway. I was just on the phone with Mike. He said they have security cameras."

"Yeah, I set those up."

"Great. Then you can get the footage for me."

"Sure."

Gunnar opened the passenger side door for her then got behind the wheel. As they drove up to the main entrance portico, she thought about the camera footage and realized she couldn't give it all to Gunnar, since what had transpired between her and Preston had started on the porch—in full view of one of the cameras.

A patient transporter was standing next to Preston, who was sitting in a wheelchair, holding his head, when Gunnar pulled up next to the curb. Annie got out and opened the back door for Preston, but he stood and got into the car without help. Annie got in next to him.

"Hey, Gunnar," she said, leaning forward. "Can you stop by my apartment? I need to grab a few things." She looked back at Preston. "Is that okay?"

"Sure. I'm fine. Sorry for all the fuss." He leaned his head back against the seat and closed his eyes.

Annie patted his knee. "It's no trouble."

"All right," Gunnar said and pulled on to the road.

THE DETOUR TO ANNIE'S apartment didn't take long. She changed into jeans and a T-shirt and swapped her espadrilles for sneakers. Then she threw more clothes and some toiletries along with food for Chester into a gym bag and grabbed her laptop. She locked the door, and Gunnar drove them back to the farm.

As they were getting out of the car, Annie said, "Let me get him settled, then I'll pull the footage for you."

"I'm fine," Preston said. "I should go check in with Alejandro."

"You're not fine. The doctor said you need to rest for the next twenty-four hours, and that's what you're going to do. I'll find Alejandro, and he can come up to the house and talk to you if he needs to."

He frowned at her, and for a moment, she thought he was going to tell her she was out of line, but he sighed and relented.

"Come on," she said in a gentler tone. "Let's put you to bed."

He grinned at her.

She chuckled. "To sleep, you freak."

"Yeah," Preston said resignedly. "I'm not really up for sexy fun time at the moment, anyway." He seemed to have lost track of the fact that Gunnar was standing right there.

Annie's cheeks heated. She glanced at Gunnar. "I'll only be a minute."

"Right." Gunnar cleared his throat. "I'm going to head down to the barn."

"I'll meet you there," she said and ushered Preston inside.

Chester greeted them at the door.

"Buddy, you stay down here, and I'll feed you in a second."

She got Preston out of his bloody clothes and settled into bed.

As she turned to leave, he caught her hand. "Thank you. I'm sorry for all the fuss." He looked adorably distressed.

Annie kissed his forehead. "It's no trouble. Get some sleep."

She went downstairs and fed Chester, who, like most terriers, finished his kibble in seconds, then she let him out front and poured herself another cup of coffee. Though it was cold, she didn't care. Chester came back to the door, and she let him in.

"You stay here again. I'll be back in a little while."

She walked down to the apple barn to meet Gunnar and Mike.

Chapter 9

Late Morning, Tuesday

Gunnar and Mike were wrapping up as Annie entered the barn. "How's it looking?" she asked.

He frowned. "Nothing is stolen. The farm manager confirmed that. Several vehicles have slashed tires, and some windows have been spray-painted, but other than that, nothing."

"So why hit Preston?"

"Maybe he knew the guy or at least saw his face," Mike said. He was pulling down the yellow tape that cordoned off the area.

"But he didn't," Annie said. "Preston said the guy hit him from behind."

Gunnar looked around the barn. It had doors on both ends and several side doors. "I don't get it. It's not like he could have been trapped in here."

Annie shook her head. "None of this makes any sense."

"I don't know," Gunnar said. "But if it's not kids, and it's not theft, then someone has it in for your guy."

Annie let out a frustrated sigh. "Why?"

Gunnar shrugged. "I don't know, Annie, but you need to be careful. People don't get knocked in the head for no reason."

"I can take care of myself," she said, bristling at Gunnar's paternal tone.

"If you say so." He gave her a pointed look. "The attacker left the piece of two-by-four that he used to hit him, so hopefully we can pull some prints from that. Since you're here, I need the footage from the security cameras."

"Right," Annie said.

Gunnar turned to Mike. "Did you speak to the farm manager's wife?"

"Yeah, she didn't see anyone on the property, either, but she was making breakfast and getting her kids ready for school, so that's not surprising."

"And no one else lives on the property?"

"No, just the farm manager's family and Farr."

"All right," Gunnar said. "You can head back. I'll be there as soon as I'm done."

"Roger," Mike said and left.

Annie realized she didn't have the keys to the apple barn's office, but Alejandro was there and talking on the phone. He nodded to Annie and Gunnar in acknowledgement. Annie pointed to the office, and he pulled a key and opened the door for them before walking away to continue his call.

She sat down at the computer and pulled up the security program. "Do you have something I can put this footage on?"

"I've got a drive in the car." He left to get it while Annie brought up the footage from the previous night.

Alejandro stepped back into the office. "If you don't need anything else, I need to call around and see if I can get someone out here to take care of those tires. I just got off the phone with the insurance company. Of course, they only want to talk to Preston. It's ridiculous," he said, clearly frustrated by the whole situation. "We never had a problem until a few weeks ago, and now it's getting worse."

"What changed?" Gunnar asked from the doorway. He handed Annie the drive.

"Nothing. I don't get it." Alejandro took off a straw cowboy hat and ran his fingers through his thick black hair. "I got a wife and kids here. Do I need to send them to her sister's?" Alejandro's warm brown eyes were filled with worry.

Gunnar sighed. "I can't tell you what to do, Mr. Flores. It does seem that all of this is centered on Mr. Farr, but if you're worried for your family's safety, you should do whatever you're comfortable with."

Alejandro frowned. "This is the best job I've ever had. We live on the property for free. My kids are in good schools, and my wife runs the kitchen. I don't understand why these things are happening. We've lived here for years with no problems."

"I assure you we're doing everything we can to address the problem," Gunnar said.

Annie switched cameras and continued downloading.

"I'm going to go check the rest of the sheds and make sure nothing's missing," Alejandro said.

"That's a good idea," Gunnar said. "Keep us posted."

"Right," Alejandro said grimly.

"He's freaked out," Gunnar commented to Annie while she downloaded the footage.

"Can you blame him? What's with that 'We're doing everything we can' line? You know and I know and he knows that you didn't take this seriously until Preston got whacked on the head."

Gunnar frowned at her. "That's not fair. We had no reason to think the situation would escalate. It's not like gang tags were used, and last time, there wasn't even any real damage. It was more of a nuisance than anything else."

"Well, it's certainly more than that now."

"And we'll do everything we can," Gunnar said, clearly annoyed.

Annie sighed. "I know. I'm sorry. This just wasn't how my day was supposed to go, you know?"

"Yeah, well," Gunnar said sourly, "mine either."

Annie handed him the drive.

He looked at the screen. "Why isn't that camera highlighted? Did you download it?"

"I'll get that to you later," Annie said without looking at him.

"I can wait. Go ahead."

"I need to check on Preston," she said evasively.

"Fine. I'll wait."

She shook her head. "I'm going to review that footage before I give it to you."

"What?" Gunnar frowned. "I want all of it. You never know what might be a clue."

"Actually, I do. I was a detective, too, remember. Besides, I'm better at picking stuff out of hours of boring footage than you are, so cut me some slack here."

"No way," Gunnar said. "I can't have you altering footage. That'll wreck things in court if this goes to trial."

"I'm not altering anything," Annie said. "I'll review it, and if there's anything there, I'll let you see the whole thing. In the meantime, it stays here."

Gunnar scowled at her, which was kind of scary. He was huge, and anger didn't look good on him. She could easily imagine him with a horned helmet and a battle-ax when he was angry.

"I want the footage, Annie."

"You really don't," she said quietly. "And even if you do, I'm not giving it to you until I see it first."

Gunnar's frown deepened. "What's on it?"

Frustrated, Annie blew out a breath. "Let's just say last night's date started on the porch, and there's no way I'm letting the whole department watch me making out with Preston."

"No one is going to care that you two are kissing on the porch."

"Obviously, it went past that."

Gunnar clenched his jaw. "For fuck's sake, Annie, I can keep it private."

Annie rolled her eyes. "Don't lie to me. Why do you keep forgetting I was a cop?"

"Annie—"

"I'm not putting on a show for you or anyone else in the department. I'll review it and check to see if there's anything that could tell us who attacked Preston. I'm obviously invested in this, so it's not like I'm going to blow through it. I'll watch it very carefully and let you know."

"And if I insist?" Gunnar asked.

"I'll tell you to get a warrant, then we'll talk."

He clenched his jaw again. "It's not really your footage. It's Preston's."

"I'm confident that he'll see this like I do, but there's no way I'm letting you disturb him right now to ask."

"Look at you, being the protective girlfriend," Gunnar said snidely.

"Well, I'm the protective something," she said, holding her ground.

They glared at each other.

Finally, he sighed. "Fine-toothed comb, though."

"Obviously. Like I said, I'm invested."

Gunnar frowned again. "Right."

They walked back up to the house in resigned silence. Annie couldn't worry about Gunnar's mood at the moment. It was time to check on Preston, then she would spend the rest of the afternoon combing through the video, looking for anything that might show who'd attacked him.

Chapter 10
Tuesday Afternoon

At the house, Gunnar got into his car and left, while Annie went inside to check on Preston. Chester came tearing down the stairs when she opened the door.

"Hi, buddy. Have you been keeping an eye on Preston?"

"He has," Preston said as he slowly came downstairs.

"How are you feeling?" He still looked pale.

"Like someone knocked me in the head," he said with a wry smile.

At least he still had his sense of humor. "Ask a stupid question..." Annie said.

He smiled for real. "I'm okay, considering. I'm actually pretty hungry."

"Eggs and toast work for you?"

"That would be great." Preston sat down on the sofa.

She started a fresh pot of coffee then made breakfast, filling him in on what had transpired while he was asleep. When she was done, she brought him a plate of food and a cup of coffee. "I'm going to review the footage from the camera directed at the house myself," she said.

"Oh?" he asked, raising his eyebrows. "Oh! Right." He grinned at her. "Can I watch too? We can make popcorn."

She chuckled. "I'm not watching for fun."

He rested a hand on her thigh. "It *was* fun, though, right?"

Putting her hand on his, she said, "Yes, it was. Eat your breakfast."

He smiled at her and picked up a forkful of eggs.

Annie got her laptop out of her overnight bag and sat down on the sofa then called up the camera footage from the network.

Preston leaned over and looked at the screen. "Can't you skip to the good part?" he asked. "This is boring."

"No, I cannot. I have to watch the whole thing."

He was right, though. The screen showed minute after minute of nothing. The most exciting thing that happened in the first hour was when Alejandro crossed in front of the camera, got into his truck, and drove away. A little while later, a cat walked across the frame. Even though she was watching with the footage slightly sped up, it was hard to stay focused. Preston had fallen asleep and was softly snoring on the other end of the sofa. Annie paused the video, picked up Preston's plate and mug, and went into the kitchen to fix herself some more coffee to wake up a bit. Chester followed her and wanted to go out. She watched him from the doorway as she drank her coffee.

Annie didn't have high hopes of seeing Preston's assailant captured on camera. Something about the whole situation wasn't sitting right with her. She considered whether the farm or Preston was the target. He didn't really seem like the kind of guy who had enemies. He was too sweet and earnest for that, so for the moment, she wrote off any personal aspect of the attack and considered who would want the farm to suffer.

Any number of property developers would love to buy the farm and build housing on it to turn a multimillion-dollar profit. On the other hand, as odious as she sometimes found the developers in Loudoun, she couldn't see any of them resorting to violence for the opportunity to buy land. After all, time and taxes were on their side already. Even if they managed to frighten Preston off his land, they could easily be outbid by another developer.

She supposed there could be some kind of business angle, but if so, she couldn't see it. Farr Reach was the only pick-your-own game in town. A couple of others were spread through the county, but she couldn't imagine that the people who ran them were vicious enough about the competition to attack him. Annie didn't know much about farming, though, so maybe that was a possibility. Perhaps farmers weren't as wholesome as their projected image.

The remaining possibility was particularly uncomfortable, considering it concerned Preston's siblings. He'd said his brother and sister were perfectly happy with the existing arrangement because they were successful and didn't need the money. Maybe that was true, but perhaps his siblings—one or the other or both—had something to hide.

She looked over at his sleeping form. He hadn't asked her to look into the problem. Private investigating had rules about what you could and couldn't do without a client's direction. But anyone could run a basic internet search on anyone else. She decided to start there.

Annie let Chester in and topped off her coffee. After sitting back on the sofa, she opened her laptop and minimized the camera footage. She couldn't remember what his brother's name was. Normally, she would have taken notes on the call, but she wasn't on the call as an investigator, so she hadn't bothered, and she regretted it. She didn't want to rummage through Preston's papers, so she let the brother go for the time being. His sister was called Ruby, so she typed it into the search box. But it wasn't as uncommon of a name as she had hoped. Loads of results came back. Then she remembered that his sister was married, so Farr likely wasn't her last name anymore. She racked her brain, trying to think if he'd said what her last name was, but couldn't remember. Frustrated, she reopened the camera footage and continued watching the boring image of the porch, hoping the name would bubble to the surface of her brain if she didn't try too hard to remember it.

Preston woke a couple of hours later and sat up, rubbing a hand down his face.

"How are you feeling?" Annie asked.

"Better," he said, yawning. "My head still hurts, but I have less of a headache, if that makes sense."

Annie nodded. "It does, actually. I know just what you mean."

He cocked his head at her. "Yeah, I guess you would. Thanks for staying. I'm sorry I've wrecked your day."

She shrugged. "That's okay, but I want to do something different for our next date."

He chuckled. "If you insist."

"I really do. Hospitals aren't my favorite places, and head wounds really freak me out."

Preston grimaced. "Yeah, sorry about that."

"It's not your fault."

He leaned over and looked at the image paused on the screen of her laptop. "Any idea whose fault it is?"

"No. I'm almost done, and it doesn't look like anyone came up toward the house, which makes sense, since you were down at the apple barn."

He sighed. "Well, I'm glad something makes sense, because nothing else about this does. Why would someone attack me? Why would someone vandalize the farm? Clearly, this isn't just local kids goofing off. This is serious. Someone's out to get me."

"Or run you off."

Preston blew out a breath of frustration. "Who would want to do that?"

"You tell me." She found it hard to imagine that he didn't have any theories as to who could be behind it. Perhaps it was a former cop's cynicism, but there had to be something prompting the attacks.

He shook his head. "No one. People love this place. It's a local institution. You know that."

Annie nodded. "Right. So what's changed?"

"Nothing. I mean, I'm thinking about doing the cider thing, but that's just starting. I planted a few more acres of berries last year, not that that would upset anyone. And Reverend Mary called a few weeks ago and wanted to talk about the slaves that used to live here."

"You mentioned her at the meeting. What's her deal?"

"She wanted to know about a church that was supposedly built near where the slaves lived in an attempt to keep them from leaving after the Civil War."

Annie raised her eyebrows. "Was there some kind of problem? Did you deny her access or anything?"

"No," Preston said, his expression indicating that he was mildly offended at the suggestion. "The part of the property where the church was supposed to be doesn't belong to me."

"You sold it?"

"I didn't, but someone did. The farm has been sold off in pieces over the years, so all that's left is the current ninety-nine acres."

"So, there's nothing there," Annie said.

Preston snorted. "Of course not. You thought Reverend Mary clubbed me on the head?"

"No. I'm just looking for connections that would explain why someone might be doing all of this."

He rubbed his head. "Your guess is as good as mine. Maybe the cops will find something on the other cameras. I'm going to go take some Tylenol." He stood and yawned, looking at the clock on the mantel. "Wait. Today is Tuesday?"

"Yeah," Annie said.

"Crap. Speaking of Reverend Mary, she's going to be here in a little while. I need to take a shower and change."

"What? Why?"

He frowned at her. "I can't meet a member of the clergy in my pajamas. I'll be back down in a few minutes. If she gets here before I'm ready, offer her some coffee. There might still be some cookies in the pantry."

"Sure," Annie said. As she watched him go upstairs, she couldn't help wondering how her sex date had turned into putting out coffee and cookies for a pastor. She sighed and went into the kitchen.

A few minutes later, as she was putting a plate of cookies onto the living room coffee table, Chester began barking at the front door. Annie opened the door to a small black woman in a gray suit with a white reverend's collar. She was carrying a large tote bag with a cardboard tube sticking out of it.

"Good afternoon. I'm Reverend Mary." She smiled and thrust out her hand. "I'm here to see Mr. Farr."

"Yes," Annie said, shaking her hand. "Preston will be down in a minute. Come on in."

"Are you Mrs. Farr?" the reverend asked.

"Uh, no," Annie said, ushering Chester out the front door before closing it. He would beg for cookies if she let him stay inside. When she turned around, Reverend Mary was looking at her. "I'm Annie Fitch, a friend of Preston's." She gestured toward the living room. "Can I get you a cup of coffee?" Annie felt awkward. She didn't have a lot of experience with clergy. Her family wasn't particularly religious.

"That sounds good." The reverend took a seat in one of the wingback chairs, and Annie brought over a tray with three mugs of coffee along with cream and sugar. The reverend added cream and sugar to her cup and said, "So how do you know Mr. Farr?"

"Oh, I just... I'm—"

"Reverend Mary," Preston said, coming downstairs with a big smile on his face despite the large white bandage on his head. "It's good to see you."

The reverend stood, and the two of them shook hands.

"I see you've met Annie."

"Yes." The reverend raised her eyebrows at the bandage. "Are you all right? If this isn't a good time—"

"I'm fine," Preston said. "Just a bit of an accident this morning."

Annie thought postponing was a good idea.

He smiled warmly. "Have a seat. What can I do for you?"

The reverend sat back down and smiled, but it didn't reach her eyes. "I went to see Mr. Nichols about the property I talked to you about last week."

"Good," Preston said. "I'm sure he was interested in what you had to say."

The reverend shook her head. "Not really. He said that property belongs to you then hurried me right out the door."

Preston raised his eyebrows. "That doesn't make sense. I thought he'd be very interested in your project."

"Well," Reverend Mary said, "I thought so too." She took a sip of her coffee and gave him a stern look. "So I sent my assistant to the county to resolve the issue."

"Resolve what issue?" Preston asked.

"The issue of who owns the property."

"But—"

"It turns out your property has been mapped quite thoroughly for a very long time."

"I'm sure that's true, but—"

"That property is yours, Mr. Farr," the reverend continued. "And I would very much like for the county archeologist to be able to access the land where the enslaved lived and had their church."

Preston sat with his mouth open, staring at her for a moment. "Ma'am, I swear to you that property belongs to Mr. Nichols."

"Would you like to see the maps?" the reverend asked.

He blinked. "Yes, ma'am. I think I would."

She pulled the tube from her bag. Annie moved the tray, and the reverend spread the map out on the coffee table. She pointed at a large parcel that crossed a creek along one edge. The creek bent near the corner of the property where it connected to another smaller parcel, but the bend was clearly within the bounds of the larger property that was Farr Reach Farm. "As you can see, the land in question is your property, Mr. Farr."

Preston shook his head. "This can't be right. I've known this farm my whole life, and I've always been told that the land on the other side of the bend in the creek is Cooke property, and we weren't to go over there." He rubbed the side of his head.

"By the Cooke property, you mean Mr. Nichols's property?" Reverend Mary asked.

"I think his mama was a Cooke," Preston said.

"Well, this is very perplexing," the reverend said, frowning.

Preston rubbed his head again, and Annie thought he looked a little pale.

"You know what?" she interjected. "He's suffered a pretty bad concussion, and I think we need to be done with this for today. It's not like we can solve it right now, anyway. Why don't you leave this with us, and we'll dig up any maps of the property that Preston has and compare them with what the county has to get to the bottom of all this. It's probably just a data error somewhere because the creek moved or something."

"Of course," the reverend said.

Preston sighed. "I'm sorry that this is so confusing, but Annie's right. We'll get it worked out."

"But not today," Annie said firmly. "You need to rest."

"Right," Reverend Mary said, rising. "I'll be on my way, then."

"Thank you," Preston said, standing and shaking her hand.

"I'll walk her out," Annie said. "You should lie down. You don't look so good."

Preston nodded and headed for the stairs.

Annie walked the reverend to the front door and shook her hand. "One of us will call you later this week," she said, hoping she wasn't overstepping her bounds.

"Thank you," Reverend Mary said.

When the door opened, Chester ran inside and right to the water bowl Annie had put down for him in the kitchen. She closed the door behind the reverend and watched Chester lapping up water while she wondered just what on earth was going on.

WHEN ANNIE RETURNED to the living room, Preston had gone back upstairs, so she opened her laptop and decided to slog through the last of the footage. Chester curled up next to her on the sofa, and she continued staring at the front porch. She was amused to witness Preston cleaning before she arrived. He beat pollen out of the cushions and wiped down all the furniture before going back into the house. Inevitably, she arrived on screen, and she relived the beginning of their evening. She thought they looked pretty good together, but no way was she going to let the video go to the police.

Annie paused and backed up the footage to before she and Preston went onto the porch. She watched it again, ignoring what she and Preston were doing, and focused instead on the surrounding area covered by the camera. To her considerable relief, nothing significant was going on. She hoped Gunnar's guys could find something on the footage he'd taken with him.

As she was getting another cup of coffee, Preston's phone rang upstairs followed by a garbled conversation and the sounds of him

getting up. As he walked downstairs, she heard him say, "Ruby...
But... Ruby, I'm fine. Seriously. No. I have a friend here... You don't...
Ruby... Yeah, sure. No. It's fine. If that's what you want to do." He
sighed as he came into the living room. "In your family, are you the
oldest or the youngest or somewhere in the middle?" he asked Annie.

"I'm the oldest," she said. "It's just my brother and me, so there is
no middle."

"Do you treat your brother like he's still a child?"

"We try not to, but he has Down syndrome, so sometimes."

"Oh," Preston said awkwardly. "I'm sorry."

"Don't be. My brother is a great guy. Everybody loves him," Annie said, smiling. "I take it that was your sister."

"Yes, and for some reason, I told her the truth about what happened this morning, and now she's coming out."

Annie raised her eyebrows.

"She's in Alexandria, so it'll be awhile."

"Is she coming to stay?"

"I hope not, but if I had to put money on it, I would say probably.
My guess is she'll call Emory on the way out here, then he'll call, and
I'll get an earful from him too." He sighed and sat down on the edge
of the sofa. "I must have been hit in the head pretty hard to tell Ruby
the truth. What the hell?"

"So," Annie said. "I should probably go then."

"I don't want you to, but I haven't told them we're dating, and
tonight probably isn't the time to bring it up. I'm really sorry. This
wasn't at all what I'd planned for today."

"So you've said." Annie smiled at him. "Just out of curiosity, what
did you plan?"

"Well, *plan* might be too strong of a word, but the reason I went
down to the apple barn so early was so I could get a little work done
then come back and have breakfast with you."

"That definitely would've been better than how we actually spent our morning."

He nodded and reached for her hands. "I don't suppose you'd let me make it up to you later this week?"

"I might be persuaded to do that."

"I never got around to making you dinner last night," he said.

"We got distracted."

"Yes, we did." He grinned. "So, I'll text you."

"Sounds like a plan," she said. "I should go."

"Yeah."

Chester was already waiting patiently, so she picked up her bag off the floor.

Preston held the door open for her. "Annie," he said as she stepped through.

She turned to look at him.

"Thank you. Seriously, I don't—"

She put her hand on his chest. "I was happy to help."

He nodded. She kissed him and went to her car, Chester at her heels. Preston waved from the porch as she drove away.

Chapter 11
Tuesday Afternoon

As soon as Annie got to the end of the drive, out of sight of the house, she made a note that Preston's brother's name was Emory. The phone rang as she waited to turn into traffic. She pressed the button to answer it through the car's Bluetooth speaker. "Hello?"

"Why haven't you called me already?" Celia said. "I thought we were BFF. How did it go with Preston last night?"

Annie chuckled. "Sorry. I got sidetracked. It was fine."

"Just fine? Was he weird about the scars?"

"No. He was fine. It was kind of an awkward discussion, but that was mostly my fault."

"Okay," Celia said. "Then... oh... was he bad in bed?"

"No!" Annie huffed. "He was good. This morning was when things went sideways." She
explained the day's events.

"Oh my god, is Preston freaked out?"

"He was trying to be all easy breezy as I was leaving, but yeah, I think he probably is. His sister is on her way over there, though, so at least he'll be with family."

"That's so crazy," Celia said. "I can't believe that happened."

"I know." Annie's head was still spinning.

"So, how did you two leave things?"

"He said he'd text me."

"Excellent!"

"Try not to be so giddy, will you?"

"Hey, I introduced you two. I'm allowed to be happy."

"Fine," Annie said. "Hey, listen, changing the subject, do you know anything about Reverend Mary?"

"Just what I've read in the paper. I don't know her personally, although I'd like to. She's done a lot for black history in Loudoun."

"She definitely knows what she wants."

"When did you meet her?" Celia asked. "And why didn't you call me?"

Annie explained about the property on the edge of Preston's orchard.

"Wow. But you don't think that has anything to do with what happened to Preston, right?"

"I can't see how it could, but it's weird that her interest and the vandalism are occurring at the same time. Still, she didn't strike me as the kind of person who would have radicalized followers."

"Oh, please. Asking developers to preserve black cemeteries and dwellings of the enslaved hardly constitutes radicalism."

"That's what I'm saying. Besides, she was nice. She clearly just wants access for an archeologist to look at the site." Annie drove past the county building on the way back to her apartment and wondered who Reverend Mary had contacted to get the map of Preston's property.

"Well, I hope they sort it out. Now I'm curious as to what's back there too," Celia said. "I wonder if my dad ever heard anything about that church."

"You should ask him. Maybe he knows something that will shed light on whose land it really is."

"Maybe," Celia said. "I'll give him a call."

"Great. Let me know what he says." Annie pulled the car into the parking lot next to her apartment. "I'm home, so I'm going to let you go."

"Talk at you later," Celia said and disconnected.

Annie put her things in her apartment then took Chester for a walk.

WHEN ANNIE AND CHESTER returned to the apartment, she got a glass of water and sat on the sofa with her laptop and ran a search on Preston's siblings. His sister owned her own marketing firm, Go Farr, and according to everything Annie could find about it, the firm was doing quite well. She was married to Ari Myers, an orthopedic surgeon working at Arlington hospital. The two were involved with a lot of charity work and, at least on the surface, seemed to be a great couple.

Annie moved on to Preston's brother, Emory, and typed in his name. As the search results appeared, she instantly regretted looking him up. Unlike Ruby, Emory had big legal-type problems.

"Shit," Annie said.

Chester perked up an ear at her. She rubbed his back and clicked on the first link, which was to an article in the *Portland Press Herald*. She scanned it and moved on to the next link.

A dozen or so articles addressed problems at a lakeside development that Emory Farr had built north of Portland, Maine, on land that had been a 1950s resort. He'd leveled the old cottages and built premium housing. Lawsuits had been filed concerning faulty or missing sprinkler systems. Annie had a sinking sensation that Preston didn't know about any of it. She picked up her cell phone and called Gunnar.

He answered on the first ring.

"Hey," Annie said. "I need to talk to you."

"What's up?"

"No, I mean in person and off the record."

"Oh." He paused then said, "Twenty minutes, King Street Coffee."

"I'll be there." Annie closed her laptop, kissed Chester on the head, and walked up to the coffee shop at the end of her street.

KING STREET COFFEE was empty in the late afternoon, so she ordered a decaf and took a seat outside under a shade tree that had just started to leaf out. A cool breeze was blowing, and Annie closed her eyes for a moment to soak in the beautiful weather. A few minutes later, Gunnar arrived, sporting a dark blue polo shirt and khaki pants. He lifted his chin at her in recognition before going in to get his own coffee.

"What's up?" he asked as he came back out and sat down in one of the red Adirondack chairs.

"Have you had a chance to look into Preston's siblings yet?" she asked without preamble.

"No, we've been reviewing footage from the security cameras all day."

"Right. Well, obviously, that's important, but you might want to check out his older brother sooner rather than later."

"Why?" Gunnar asked and sipped his coffee.

"Because he's involved in a shady development deal in Maine and has a ton of legal problems, which I'm guessing are costing him a fortune."

Gunnar frowned. "Why didn't your boyfriend mention this?"

"It's possible he doesn't know." She hadn't asked Preston because she hadn't wanted him to know she'd been cyber-snooping on his siblings.

Gunnar's frown deepened. "Then how do you know?"

Annie glared at him. "Um, Google?"

He snorted.

"Hey, I was looking up the family of the guy I'm dating. Not only is that perfectly legal, it's practically expected in this day and age."

"Uh-huh. Did you watch the footage from the other camera yet?"

"Yeah, there isn't anyone on it. I take it you guys haven't found anything either."

"Not yet, but we've got two more cameras to go."

Annie sighed. "But you'll look into the brother?"

"Of course," Gunnar said. "Are he and your boyfriend on the outs?"

"Why do you keep doing that?"

"What?"

"Calling him my boyfriend."

Gunnar raised his eyebrows in surprise. "I'm sorry. Is he not your boyfriend?"

Annie sidestepped the question because she didn't know how to answer it. "He's the victim of a crime. You can use his name."

Gunnar quirked his lips. "Do Mr. Farr and his brother have a strained relationship?"

"I'm not sure. He did kind of talk down to Preston during the conference call about the security system. But not in a mean way—more patronizing than antagonizing, if that makes sense. I mean, there is a big age difference."

"But you think the brother is involved?"

"Maybe. His legal problems speak to motive, don't you think? If he can convince Preston the farm isn't worth the hassle, they can sell the land, and the proceeds are split three ways."

"Which would be millions of dollars," Gunnar said. "That gives the sister motive, too, then."

"True, but she seems to be thriving, at least on the internet."

"Right. I'll look into her, anyway."

"Okay, but seriously, please don't mention we had this conversation in any sort of official report that might eventually make its way to Preston."

Gunnar took a long drink of his coffee and looked at her over the rim of the cup. He set it down and said, "You haven't talked to him about any of this?"

"No. It's a police matter. I shouldn't be involved," Annie said as she looked at a car driving past.

"And you think it might mess things up with him if he knew you pointed the police toward his brother," Gunnar said with a wry smile.

She sighed. "I'm thinking that might be bad for our relationship, yes."

"Yeah." Gunnar stood. "I was going to check out the siblings, anyway, but I'll bump them up on the priority list. Brother first."

"Thanks, Gun."

He nodded. "Yep."

Annie watched the big man walk away and smiled. Gunnar was a good guy and a good cop. He would figure out the mess at the farm.

Chapter 12
Tuesday and Wednesday

A nnie had turned her phone off while she talked to Gunnar, so on the way home, she turned it back on to find a message from a local law firm that hoped to engage her in a financial investigation on a client. Small local law firms that couldn't afford to keep a full-time investigator often called her. She'd just started to call them back when a text message came through.

Preston: *Can you come back and bring the dog? Ruby is allergic.*

Annie texted back, *???*

She won't stop fussing over me. I asked her to look for a map of the property in the study. I'm hoping that takes a long time.

Annie typed in the fingers-crossed emoji. He was probably joking about returning with Chester, but she hoped he was serious about Ruby looking for old maps of the farm. *If she finds one, let me know what it says.*

Will do. I'm going to go upstairs to pretend to be sleeping.

She sent him a smiley face emoji, and he sent one back. Embarrassed by how giddy the exchange made her feel, she shook her head. Her thing with Preston might go nowhere. The day's urgent activities being so soon after sex the previous night made it feel like they were closer than they actually were. She reminded herself not to be ridiculous. Her feelings might be nothing more than a heady combination of hormones and adrenaline. Only time would tell if they were real.

Feeling a bit more centered, Annie went back into her apartment and checked her PayPal balance to see if two of her outstanding invoices had been paid. Alas, neither had. She sent a gentle reminder to Charlie at Peterson, Prescott, and Warbler. Charlie was not the regular billing clerk. Louise, the bookkeeper, was scrupulous about payments to contractors like Annie, but she was on maternity leave. Charlie had scruples, but he was a paralegal. Covering in Louise's absence had become his problem, and he was struggling to keep up with both jobs.

The second outstanding invoice was more worrisome. Annie had been hired by a distraught mother to locate her missing son. It hadn't taken her long, since said son kept using his credit card and his phone. He also kept using heroin with no intention of stopping anytime soon. Annie had tried to convince him to at least talk to his mother on the phone but to no avail. In the end, she'd taken a selfie with him to prove she'd found him then returned with the bad news to his mother. As with all her clients, Annie had gotten the first half of the payment up front, but the mother was turning a deaf ear to her requests for the remainder of the balance. The woman blamed Annie for not bringing her adult son home, even though Annie had explained before she took the job that she wasn't a kidnapper for hire. All she could do was locate him and talk to him. She sighed and stared at her computer screen. She didn't want to take the woman to small-claims court, but she would if she had to. For the moment, she sent another less kindly reminder.

THAT NIGHT, ANNIE READ *The Hemingses of Monticello: An American Family* in bed. She and Celia were both reading it and planned to discuss it when they were done. The story of Thomas Jefferson's complex relationship with the enslaved Sally Hemings and the lives of their offspring was fascinating, but the book was densely written history. Annie's typical taste in reading was more along the lines of fiction by Margaret Atwood or John Irving or nonfiction of a lighter nature like books by Mary Roach or Henry Petroski. Annie liked it when she and Celia talked about books, but at almost eight hundred pages, her current one was slow going. Celia was way ahead of her, and she was trying to catch up.

Her phone chimed again, and she picked it up from where it was charging on her nightstand. Next to her, Chester raised an ear. Preston had texted again.

Ruby found the map. It looks like that is my property.

Wow, Annie replied.

I'm going to walk over there and have a look tomorrow. Want to come? Dinner after? I owe you a steak.

Annie sent a smiley-face emoji along with *Sure. What time?*

How about 4:30?

Okay. See you then.

Her phone chimed again a minute later. *Bring Chester.*

Another chime. *And a bag, in case you want to stay over.*

Annie replied with, *Do you want me to stay over?*

Absolutely! Preston answered.

Will your sister be having dinner with us?

God no! She's leaving in the morning.

Annie sent a winking emoji. *Good night.*

Preston replied with a kissing emoji.

She fell asleep smiling.

WHEN ANNIE PULLED IN front of the garage next to Preston's house late the next afternoon, Preston and Alejandro were talking with another man in the yard. She let Chester out of his crate but didn't bother with his leash. The property was huge, and Chester had always been good about coming when called. Since they'd rescued him, the little terrier hadn't ever strayed far from her. As she walked toward the men, the conversation ended, and Preston came over to her.

"Hey," he said, smiling.

"Hi. How are you feeling?"

"Totally fine."

"Great. No headache?"

"A little bit of one this morning, but Tylenol took care of it. Are you ready to go exploring?" he asked.

"Yep, let's do it."

"I'm glad you dressed for it. I forgot to mention how overgrown it is on that side of the creek."

Annie had put on waterproof hiking boots, old jeans, and a long-sleeved T-shirt to brave the brambles. "I figured. Though I hope I don't regret the long sleeves. It's turned out to be a warm day."

"I think you'll be fine. I hear you on the heat, though," Preston said. "It seems like spring and fall get shorter and shorter every year, so we just go from winter right into summer." He reached into the UTV that was parked in front of the garage and handed her a pair of work gloves and a sheathed machete on a wide belt made of webbing. "You'll probably want these too."

"Thanks." Annie tucked the gloves into her back pocket and put on the belt over her jeans.

He pulled a bottle out of the glove compartment and sprayed himself with it before handing it to her. "Tick spray," he explained. "Don't want you getting Lyme disease." He winked at her. "But we should still do a thorough tick check on each other when we get back."

"Uh-huh," she said, smirking.

They set off on foot toward the creek. Preston periodically pointed out features of the farm and told her about some foolishness he and his friends had gotten up to when they were kids. The creek was low and slow-moving, with bugs skimming across the surface.

Preston went first, crossing over on smooth, flat rocks that stuck out above the water. Annie and Chester carefully followed. Preston smiled and leaned over to give her a hand up the bank on the other side. They looked around. That side of the creek was so overgrown that it was dark beneath the trees.

"So, where is this old church supposed to be?" Annie asked.

Preston pushed back his ball cap and rubbed his head. The white bandage stood out against his tanned skin. "I'm not sure. The oldest map Ruby found was from the turn of the last century. It was hand drawn, but I don't think it was done by a professional with surveying tools or anything. That's the only map that shows the church, and the landmarks aren't very clear. It was definitely on this side of the creek, though. But where in all this, I'm not exactly sure."

"We just wade in, then?" Annie asked, looking doubtfully at the undergrowth.

"Yep. Follow me." He drew out his machete, ready to hack through anything.

After they entered the trees, the air was noticeably cooler. The undergrowth was thick, and heavy vines draped off a lot of the trees, which made walking difficult. Their exertion quickly mitigated the drop in temperature, and they both began sweating.

"What are these vines?" Annie asked as she helped Preston pull away the ones he'd hacked in two.

"Mostly Virginia creeper with some porcelain berry thrown in. Could be worse—could be kudzu. It's not going to be easy for the archeologist to get through this stuff, though." He looked around as they crested an embankment to find a relatively flat area. "What do you think?"

"We could split up," Annie suggested. "You go that way, I'll go this way, and we can cover more territory and hopefully find the building—or the building-shaped vines."

"All right. That sounds good. It's not like it's that big. It's probably only an acre or two. If it weren't for all this mess, we could probably see it from here."

Annie nodded and started to the left, Chester at her heels.

"Shout if you see anything," Preston said.

"Will do."

Using the machete as little as possible, Annie made her way carefully through the undergrowth over a slight rise. The machete felt awkward in her left hand, but she didn't have the grip strength in her right hand to use it. The Virginia creeper had overgrown small trees and shrubbery and made progress slow.

Chester let out an excited bark. He'd caught the scent of something in the undergrowth and went racing after it.

"Hey!" Annie shouted. "No! Get back here! Chester! No!" The little terrier ignored her and continued the chase. She struggled to hurry after him in the vines but lost sight of him as he went burrowing for whatever unfortunate creature had caught his attention.

"Chester! Chester! Dammit, dog," she muttered, continuing after him and looking to catch a glimpse of white. Then she heard a sharp cry followed by another. "Chester!" she shouted again, that time with more concern.

When he started to whimper, she redoubled her efforts to get through the undergrowth, struggling through the vines. Her leg screamed at the extra exertion. After what seemed like an eternity, she came to an open area that was less overgrown. In front of her stood an old clapboard church, boarded up and weathered, with its white paint peeling. Chester was tangled in a thicket at one end of the building. He'd probably gotten his collar snagged and panicked.

"It's okay, buddy," she said, approaching and kneeling to help him. "I've got you." But when she looked closely, she saw that he was bleeding, and a rope of rusty barbed wire crossed his body. She gasped. "Oh, buddy! What have you gotten into?"

Annie tugged gently on the wire, and Chester let out a piercing cry of pain.

"I've just got to get you untangled." It was hard to see with all the leaves and vines, but another wire was wrapped around his foot. She realized he was stuck against the stone foundation of the church. As she yanked away the surrounding brambles, she saw a boarded-up window. "It's okay," she said again, trying to calm herself as much as the dog. Chester was bleeding and whimpering, and she couldn't pull one wire without tightening another.

"Preston!" she shouted. "Preston! I need help over here!"

A barb was caught on the tag ring of Chester's collar, and he'd probably panicked to get away and tangled himself further. She unfastened his collar, and that helped. Then she tried untangling Chester's foot, but as she pulled his leg free of the wire, another barb tore through her shirt and down her arm. "Fuck!" she growled. The rusty wire seemed to be everywhere—up against the building and coiled on the ground. It seemed to grow like the vines.

The sounds of Preston coming through the trees moved closer. "Annie?" he called.

"Over here!" she shouted.

Chester was squirming and whimpering, trying to free himself, but he was making it worse.

"Don't move, buddy," she told the dog. "I'm getting you out. Don't move."

Preston made it to them. "Oh, shit!"

"I know. I know," Annie said. "Look, can you hold this piece back? Watch your hands. It's barbed wire."

"What the hell is barbed wire doing out here?" Preston asked.

"You tell me," she said.

"I have no idea."

"Well, it's all over the place. It's okay, buddy," she said soothingly.

Annie stood and pulled the piece that was wrapped around Chester's body, while Preston held the other piece to keep it from tightening. From her standing position, she could see into the church through where one of the boards covering the dust-crusted window had slipped down. She could see pews, and one had something lying across it.

Suddenly, Chester cried out and slipped free. She dropped her end of the wire and pulled him into her arms, pressing her face to his fur.

The little dog trembled.

"We've got to get him out of here."

Preston nodded. "Do you want me to carry him?"

"No, I've got him, but I might need your help getting through this mess."

"You got it."

Preston took her arm or sometimes the back of her jeans as they struggled back to the trail he'd cut through the vines and down to the creek.

In the full daylight, Annie could see that Chester was bleeding from several gashes. The red blood against his white fur made her feel panicky. It looked bad. "We've got to get him to the vet."

"Come on," Preston said. He pulled his cell phone from his pocket and made a call. "Alejandro, can you pull the truck up to the edge of the orchard near the creek? We've got an injured dog here... Okay. See you in a few."

They made their way carefully across the creek then hurried up the hill to where a dirt road connected to the central gravel road of the farm. Annie kept her hand pressed tightly over the worst of Chester's wounds, trying to slow the bleeding.

Alejandro had the truck running when they got to the edge of the orchard.

"Thanks," Preston said to him as he opened the passenger door for Annie.

The two men traded places, and Preston drove out of the orchard and down the farm road. Annie gave him directions to her vet on Market Street.

When she went in, a couple of people were in the waiting room with their dogs, but the vet tech took them right back and called Dr. Alice Tran out of another room for the emergency. Annie was relieved to see her. She'd always been good with Chester, and he liked her.

"What happened?" Dr. Tran, a slim Vietnamese woman, asked as Annie set Chester on the stainless-steel table.

Annie and Preston talked over each other, explaining, while Dr. Tran assessed Chester.

"Well, the good news is that it looks worse than it is. But he's going to need a lot of stitches." She looked at Annie. "Leave him with me while you go get your arm looked at."

"What?" Annie asked.

Dr. Tran pointed at Annie's arm. "That looks like it needs stitches too. And depending on when you last had one, you might need a tetanus shot." She grabbed some paper towels and handed them to Annie. "You should keep pressure on that."

"I can wait and go after," Annie said.

"This is going to take a while," Dr. Tran said. "I'm going to need to lightly sedate him. Go ahead. He'll be fine."

"I don't know."

"Come on, Annie," Preston said. "The hospital is our spot. They'll be thrilled to see us."

She looked at him and smiled weakly. "But you'll call as soon as I can come get him?"

"Of course," Dr. Tran said.

Annie nodded. She leaned down and kissed Chester's head. "I'll be back soon, buddy. You be a good boy."

She followed Preston back toward the parking lot, but the second they stepped out of the veterinary clinic, she burst into tears.

Preston turned and put his arms around her. "It's okay. He'll be fine."

She nodded against his chest. "He's just so little, and he's already lost an eye."

"I know," Preston said soothingly. "I know."

She leaned into him and let herself cry for a minute before pulling away and wiping her face with the back of her hand. "I'm sorry."

"Don't be." Preston smiled sympathetically. "It's been a rough day."

She nodded and blew out a shaky breath. "Yeah."

"Come on. Let's get you stitched up."

Annie shook her head. "We *have* got to find something better to do on a date."

Preston laughed. "Right?" He opened the door for her, and she got inside.

As he started the truck, Annie said, "I don't want to go to the emergency room. I'm going to call my doctor and see if she can take care of this."

"If she can't do it, I could take you to that urgent care off Battlefield Parkway."

Annie nodded and dialed her doctor's office. She explained the situation to the receptionist and waited while the woman talked to the doctor. A minute later, the receptionist returned to the phone and told Annie to come in.

"Great," Annie said and gave Preston directions to her doctor's office.

When they walked in a few minutes later, the receptionist stood wide-eyed. "Oh my god! You said it was just a cut!"

"It is," Annie said. She looked down at her arm and realized she had blood all over her shirt and the thighs of her jeans. "Most of this is my dog's blood."

"Oh no! Is he okay?"

"He will be," Annie said.

"Good. I'll let Dr. Ferris know you're here."

"Let's sit down," Preston said.

"You go ahead. I don't want to get blood on anything." She had bled through the paper towels Dr. Tran had given her.

A nurse appeared at the door that led back to the exam rooms. "Annie, Dr. Ferris will see you now."

"You want me to go with you?" Preston asked.

Though it was sweet of him to offer, it didn't seem necessary. "No, I'll be fine."

"All right." He took a seat while Annie followed the nurse.

AFTER CLEANING THE cut and giving Annie a shot to numb the area, the doctor began stitching. "No one ever thinks to come to me for stuff like this," she said happily. "It's a nice change."

"I'm so glad I could liven up your day," Annie said dryly.

The doctor smiled at her and put in the last stitch. "All right, I'll irrigate these two punctures, and you're good to go."

Annie didn't even remember getting the puncture wounds. "I don't need a tetanus shot?" she asked.

"No, you had one back in December, so you're good."

"Silver lining. Not a lot of those with being shot."

"Indeed." Dr. Ferris explained how to take care of the punctures and the stitches as she worked. "Any questions?" she asked when she was done.

"No, I'm good," Annie said.

"Great. I'm done, then. You have a good day. Get some rest."

Annie nodded and got off the examination table. "Thanks."

After she made her copayment, she and Preston returned to the vet. Chester was still sedated, but Annie didn't want to leave.

"If you want to go back, I'll go with you and get my car," she told Preston.

"No," he said. "I can wait with you."

Annie asked to go ahead and pay the bill so that when Chester was ready, they could just leave. When she got her credit card back, she and Preston took seats in the waiting area. Exhausted, Annie blew out a long breath. "What a day."

"I know," Preston said. "I had no idea there would be all that barbed wire back there."

Annie shook her head. "It's weird. It seemed like it was everywhere."

"It doesn't make any sense. Why would there be barbed wire so close to a church?" He scratched his cheek as he considered the problem. "Maybe it was a fence, and the vines pulled the barbed wire off the posts as they rotted. Then the vines grew, and the trailing wire ended up in the brambles."

"Vines can pull down barbed wire?"

"Some of them had trunks that were three inches thick. They've been growing unchecked for a long time." Preston frowned. "Well, whatever it's doing there, I'm clearing up that mess. I can't have an archeologist going back there to look at the site if it's covered in barbed wire. That's a liability nightmare."

Annie nodded. "Then I want to help."

"No, you don't. It's going to be a lot of work, and you're already hurt."

"It's just a scratch," she said. "And besides, it'll be cathartic." She really wanted a better look at what she'd seen lying on that pew in the church. It looked almost funerary, but she'd only glimpsed it for a moment through dirty glass. It might be nothing, but something about it made her uneasy. She didn't want to say anything to Preston, though, unless she was sure.

"If you say so," he said. "I'll ask Mr. Nichols if we can go through his property so that I can get a brush mower back there after we get rid of the wire. If Alejandro and Gerardo help me, clearing it won't take long."

Annie shook her head. "I don't think it's such a good idea to take a bunch of equipment back there."

"Well, I don't want to pull all that stuff by hand, Annie. That would take days."

"Yeah, but if it's a site with historic significance, shouldn't you talk to the archeologist first?"

"Maybe," Preston said, rubbing his head.

Annie shrugged. "They might have a certain way to handle things like that."

"I guess that's true. I still think I need to deal with that barbed wire before I have anyone from the county back there, though."

"We'll go have a better look tomorrow, when it's less of a panic situation."

He nodded. "That sounds good."

"Look who's ready to go," a vet tech said as he carried Chester out into the waiting area.

Chester groggily lifted his head to look at Annie as she approached and took him from the tech's arms.

"Hey, buddy," she said, kissing the top of his head. He looked a bit like a Franken-dog, with the black stitches on his leg and side standing in stark relief against his white fur.

The vet tech took a paper bag from behind the counter. "These are his antibiotics. Give one pill with food twice a day."

"Thank you," Annie said.

"Anytime. We'll call and check on him tomorrow."

Annie nodded. Preston held the door for her, and they went back out to his truck. She held Chester as they drove back to the farm.

When they got back, Annie put Chester in her car and turned to Preston. "Thank you for everything."

"I'm just glad he's going to be okay," he said.

"Still, you're good in a crisis."

He shrugged. "I know you want to get him home, but will you let me bring you dinner? I could pick up Thai food or something."

As if to answer, her stomach growled. She smiled at him. "You sure you don't mind?"

"I want to," he said. "I'll see you in a little bit."

WHEN ANNIE GOT HOME, she settled Chester into his dog bed in the living room. She was afraid to put him on the sofa with her because she didn't want him to hurt himself if he decided to jump down. He fell back asleep almost immediately.

Annie read through the instructions from the vet and left them on the counter next to his food. Despite how he looked, it could have been a lot worse. She found herself thinking again about what she'd seen through the window of the church. She'd caught such a brief glimpse, and she struggled to remember exactly what she'd seen to figure out what was making her uncomfortable. The best she could come up with was fabric stretched out on one of the pews, which didn't seem like a big deal. But something was missing—something she'd seen without really registering it.

She looked down at Chester, who had curled into a little ball and was softly snoring. A sense of relief flooded her, and she closed her eyes and sighed. She was exhausted and so filthy that she was definitely in need of a shower. With a monumental effort, she got to her feet.

Her T-shirt and jeans were a total loss, so they went right into the kitchen trash before she headed to the shower. She taped a plastic bag over the bandage on her arm, but the soapy water found every other cut and scrape she'd acquired in the woods—and it felt like there were a million of them.

When she went back into the living room, Chester was still sound asleep. She lay on the sofa and watched him breathing.

Sometime later, a knock on the door woke her. Annie wiped a hand down her face and got up. Every muscle in her body, along with the cuts and scrapes, screamed for her attention. Chester lifted his head but didn't bark or run to the door. She rolled her neck and shoulders to ease the stiffness, but she couldn't do anything about the limp as she went to let Preston in. He was standing there with a bag of food.

"Hungry?" he asked.

She nodded, not trusting herself to speak yet.

Preston stepped inside. "I forgot to ask what you wanted, so I went with the basics. Do you prefer pad Thai or drunken noodle?"

"Either," she said, sticking with one-word answers until she was fully awake.

She went into the kitchen and got them each a glass of iced tea. She drank part of hers while Preston unpacked the food.

"Come on. Let's eat," he said as he put paper plates and plastic forks on the table.

Annie decided real forks were in order, so she brought over two and sat down. Chester lifted his head again but stayed in his bed. Annie sighed. Chester always ran to the door or came over when there was food.

Preston pushed a plastic container of pad Thai toward her. "You should eat. How are you feeling?"

"Tired but okay." She piled some of the noodles onto her plate and drank some more tea. "How about you? How's your head?"

"I'm fine." Preston cocked his head at her. "Are you sure you want to go back over there with me?"

Annie nodded.

He shook his head. "Pulling that wire is going to be nasty business. You should let the guys and me handle it."

She shrugged. Feeling clearer headed, she said, "Fine. I'm not a hero. You guys can do the hard work, but I still want to go back over there. I'd like to go into that building just to see what it's like."

Preston nodded. "Yeah, I know what you mean. I tell you what. We'll walk over there again tomorrow and see if we can figure out how much wire we're dealing with. And we'll go in the old church."

"That sounds good." She looked affectionately over at Chester, who was sleeping again. "I think my little buddy can stay home, though."

"Definitely," Preston agreed before shoveling in more noodles.

They ate in silence for a while, both hungry after the day's exertions.

"I can't believe that building has been over there all this time, and I never knew it. It's like discovering a hidden room in your house or something. Does that make sense?"

"Sure. I imagine you thought you knew every inch of your property. Of course, you didn't know that was yours, so not surprising, really."

"Yeah. I don't understand that. Why was I told it wasn't ours if it was? That doesn't make sense." He pushed the container of pad Thai toward her. "You want some more noodles?"

"Yes," she said, taking a scoop. "They're really good."

"I know, right? I can't tell whether they're exceptional, or I'm just starving because we skipped lunch."

"We did, didn't we? I—"

The tags on Chester's collar jingled.

She looked over to see the terrier on his feet but still looking out of it. "Hey, buddy," she said, getting up. "You want to go out?"

The dog looked up at her then slowly made his way to the door.

"I'll be right back," Annie said to Preston before getting the leash to take Chester out.

As she stood in the vacant lot down from her apartment while Chester tried to settle on a spot, she stretched her leg, rubbed her hand, and thought about the last few days. Things with Preston seemed to be on a fast-moving train—too fast for her to be entirely comfortable, but she also really liked him. He was a solid guy, thoughtful, considerate, and good in bed. It wasn't as if they'd professed undying love or anything. They'd just spent a lot of time together recently, and nothing was wrong with that.

Chester finished, and Annie walked him slowly back to the apartment. She wondered if Preston would stay the night. If he didn't offer, she wondered if she should ask him to. Sighing tiredly, she opened the door. Since she'd eaten, she wanted nothing more than to go to bed. Preston was clearing the table when she came inside.

"Thank you for doing that," she said. "And for getting it in the first place."

"No problem," Preston said. "You must be wiped out."

She nodded and reached down to unhook Chester's leash. He went right back to his bed.

"How are you feeling?" Preston asked.

"I'm fine, just exhausted. It's been a long day."

He nodded and stepped toward her. "Do you want me to go, or do you want me to stay?"

She blew out a slow breath, not sure of the answer. To her embarrassment, her eyes filled with tears. She was exhausted and less in control of her emotions than she had been before she was shot. The brain trauma had changed her personality somewhat. She'd adapted to being less driven, and in some ways, she enjoyed the different pace of her life. Other aspects, though, like the inability to stop herself from crying, made her crazy.

"Hey," Preston said, putting his arms around her. "It's okay."

"Good grief," Annie said, pulling back. "What is wrong with me?"

"You're tired. I'll get out of here so you can go to bed."

Annie nodded. "What time do you want to get started tomorrow?"

"I need to call the guy with the bouncy house at eight to make sure that's scheduled for opening day, then I need to make sure Alejandro has everything to get the rest of the playground in order. So probably nine o'clock, but you really don't have to come."

"I'll be there."

Preston leaned in and kissed her softly on the lips. "I'll see you in the morning, then."

She nodded. "Yes, you will."

Chapter 13

Thursday

Annie slept in the next morning, as did Chester. She felt very groggy on waking, and every muscle in her body screamed—especially her right leg. The emotional stress and physical exertion of the previous day had taken a huge toll. She made coffee and started a series of stretching exercises to wake up her brain and body. When she got out of a long, hot shower, Chester had finally woken up. He seemed far more alert than he had the night before, and he devoured his breakfast. The stitches on her arm felt tight, but when she changed the bandage, the cut looked fine, so she rewrapped it and took Chester for a short walk, hoping the exercise would loosen up her leg some more.

When they returned to the apartment, her phone chimed with a text from Preston.

Issues for opening day. Can we push this back to this evening? Maybe 6:30?

Sure. No problem, she replied.

Somewhat relieved that she wouldn't have to make that trek for several hours, she got comfortable on the sofa to relax and play video games for a while. She didn't have any pressing work and could use the break. After lunch, she took Chester for another walk and did some more stretching before taking a nap.

Feeling better after relaxing all day, she went through her drawers that evening, looking for clothes she didn't mind ruining. She found an old pair of jeans in the back of her closet and added a faded T-shirt and a denim jacket that had paint on it. Then she kissed Chester on top of his head and left for the farm.

Preston was in front of the garage, talking to Alejandro, when Annie pulled in. Preston smiled when he saw her, said something else to Alejandro, then walked toward her.

"Hey." He looked her over. "Nice outfit."

"These are my nicest crappy clothes."

Preston chuckled. "I've got some long leather gloves you can use to protect your forearm, but you won't need them for anything else. We're just going to assess the situation, then if need be, the guys and I can go over there later this week. I don't want to pull them off getting the playground ready for the pickers until I have to. The first berries of the season are going to be ready pretty soon. You sure you're up for this?"

"Yeah." She followed him to an old Honda ATV that she hadn't seen before.

"We're losing daylight, so I figured we'd just drive to the creek."

"Sounds good."

She got on behind Preston, and he drove over to the bank of the creek where they'd been the previous day. The ATV provided a bumpy ride, but it was kind of fun to be wrapped around him. Before she got off, he opened a box on the back and pulled out a tool bag and a pair of leather gloves long enough to cover her forearms.

Annie pulled on the gloves and held out her arms. "Usually, long gloves like this are satin and a bit tighter, but these are nice too."

Preston grinned at her. "They're fancy to match your outfit."

She smiled back at him as they started across the creek. "I'm surprised you wanted to deal with this today, with everything you've got going on."

"Well, it's because I've got so much coming up that it's pretty much now or next winter, and I don't want to put off Reverend Mary for that long," Preston said as he shifted the tool bag to his other hand.

"I'm not sure you could if you wanted to. She seems pretty determined."

Preston nodded. "Yeah. I understand where she's coming from, though."

"Me too. A lot of history has already been lost in this county."

"True. As someone trying to hold on to some of it, I appreciate her efforts. They might even help me." He held out a hand to help Annie up the bank. Her leg was unhappy to be making the trek again. "If they find significant archeology on the property, that might be an additional draw to bring people out to the farm. And while they're here, maybe they'll want to buy a pie or a peck of apples."

Annie gave him the side-eye. "How capitalist of you." When he frowned at her, she winked at him. "But I get it. It takes money to keep this place going."

"A lot of it," he said. "But on the other hand, I know my ancestors owned slaves. The slaves made this place work, and I have their blood, sweat, and tears to thank for what I have as much as anything my ancestors did. The tragedy of that isn't lost on me. It really isn't, so I'd like to help Reverend Mary, because it's the right thing to do."

"But if it brings in a little extra cash, that would be nice too," Annie said, teasing.

"Yes, it would. Stop picking on me." He took her hand and helped her through the vines.

Her inclination was to say she could do it on her own, but the truth was that she found it harder than she had the previous day. In the fading light, it was even darker under the trees and harder to see where to step. Holding Preston's hand as she stepped through the undergrowth, she was again impressed by what a thoughtful guy he was.

When they reached the clearing and the church, Annie's good humor fell away as she remembered Chester's pained yelps. She blew out a calming breath and looked around. While the slope down to the creek was packed with vine-covered trees, the area where they were standing was much more open. The undergrowth was low, and the few trees were younger than the woods around them. The small clapboard church stood squat and weathered at one end of the clearing. Its white paint had mostly peeled off, and its small cupola was sagging. A simple rotting wooden cross hung above the entrance. The windows were all boarded up, except the one at the back, where one of the boards had fallen off. Annie looked at the ground around the church and wondered what the archeologist would be able to find. At least on the surface, the church seemed to stand alone, but it made sense that in the past, homes had been nearby.

Preston set down his tool bag and continued ahead of her to the spot where Chester had gotten tangled. He pulled at a strand of barbed wire and followed it. He only went a few feet before he reached the edge of the building. "Man, this is a mess," he grumbled.

Annie came up behind him.

"Can you follow it on that side and see if you can find an end? I'm going to go this way."

Annie traced the wire, pulling away brambles as she went, careful to avoid the barbs, but it was tricky because other strands were tangled around the one she was following.

"Aha!" Preston shouted from around the corner of the building.

"What?" she shouted back.

"I found a broken fence post with three strands of wire stapled to it. Someone had something penned up back here."

Annie walked toward him, closer to the window with the missing board. Before she could peer in, Preston came around the corner with a rotted post in his hand. The end was broken off, and barbed wire trailed behind him.

"This is more than we can deal with today. I'm going to go see Mr. Nichols and find out what was back here and how big the fence was. Then I'm going to get the guys over here to help."

A dog bayed in the distance, but she couldn't tell where the sound was coming from. She no longer had directional hearing, because she didn't hear well out of her right ear since the shooting.

"Come on," Preston said. "Let's have a look in the church."

As they walked toward the building, she noticed that the foundation looked like local stone. It didn't have a smooth finish, as though the builders had used what was to hand but weren't really stone masons.

"Careful where you step," Preston said.

When they reached the front of the building, he looked up and pushed his baseball cap back on his head. Four stone steps led up to a door that, like the windows, was boarded.

Preston made his way over to the tool bag and sorted through it then eventually came up with a crowbar. "Look," he said. "I found the key."

"Nice," Annie said.

He jammed the wedge between a board and the door and yanked. The old boards came away easily. When the door was clear, Preston turned the handle. The door didn't budge.

"Huh," Preston said. He tried again, pushing harder. He stopped and looked more closely at the door. "What the hell?"

Annie stepped onto the threshold and looked. Nails were sunk into the door, up and down both sides, securing it in the frame. "It's nailed shut?"

"Yeah. That's annoying. Maybe they had problems with kids coming back here. But it's kind of overkill to nail it shut and board it up, too, don't you think?"

Annie shrugged, but she started to feel uneasy. Someone had gone to a lot of trouble to keep people out of the building.

Preston let out a sigh of frustration and returned to his tool bag for a hammer. He handed it to her. "You start on that side, and I'll get this one."

Annie started pulling out rusty nails. Though there were a lot of them, they came out quickly. The evening was warm, and soon Annie felt sweat start to trickle down her back. Gnats began to swarm, and she swatted them away. The dog bayed in the distance again.

As they pulled nails, Preston chuckled.

"What?" Annie asked.

"I hope this is worth it. I'm starting to feel like we're looking for the Ark of the Covenant or the Holy Grail or something."

"That would definitely draw visitors to the farm."

Preston laughed. "Yes, it would."

He was pulling nails twice as fast as she was. When he finished his side, he started helping on hers.

When he had pulled out the last one, he looked at her. "Ready?"

"As I'll ever be," she said with a shrug.

Preston pushed open the door. It scraped along the floor but opened wide enough for them to easily step through. The building only had one room, and the only things that distinguished it from a house were the high ceiling and the pews. The air smelled heavily of dust and abandonment. Clearly, no one had been in there in a long time.

"Wow," Preston said, looking around the dark room.

The only light was from the doorway and the one window that had lost a board. Plain wooden benches lined the room, five to a side, but the front row had proper pews with backs. In front of the pews stood a lectern with a yellowed cotton cloth draped over it. A cross was embroidered on the cloth.

"Wow," Preston said again, looking up at the ceiling. The interior had rough plank walls. They had been whitewashed at one point but had faded and just looked like dusty wood.

Annie moved toward the front pew she'd seen from outside. Light from the window highlighted the bench. "Oh god," she whispered, feeling suddenly cold.

Laid out on the bench was a skeleton. Blond hair was still attached to part of the skull, and a dusty white blouse and a green gingham skirt covered the bones. The cloth she'd seen from the window was the skirt, stained brown. A leg bone stuck out from beneath it and led to a pair of black-and-white saddle shoes, one of which was still on the bench. The other was overturned on the floor, foot bones scattered around it.

"What?" Preston asked, coming up behind her. "Oh god!" He pulled off his ball cap and twisted it. "This is terrible."

The whine of what sounded like a riding mower came toward them, and the baying dog sounded a lot closer. A moment later, a lanky brown-and-white hound came in through the open door.

"Hey," Annie said in a friendly voice. She stepped toward the dog to keep it away from the bones. "What are you doing here, buddy?"

The hound came to her. She held out her hand, and the dog sniffed it.

"Go on, bud. You need to get out of here now," she told the dog, hurrying it toward the door.

The engine sound stopped. When she looked up, an elderly black man with neatly cropped white hair carefully stepped through the underbrush toward the doorway. He was wearing a brown suit with a white dress shirt but no tie, and in one large hand, he held a single-barrel shotgun, its muzzle pointed to the ground.

Annie froze. Blood roared in her ears, and she flinched as she remembered the blast that had shattered the door frame and peppered her shoulder with searing pain. She blinked. Annie wasn't in that madman's house in town. She was in a little church in the woods, and she could hear birdsong and the call of some insect. She could smell the dusty room around her.

"What the devil are you doing here?" the man asked in a gruff half shout.

"Mr. Nichols?" Preston asked, stepping in front of Annie and out the door.

The two men faced each other. Annie could barely hear either of them. The roaring in her ears was so loud, and all she could see was the gun. She began to tremble. The dog pressed its cold, wet nose into her other hand, and she sat down hard on one of the pews. It felt solid beneath her. She gripped the plank with both hands, feeling the rough wood and grounding herself in it.

"Aren't you one of the Farr boys?" Mr. Nichols asked, narrowing his eyes, as if he couldn't see well.

"Yes, sir. I'm Preston Farr." He pointed with his thumb over his shoulder. "Do you know what happened in there?"

Mr. Nichols's jaw dropped. He stood there staring at Preston for several moments. "You a damn fool. Come on, Lottie."

The old man stepped carefully back through the underbrush, supporting himself with saplings and tree trunks as he went. The dog left Annie and trotted behind him as he walked back to the riding mower, which was just visible through the trees. The old man started the engine and drove away. Preston stood there watching, as if he didn't quite know what to make of the encounter.

Annie tried to slow her breathing, letting a wave of nausea pass. She hadn't come face-to-face with a gun since she'd been shot the previous winter.

"What the hell was that about?" Preston asked. He looked back at her. "Are you okay?"

"Yeah," Annie said weakly.

"You don't look okay."

"I'm fine," she said, embarrassed by her response. "I just... he had a shotgun."

"But he didn't point it." He came inside and sat next to her, putting his arm around her. "It may not have even been loaded. He's really old. He probably just had it for intimidation in case someone was causing trouble back here. I'm surprised he could even carry it all the way out here. Although I guess he rode the mower most of the way." He glanced back toward the bones.

"Right," Annie said, desperate to pull herself together and think about something else. "How old is he?"

"I guess he's in his late eighties. Actually, he might be in his nineties." He got up and went over to look at the remains.

Annie blew out a calming breath and followed. The saddle shoes and gingham skirt made her think of the fifties. She wondered if Mr. Nichols was connected. "We need to call the police," she said.

"What? Wait a minute."

"Wait a minute for what? There's a body here... or what's left of one. It's obvious she didn't die of natural causes. Either way, we have to call this in." She felt stronger in cop mode.

"Shit," Preston said, rubbing his head. "Shit. I don't need this kind of publicity. As if the damn vandalism weren't bad enough."

"Come on. Let's get out of here and call the police," Annie said firmly, taking his arm. He followed her without protest.

Once outside, he sat down on the front steps of the church and pulled out his phone but didn't make the call. "The timing is just unbelievable. Emory is going to have a stroke."

"Why?" Annie asked, sitting next to him.

Preston sighed. "He called last night. Ruby told him I'd been attacked. He completely lost his shit."

"I'm sure he's just upset."

"I get that. It's not like I'm happy about it, but now, he's even less interested in ceding the development rights to the county."

"Why?" Annie asked, although she was fairly certain it was because Emory hoped to sell the farm off to solve some of his financial problems.

"He's worried no one in the next generation will want to farm it, and we'll have prevented them from selling it for serious money if we lose the development rights."

"Oh."

Annie couldn't help thinking that Emory might be right. That the family had held on to the farm as long as they had seemed like a miracle. Still, Preston hadn't mentioned Emory encouraging him to think about selling the farm, so maybe he wasn't interested in that money. She wished she'd met the guy in person. It was hard to get a feel for someone on a video conference call.

"He has a point. But he doesn't see the historic significance. He just doesn't think that way. Ruby was all for ceding the development rights before, but after this, I'm afraid she'll side with Emory."

"Not necessarily," Annie said, squeezing his arm. "We don't know who that is in there. This could be some historic case that's finally solved. It could draw positive attention instead of negative attention. You never know with these things."

"Because everyone loves to take their children to sites of historic murder," Preston said, frowning.

"People take their kids to sites of historic murder all the time. The key word is 'historic.' Look, I don't know what happened to that woman in there, but it didn't happen last week. You're worrying prematurely. Wait and see what happens." She slipped her arm around his waist. "I understand you're worried about the publicity, and I know this whole thing has you a little freaked out, but we still have to call the police. That woman died in there. It's not fair to her or whoever her family is not to report it."

"I know. I just... Why did we come over here?"

She sighed. "Because we did." She pulled out her cell phone and called Gunnar's personal number. "Hey," she said when he answered. "So, I'm in kind of a weird situation."

Chapter 14
Thursday Evening

Preston walked back to meet Gunnar so that he could lead him to the church. Annie stayed on the front stoop, listening to spring insects call as the sun sank lower. It wouldn't be long before dark. She thought about Mr. Nichols appearing with the shotgun and the chill that had come over her.

When she'd recovered sufficiently from the first time she'd gotten shot, she'd spent months talking with a therapist. Actually, she'd spent months with all sorts of therapists: physical therapists, occupational therapists, and a psychologist. *Shouldn't they be called mind therapists?* She rubbed her eyes.

But the second time she'd gotten shot, she hadn't gone back to see the psychologist. She'd learned grounding techniques to push back the trauma in order to function the first time, so she hadn't felt like she'd needed to go over those again. Suddenly, she wasn't so sure. She couldn't freeze in situations like this—which she could face at work. Although it felt more like her cop job than her PI job. She thought wistfully of all the background checks she'd been doing. She didn't miss dealing with bodies.

Annie took off the gloves and her jacket, sighed, and closed her eyes. She had a headache from pushing herself too hard for the last few days. Her doctors had cautioned her about getting too tired or stressed—or even a little dehydrated. Her brain didn't handle any of those things well due to the trauma. Annie shook her head. She was all of those things at the moment.

Opening her eyes, she stood to get a bottle of water out of the tool bag Preston had brought. No reason she shouldn't hydrate while she had the chance. As she sat drinking water, she noticed that on the other side of the church was a huge patch of purple flowers dotted here and there with daffodils. They seemed weirdly random in the undergrowth. She walked toward them and realized fieldstone markers were among the flowers and sunken places in the ground. The area was a graveyard.

Annie returned to the front stoop of the church to drink her water. She was surprised to hear someone coming through the woods. It seemed too soon for it to be Preston and Gunnar. Instead, a man came through the trees in front of her but not from the same path Mr. Nichols had taken. The man was a tall, lanky white guy, and he was carrying a gas can. He seemed familiar. When he saw Annie, he dropped the gas can and started to run.

"Hey!" she shouted and started after him, but she couldn't run with any speed on a good day, and it wasn't a good day.

She tripped and caught herself on a sapling. The guy was way ahead of her. Unwilling to risk hurting herself by trying to follow him through the trees in the gathering dark, she let him go.

Annie had just returned to the church when she heard the guys coming up the makeshift path. They crashed through the undergrowth, sounding like bears. When they reached the clearing, Preston was sweaty and dirty and looked very stressed. Gunnar came up behind him, red in the face and a little winded. Mike Hartt brought up the rear, looking cool and unbothered, as though he were just on a casual stroll. Annie had taught Mike at the academy, and he'd had that cool, calm exterior from the beginning.

"Hey," she called.

"Hey, let's see what you've got," Gunnar said, getting right to business.

"Actually, I've got a lot more than I thought. I just chased off a guy carrying a gas can." She was sure she'd seen the guy before, but she didn't want to say anything until she could place him.

"What?" Preston asked.

"Where?" Gunnar added.

Annie pointed through the trees in the direction the guy had run. The red gas can was on the ground at the edge of clearing. "He dropped the can. It might be good for prints, if he's your vandal, but I think he had gloves on."

"Mike, could you go bag that?" Gunnar asked.

"Sure thing," Mike said, trotting over to the can.

Preston and Gunnar followed Annie into the church and to the front pew, where the bones were. Gunnar leaned over and took a long, careful look. Preston stayed near the entrance. Annie felt for him. He'd had a hell of a week.

When Gunnar stood up straight, he shook his head. "Well, I guess I'm going to call the medical examiner to come collect this. What do those clothes look like to you? Forties? Fifties?"

"That's what I was thinking," Annie said.

"How could she have been here that long without anyone noticing?" Gunnar asked.

"Oh, someone knew she was in here." Annie explained about the door, surprised that Preston hadn't mentioned it on their trek up to the church.

Mike came into the church with the bagged gas can. He looked at the bones and shook his head. "Jesus."

"Come on," Gunnar said. "We should clear the scene, such as it is." They all trooped out of the little church, and Gunnar stepped away to call the ME.

Mike turned to Annie. "I've never seen anything like that."

Annie shook her head. "Me either. Not that old, anyway."

Preston was quietly twisting his ball cap.

She reached over and touched his forearm. "It's going to be okay." He looked at her with disbelief.

"All right," Gunnar said, walking back over to them. "They're on their way, but it's going to take a while. They're coming out of Manassas." He turned to Mike. "I'm going to leave you here to secure the scene and set up lights." He turned back to Annie and Preston. "Let's go back to the house, and you two can tell me what brought you here." He took a handkerchief out of his pocket and wiped his forehead. Sunset hadn't done much to improve the humidity.

"Sure," Annie said. Preston didn't say anything, and she realized he was staring off into the distance. "Hey, come on. Let's go back to the house."

He looked at her. "Yeah, okay."

She picked up the gloves and her jacket from the church steps, and the three of them started walking toward the creek. Preston and Gunnar each had a flashlight.

"What did you do to your arm?" Gunnar asked her.

"Nothing. It's just a scratch."

"Big bandage for a scratch," Gunnar observed.

"That's because the scratch took twelve stitches," Preston said.

Though it irritated her that Preston had spoken for her, it heartened her that he was paying attention. He'd been very quiet since finding the bones.

"I caught it on some old barbed wire over here yesterday," she explained.

Gunnar looked surprised. "You came over here to clean up barbed wire?" He arched an eyebrow at Annie.

"No." Preston explained Reverend Mary's request.

"So, you're saying you didn't know that church was there?" Gunnar asked.

"Right," Preston said. "I always thought this was part of Mr. Nichols's land. I've never been over here."

"Nichols is the neighbor?"

"Yes. He actually showed up today while we were in the building. I guess his dog alerted him that someone was back there."

"Did he know who that woman was?" Gunnar asked.

"I don't know. He's really old. I asked him if he knew what happened, but he didn't go into the building. Now that I think about it, he might not have known what I meant."

"How did he respond?" Gunnar asked.

"He said I was a fool, and he got back on his riding mower and left."

Gunnar looked at Annie. "That's weird."

Annie gave him a look that told him she agreed. "He had a shotgun with him. Not that he pointed it or threatened us, but he did have it."

"He's really old," Preston said again. "He's got to be in his eighties or nineties."

"And he came all the way back here? That's pretty spry for an old guy like that."

Preston nodded. "Yeah, well, he drove most of the way, and when he got off the mower, he wasn't exactly sprinting, but he didn't use a walker either. He didn't even have a cane."

"Right," Gunnar said. "I'll talk to him and see if he can shed some light on what happened in that church."

"Okay," Preston said.

"You have no idea who that could be?"

Preston shook his head.

They crossed the creek, and Annie and Preston got on the ATV to head back to the house. The engine was too loud to talk over, and Annie was grateful for the break. Gunnar got in his car and drove around.

WHEN THEY WENT INTO the house, Preston offered Annie and Gunnar iced tea.

"I'll get it," Annie said.

Preston and Gunnar took seats in the living room while she went into the kitchen.

"I was intending to come out and talk to you later today, anyway," Gunnar said to Preston while Annie filled three glasses with ice.

"Oh?" Preston asked. "Have you figured out who hit me?"

"We have some good leads. One of the cameras gave us a partial plate for a vehicle that was parked at the edge of the property. You were smart to install HD cameras. We can really zoom in on details with those."

Preston smiled at Annie as she came in with the glasses of tea on a round tray. "That was Annie's idea."

Gunnar nodded and cleared his throat. He took a sip of tea before continuing. "I wanted to ask you about your brother."

"Emory? What about him?"

"You said he and your sister didn't have any interest in selling the land because they were both doing well financially."

"That's right," Preston said.

"Only it isn't. We looked into both of your siblings, and your brother is in a world of trouble in Maine over a code-enforcement scandal for one of his housing developments."

"What?" Preston asked, setting down his tea. "That can't be right. I just talked to him. He didn't say anything about it."

"It's been going on for the better part of a year. There are multiple lawsuits as well as possible criminal charges, and it's put a lot of financial pressure on him," Gunnar continued.

Preston looked at Annie. "I don't understand what this has to do with—"

"The thing is, the police in Maine already have a warrant for his emails and phone records, so we were able to piggyback on that and ask if anything connected him to Virginia," Gunnar continued.

"Well, he talks to Ruby and me fairly regularly," Preston said.

"Yes, sir. But he also called another number in Virginia, and it was to a gentleman known to the police."

Preston shook his head. "That's not—" He looked at Annie for support. "What gentleman?"

Annie took Preston's hand.

"I'm not at liberty to say," Gunnar said.

Preston's voice rose. "What?"

"It's okay," Annie said calmly.

"No, it's not," Preston said, pulling his hand back and standing. "My brother would never—"

"The gentleman in question drives a black Chevy Colorado with a plate that has the same last number that was caught on camera. If he's the guy Annie chased in the woods, she can probably identify him."

Preston shook his head again and walked out of the room. Annie gave Gunnar a concerned look before following Preston. He had gone through the kitchen and out the front door and was standing in the yard, staring at the tree-lined drive.

"Hey," she said, stepping out and closing the door behind her.

He shook his head. "Emory wouldn't hurt me."

"I'm sure that's true," Annie said, although she wasn't sure of that at all.

"What the hell is happening?" Preston asked. He pressed a hand over his eyes. "First, my wife left, then Nannie died." He threw up his hands in exasperation. "I thought when I took over this place, it was an opportunity for a fresh start, you know? Sure, it needed work, but I was up for that, and Ruby and Emory were supportive. More than supportive—they wanted me to do it. But we found bones this morning. And now that cop says Emory is sabotaging me? I'm starting to feel like Job here." He seemed to deflate after the outburst.

Annie felt terrible for him. "What can I do?"

Preston pulled her into his arms and pressed his face into her neck. He held on tight, and she hugged him back. She was pretty sure she was in over her head with him, but it felt good to be needed. Ford had always been so indifferent about their relationship—it never seemed to matter to him whether they were on or off. He always seemed able to walk away with such casual disregard, seemingly unconcerned that she might not be there when he got back. But she always had been. She snapped back to the present, rubbing her cheek against Preston's. His skin was warm.

"You're okay," she said. "We'll get this all sorted out."

He pulled back. "I'm sorry."

"Don't be. It's been a rough few days," Annie told him.

"Still," he said, tucking an errant strand of her hair behind her ear. "I need to talk to Ruby." He looked back at the house. "How long is he going to be here?"

"Probably until the ME arrives from Manassas, so maybe another hour."

Preston frowned and looked down at his dirty, sweat-stained clothes. "I'm going to go take a shower and call Ruby. You mind entertaining your big friend while I do that?"

She smiled at him. "I think I can handle that."

He kissed her forehead. "Thanks."

When they went back into the house, Gunnar was pacing between the kitchen and the living room, talking on the phone. "Right," he said. "No hurry. The ME isn't even on site yet." He returned his phone to his pocket. "Bernie is going to come out in a little while, but she's got to get some more lights for the scene."

Preston looked at Annie.

"Bernie is the crime scene tech," Annie explained.

"You think she'll find anything after all this time?" Preston asked.

"It's hard to know if there's anything left to find, but it's worth having her give the place a once-over."

"Okay," Preston said to Gunnar. "If it's all the same to you, I'm going to take a shower and change the bandage on my head."

"No problem," Gunnar said. "I'll be out of here as soon as the ME arrives."

Preston nodded and went upstairs.

As soon as they heard the shower start, Gunnar turned to Annie. "Why are you messed up with this guy?"

She frowned. "I'm not *messed up* with him. I'm dating him, and he happens to be a nice man."

"Really? Then why is his brother paying someone to go after him? Why does he have dead bodies on his property?"

"You and I both know that body has probably been there longer than he's been alive. I don't know what the deal with his brother is, but that's not Preston's fault."

Gunnar shook his head. "I don't want to be too on the nose here, but the apple doesn't fall far from the tree."

"Oh, please, that's crap, and you know it," she said, rolling her eyes. "You're just jealous because I'm happy."

Gunnar's jaw twitched as he stared at her. "That's not why I'm jealous."

Before Annie could respond, his phone rang. He stood to answer it and walked away from her as he talked. She sat back on the sofa and stared at his back, stunned by what he'd just said.

He came back and sat on the sofa. "That was the ME. They're ten minutes out."

She wondered if he was going to pretend he hadn't said what he'd just said.

His cheeks colored slightly under her scrutiny. "I'm sorry. I just... I wish you'd told me you'd broken up with Ford."

Annie let out a soft snort. "I probably would have if it had been that cut-and-dried. It was less a case of breaking up and more a case of getting ghosted."

Gunnar shook his head. "That's rough."

"It has been."

"You could've talked to me," Gunnar said quietly.

Annie shook her head. "You've had your own problems. Besides, it took me a while to realize, you know, because of the kind of job he has."

"Right." Gunnar nodded. "And you like this guy?"

"Yeah. He's nice. Easy to be around."

"Huh. And what about this situation with his brother? Do you think he'll press charges?"

"He doesn't have to. He was assaulted."

Gunnar held up a palm. "You and I both know that if he isn't a cooperating witness, the DA isn't going to prosecute. It'll end up being case closed exceptional."

"That's crap," Annie said. "You saw what that guy did to him. He could have cracked his skull. He could've killed him."

"I know that, and I know you're upset. But there's what you know to be true and what you can prosecute—and if Preston isn't willing to cooperate against his brother, there isn't much we can do."

Annie shook her head, disgusted that the guy who'd assaulted Preston would likely walk. She was fairly certain Preston wouldn't want to embroil his brother in a criminal trial. "What about gas-can guy? If he's the same guy who hit Preston, was he going to burn the church, or was he just approaching the farm from the other side of creek? Are we sure Emory is behind all this? And if he is, what the hell does he know about those bones?"

Gunnar cleared his throat. "Look, I don't know how old those bones are going to turn out to be, but if it's like we think, then there aren't going to be quick answers coming back from the lab. I'll walk the ME over to the church, then I'll drop in on Mr. Nichols and see if he can't shed some light on this. Then maybe we can close this, and your boyfriend won't have to worry about who the dead woman was. As for gas-can guy, come by the station in the morning, and you can look through a photo lineup."

Annie nodded. "Right. I guess that's something, anyway."

His phone rang. "I've got to get this. Try to take it easy," he said before going out the back door.

Annie sat on the sofa for another moment, trying to collect her thoughts before going upstairs.

The door to Preston's bedroom was closed. She started to knock but heard him say, "What do you mean, you're almost here? You can't just—what? No. Ruby... that isn't a good idea. Take him to your house. I'll meet you guys there. Fine, then how about Reston? Because I don't want him anywhere near here! Can you just trust me on this? Meet me at the town center in front of the movie theater. Good, then. Yeah, bye. Damn it!"

Annie tapped cautiously on the door. "Preston?"

"Yeah, come in."

She opened the door. He was standing in the middle of the room with a towel around his waist and his phone in his hand. She smiled at how pale his chest was compared to his arms and face. He had an impressive farmer's tan.

"Is everything okay?" she asked.

He tossed his phone onto the bed. "Is that cop still downstairs?"

"He's outside, taking a call. Why?"

"My crazy brother decided to get on a plane and come down here, and now he and Ruby want to meet. She was going to bring him here. Can you imagine what a clusterfuck that would be?" He sat on the edge of the bed and rubbed his head. "What the hell am I supposed to do? What if that cop was right? What if my brother hired a guy to vandalize the farm? What if he paid him to hit me?"

Annie sat next to him. "He's not my brother, so I'm inclined to say have him arrested."

He looked at her with tear-filled eyes. "I can't do that. Emory's always been there for me. He stepped in to do all the dad stuff after our dad died. I can't just... How could he..." He shook his head and covered his face with his hands.

Putting her arm around him, Annie pressed her cheek to his shoulder. "What can I do?"

He blew out a sigh of exhaustion and held her tight. "Nothing. I've got to go talk to them." He let her go and shook his head again. "How am I even going to say any of this?"

"All you can do is tell them what happened and what the police think and see what he says."

"Shit," he said softly.

Annie kissed his cheek. "I'm so sorry." She felt terrible for him but wasn't sure she could do anything about it. She wished she could be a fly on the wall for the conversation with his siblings.

"It's okay. I'll be fine. Don't worry about it. I'll text you later."

She pulled back. "I guess I should get going, then."

He nodded. "Me too. I just need to get dressed."

She showed herself out. As she walked to the car, Gunnar put his phone into his pocket.

"I need to head out," she told him.

"I'm going back over to the church, anyway. Bernie should be here in a few minutes."

"Great. I'll talk to you later, then."

"Yep." He waved as she drove down the drive.

Chapter 15

Thursday Night into Friday Morning

After answering some client emails and having a simple dinner, Annie settled on the sofa to read with Chester beside her. She wasn't up for heavy history and was too cheap to rent a movie just for her, but she wasn't in the mood for television either. She opened Greg Keyes's *The Infernal City*, a book set in the *Elder Scrolls* video game universe. She'd read it before but found it comforting to return to the game world where she'd spent so much time, especially at the moment, when she didn't have the energy to actually play. Like many fans of the series, she was desperate for a new game, but nothing but a teaser trailer had been released, and it was tantalizing but not terribly informative. She sighed and read on. Chester curled up by her crossed ankles and nodded off.

Annie was deep into the story when a knock on the door startled her. Chester jumped up, barking.

"That's enough," Annie said to him. She got up and opened the door.

Preston stood on the patio, looking as lost and forlorn as she'd ever seen anyone look. "Hi," he said, not quite meeting her eye. "I'm sorry. I know it's late."

Annie stepped back from the door. "Come in."

"I should have texted before I came over. I'm sorry for just showing up."

"Don't be. What happened?"

"We met in Reston Town Center. Ruby wanted to go to dinner, but I couldn't sit in a restaurant with him and not say anything, so I told them what that cop said right there in front of the theater." Preston rubbed a hand over his head. "Christ, he... he just started crying." His voice cracked. "I've only ever seen Emory cry once—at Dad's funeral." He shook his head. "I can't believe this." A tear slipped down his cheek, and he brushed it away. "I'm sorry. I shouldn't have come over here. I'm sorry." He turned to leave, but she caught his hand.

"No, it's okay."

She put her arms around him, and he seemed to melt into her and held her tight. They stayed that way for a while until he pulled himself together. When he finally loosened his hold, Annie stepped back.

"Take a seat." She went into the kitchen and pulled a bottle of Jameson from the cabinet under the sink and poured two fingers into a juice glass and brought it over to him.

Preston took a sip. "Thanks." He stared at the glass. "Emory kept saying we didn't understand and that no one was supposed to get hurt. Ruby is..." He shook his head. "Apoplectic. I've never seen her that angry. Emory was supposed to stay with her and Ari, but she told him to call a cab to take him to a hotel, then she just left, which was probably for the best. God, she was angry."

"Did you ask about the guy with the gas can?"

Preston shook his head. "We didn't get that far. Ruby stormed off, and Emory just kind of stood there. Fuck." He took another swallow of his drink. "He swore he never told that guy to hurt me. He was just supposed to cause damage around the farm to make it more appealing for me to get out from under it."

"Do you believe him?" Annie asked.

"I don't know. I think I do. Ruby threatened to call the cops." He took another drink of whiskey.

"I can understand that," Annie said.

He shook his head again. "He's got a wife and three kids, Annie."

Like a lot of criminals, Annie thought. "Okay."

"I can't put him in jail. He's my brother."

"What about Ruby?"

"She'll calm down. She loves Emory's kids. She and Ari don't have children. Ruby took my niece to Paris for her sixteenth birthday last year. Honestly, I don't think she could do that to them."

"What about the bones?"

"No." Preston rubbed his head again. "I told you—we didn't get that far." He finished off the whiskey. "I'm sorry to dump all this on you. It's too soon, I know, but you're easy to talk to. And you already know what happened because you were there. I'd have to explain so much to anyone else."

Annie smiled at him. "I don't mind. At least this way I know how you are in crisis." But she wanted to know if Emory had sent the guy with the gas can, because if he had, then he probably knew the bones were in that church.

He snorted a laugh. "Yeah, I guess that's something."

Annie shrugged and smiled at him sympathetically. "Sometimes, it's everything. My father always says you test character like you test metal: apply heat."

Preston nodded and laced his fingers with hers. "You're pretty good in a crisis yourself." He smiled at her. "And you're beautiful."

She shook her head. "I'm a bit banged up for beautiful."

"Nah," he said. "You're perfect."

She chuckled. "Now you're just trying to get me into bed."

He raised his eyebrows hopefully. "Is it working?"

"What do you know... it is." She pulled him up and led him back to her bedroom.

ANNIE WOKE TO THE CRACK of a shotgun blast and searing pain. She sat bolt upright in bed, gasping, as adrenaline coursed through her veins—more effective than caffeine at bringing her fully awake.

"Hey." Preston's voice came from behind her, and she jumped. "Are you okay?"

She turned to him, trying to get her heart rate and breathing to slow down. Nodding, she said, "Just a nightmare. Sorry if I woke you."

He scratched at the stubble on his cheek. "You didn't. I woke up about an hour ago and couldn't fall back asleep. You want to tell me about your dream?"

She shook her head, got out of bed, and went into the bathroom to splash water on her face. Several weeks had passed since she'd had a nightmare. She blew out a calming breath and went back to bed.

Preston had propped the pillows against the headboard and was waiting for her. "Better?" he asked.

"Yeah," she said, climbing back into bed.

"Come here."

She slid over next to him and rested her head against his chest. Preston put his arms loosely around her and kissed the top of her head. He didn't say anything, just held her. She couldn't help but think about all the times Ford had done the same thing and wondered where he was and if he was really done. After all those years as lovers and friends, that he would walk out with no explanation seemed impossible. Yet there she was, in bed with Preston, with no idea what country Ford was even in—much less how he felt about her. The lack of closure was what ate at her. Cutting her off like that was cruel. Even if he didn't love her anymore, she didn't think she deserved to be cut adrift with no explanation.

Preston's breathing shifted, deepening. He'd fallen asleep. She kissed his chest softly and closed her eyes. He was a good man—kind and worthy of her affections. She could do a lot worse.

ANNIE AWOKE SOMETIME later to the sounds of someone moving around in the kitchen and the smell of coffee. She wanted to go back to sleep. Though she wasn't sure what time it was, it was too early.

A few minutes later, the mattress sank, and she opened one eye to find Preston sitting on the edge of the bed, looking at her.

He set a cup of coffee on the nightstand. "Hey."

She made a noncommittal noise and reached for the coffee.

"You want something to eat?" he asked. "I need to get back to the farm, but it would be nice to have breakfast first."

Annie nodded.

He gave her an odd look. "Are you okay?"

She took another sip of coffee and rubbed the back of her neck. Every muscle in her body was feeling the effects of the last few days. Her shoulder, in particular, ached from overexertion, and her right leg was very tight. She didn't want him to see her moving around like an old lady. "I'm fine," she said slowly, careful to enunciate.

"You want to walk up to Leesburg restaurant or eat here?"

When she tried to think what she had on hand to eat, she couldn't remember the contents of her refrigerator. She realized she'd been thinking about it too long when Preston prompted, "Annie?"

She sighed. "I need a minute," she said thickly.

"Oh. Sure," he said and went back into the living room.

Annie eased out from under the covers, sat on the side of the bed, and finished her coffee. When she was done, she pulled on some clothes, ran a brush through her hair, and walked slowly into the living room, with Chester at her heels. Preston was pacing around. He stopped when he saw her.

She sighed and stepped into the kitchen to pour another cup of coffee. Trying to push down her embarrassment, she reminded herself that this was her life, and she needed to own that.

He stood at the bar that separated the kitchen from the living room. "Are you okay?"

She took another sip of coffee and leaned against the counter. "Mornings aren't my best time. The brain trauma makes it hard to wake up, and my leg tightens up overnight. It's not usually this bad, but I've overdone it the past few days."

"And that's my fault," Preston said, concern wrinkling his brow.

Annie shook her head. "No, it's not. I'm a big girl. I make my own choices." She couldn't meet his eyes. Pity wasn't something she could stomach.

"I tell you what... why don't I go get us some breakfast and bring it back?"

"That'd be great," she said.

"Preference?"

"Shoe's Cup and Cork on King Street has good sandwiches."

"What do you want?"

"Whatever you're getting is fine. Actually, I'm supposed to take my neighbor lunch today. Could you pick up a couple of chef salads too?"

"Sure," he said.

"Let me get you some cash."

"I think I can handle it," he said. "I'll be back in a little bit."

Annie was relieved when he left. She took some aspirin then took Chester out to pee. She fed him then got into the shower. Normally, she wished she had a bigger shower, but that day, she was grateful that it was small enough that she could lean against the wall and let the hot water ease the stiffness in her muscles.

By the time she got out of the shower, the coffee and aspirin had kicked in, and she felt better and much clearer headed. A knock came at the door, and she let Preston in.

"You look better," he said, setting the bag of food on the counter.

"Yeah, sorry about earlier," Annie said. "I'm not used to having anyone here when I wake up." That wasn't exactly true. Ford had stayed over all the time, but he'd been there through her entire recovery, so it hadn't bothered her for him to see her in the morning.

Preston tucked a strand of damp hair behind her ear. "I'm sorry. I kind of invited myself to stay over last night."

She wrapped her arms around his waist. "I enjoyed having you."

"Good." He winked at her. "I enjoyed having you too. Now, let's eat. I'm starving."

"Me too."

As they settled down to enjoy their breakfast sandwiches, Annie asked, "So, what's on your agenda today?"

"I've got the guy with the bouncy house coming this morning, and I guess I'll have to deal with Emory at some point."

"Yeah," Annie said, looking up from her sandwich. "Have you decided what you're going to do?"

He nodded. "Nothing."

She raised her eyebrows at him.

"It's over. I'm not selling the farm. Ruby will side with me on that. Emory's been caught out. He's ashamed and embarrassed, and that's that. He'll just have to figure out a way to deal with his legal problems on his own."

"You sure that's the right course?" Annie asked. She didn't want to nag, but it seemed so wrong to just drop it, not to mention that they still didn't know if he was responsible for the gas-can guy.

"Yeah. I know you don't know him, so I understand why you'd be worried about that, but seriously, it's okay. It's over."

"Except I've got to go look at photos this morning to see if I recognize the guy with the gas can."

"Shit," Preston said quietly.

"And if he's the same guy that owns the vehicle with the partial license plate from the cameras, what then?"

Preston wiped a hand down his face.

"It seems pretty clear he was planning on burning something, but the question is, What? I mean, if he was planning on burning down the church, that implies your brother knew what was in there, but if he was just approaching the farm from the side with fewer cameras, then... well... that doesn't sound like your brother called him off after he hit you."

Preston shook his head. "Fuck. I don't know what to do. I can't just... Shit."

"How would you feel if I did a little digging?"

"Aren't the police handling it?"

"Sure, but the bones will go off to the lab, and they won't get a report for months. Meanwhile, you're stuck not knowing. Besides, in order to identify them beyond the basics of age, gender, et cetera, they need something to compare them to. The likelihood of DNA already being in a police database from a historic crime is really slim."

"But I thought that big cop said he'd go talk to Mr. Nichols."

"I'm sure he will," Annie said. "And if Mr. Nichols knows something, then he might very well solve the case. But if Mr. Nichols doesn't know anything, then he'll likely let it go until he gets the lab report. Realistically, it's probably going to end up a cold case. If those bones really are as old as the clothes imply, the odds that anyone connected can be found aren't good."

Preston sighed. "Well, let's see what he comes back with. I don't want you wasting your time on this."

"I wasn't suggesting I stop work on anything else," Annie said. "But I can give it more time than Gunnar can. I can call him later, if you'd like."

"Sure." He looked at his watch. "I need to get going." He gave her a quick kiss on the lips and got up but stopped and looked at her. "What would looking into it entail? How would you start?"

"I'd probably start by talking to the Nichols family to find out if any of them know anything about that church. I'd also like to talk to your family to see what they know about it."

"None of us knows anything about it," Preston said.

"I don't mean your brother and sister," Annie clarified. "I mean aunts, uncles, and other older relatives."

"Oh. I guess you could talk to my uncle."

"Great. Where does he live?"

"DC. But I don't have time to take you out there. The berries are coming in now. I've got about a million things to do to get ready, and I've lost a lot of time lately."

"You wouldn't have to go with me. I actually have a client I need to see in DC. I could stop by after."

"I should probably call him first," Preston said, his forehead wrinkling in concern.

"If you want, or I can. I'm not planning some 'gotcha' interrogation. I'm just going to ask if he remembers anyone going missing or running off—rumors, gossip, that sort of thing. I need a starting point, then I can start combing through old newspapers, looking for articles. I could even try the police archives to look for missing persons, but I need a rough date as a starting point."

"Sure, call him." Preston looked relieved, and she wondered what he'd thought she'd intended. He pulled out his phone and shared his uncle's address and phone number with her.

"Great. Thanks," Annie said. "I'll let you know if I find out anything."

Chapter 16

Friday Morning

After Preston left, Annie texted Gunnar: *Are you at the station?*
Yes, he replied.
I'll bring coffee.
Gunnar sent a thumbs-up emoji.

She made the coffee herself and put it into a Thermos. After a short drive to the other side of town, she walked into the police station and signed in at the front desk.

Officer Jack Stone sat behind a long reception desk with a sliding bulletproof window, which was open. "How's it going, Little Big Man?" he asked.

Leesburg police officers didn't officially have partners, but she and Gunnar had worked a lot of cases together. Gunnar, for obvious reasons, had been called "the Big Man" since he'd joined the force. When Annie had made detective and started working with him, her nickname followed. As the only female detective back then, it had irritated her, but she'd never said anything. She'd eventually taken it in stride. "Just fine, Jack. How's it with you?"

"Still married, so it's all good," Jack joked.

She smiled. "Fourth time's the charm, then?"

"I guess." He laughed. "You here to see Gunnar?"

Annie nodded. She held up the Thermos of coffee. "I thought I'd bring him something decent to drink before the swill you guys make eats right through his stomach."

"Ridiculous," Jack said, laughing. "That stuff puts hair on your chest."

"And now you know the real reason I left."

Jack snorted. "Go on back, then. You know where he is." He released the lock on the door.

She stepped through to a long hall that led to the area where the detectives worked. New framed awards for the station along with some informational posters had been hung on the white walls since she'd last been there. Otherwise, the station looked like any other office building. She smiled, thinking about all the gritty police stations featured on TV shows. Leesburg's was clean and quiet, which, as far as she was concerned, was exactly what a police station should be. Gunnar was hanging up the phone when she entered the large room full of gray-and-black corporate-style cubes.

"Hey," he said, standing in his corner cube. "Let's go sit in the conference room."

Annie followed him back down the hall.

He took a seat in one of the rolling chairs at the big table.

"These are new," Annie commented.

"Yeah. It's about time we got new chairs around here. The old ones were falling apart."

A cabinet stood in a corner of the room, and on top of it were a coffeemaker and several Styrofoam cups. She took two and sat down to pour them coffee from her Thermos.

"Ooh, you brought the good stuff."

"I decided I couldn't handle station coffee this morning."

"I hear you."

Annie chuckled, and they sipped their coffee. "Did you get a chance to speak to Mr. Nichols yesterday?"

"I walked over to his place after the ME finished up. It's not far from the church to his house—only like a quarter mile."

"What did he say?"

"Nothing. When I got to the house, his daughter was there, frantically looking for his wallet. Apparently, she takes him out for an early dinner every Thursday. When she got there yesterday, he was in distress. She called 911, and they took him to the hospital. She forgot to grab his wallet with his insurance card, so she'd come back to get it. That's when I showed up."

"Oh," Annie said. "How's he doing?"

"Not well."

Annie sighed. "I'm sorry to hear that. I was hoping he'd be able to shed some light on the bones in the church."

"Me too. We should get an age on the bones pretty quick. As for an identity, the likelihood—"

"I know." Annie shook her head. "I know."

"I'm sure your boyfriend is eager for answers, but I can't really focus on this right now, unless those bones turn out to be more recently deceased than they appear. I'm on a gang taskforce that's taking up huge amounts of my time, and between that and my regular caseload—"

"It's okay. I talked to him last night to try to set reasonable expectations."

"Good. Obviously, as soon as we hear from the lab..."

"I know you'll do your best," Annie said. "In the meantime, I thought I might poke around a bit and ask some of the older residents like Miss Mabel to see if they remember anything from back then that might be relevant."

"Be my guest. It's not like this is exactly an active investigation."

"Obviously, I'll share anything relevant."

"Great," Gunnar said. "Keep me posted." He sipped his coffee then picked up a folder on the other side of the table. "On the other hand, the vandalism *is* an active investigation. You ready to look at the photo lineup?"

"That's why I'm here."

"I pulled some known offenders with license plates that have a matching last number to what we saw on the camera." He opened the folder.

Annie nodded and stood to look at the photos arranged in groups of six. In the third grouping, she found her guy. "That's him. I knew I recognized him."

Gunnar looked at the guy. "Oh yeah, Ernie Henley. Repeat offender. Vandalism, theft, and now assault."

"Moving up in the world," Annie said grimly.

"Yep, we'll pick him up." He looked at her as she sat back down. "How are you feeling? You seem kind of... stiff."

"I'm fine," she said. "Might have overdone it a bit, running around in the woods."

"Should you be dating a farmer?" Gunnar teased. "Seems like a lot of manual labor."

She rolled her eyes. "I'm not exactly working the fields."

Gunnar chuckled and shook his head.

"How are things with you, then?" Annie asked.

He shrugged. "Still getting divorced."

Annie grimaced. "How's it going?"

"Surprisingly well. Ellen is being exceptionally reasonable. I think she's seeing someone and just wants this to be over."

Annie felt bad for him. Gunnar was a good guy. She'd never understood why he was so unlucky in love. "What do you want?"

He stared into his coffee cup, like the answer might be there. "I don't know. I guess I just want it over too. I can't fix it, so there's no point in prolonging the inevitable."

"No," Annie said. "As soon as possible is probably for the best."

"Yeah." He seemed to sag in defeat, making him look smaller.

She leaned over and squeezed his forearm. "I'll get out of your hair. Call me if you want to talk. I'm around."

He gave her a weak smile. "Thanks. I appreciate that."

"Any time."

He wouldn't call. They both knew that.

She stood to leave, and Gunnar got up and walked her to her car. She used the key fob to open the door.

It chirped, and Gunnar said, "Annie, be careful. You don't really know this guy, and that brother of his is seriously shady."

Annie nodded. "Relax. It's not like I'm marrying him."

"Still." Gunnar opened the car door.

"I know," Annie said, getting in. "I'll be careful."

"Good," he said and shut the door.

AS ANNIE DROVE HOME, her phone rang. A temp agency she worked with wanted her to do basic background checks on ten potential employees. Jobs like that weren't terribly interesting, but they paid well and didn't take long. The work was really just a database search to confirm the applicants were who they said they were and didn't have outstanding warrants or liens against them. She accepted the job via email and spent the rest of the morning working on it.

At noon, she took a break, retrieved the salads Preston had bought for her at Shoe's, put Chester on his leash, and headed to Miss Mabel's two-story brick townhouse. A remnant of the street's earlier times, the house was narrow and had three bedrooms, one bathroom, and a long, skinny backyard. Miss Mabel and her husband had raised their family there. At seventy-nine, Miss Mabel still lived in the home—assisted by her children and neighbors like Annie.

Miss Mabel had opened the windows to enjoy the warm breeze. Typical of Virginia, what was lovely spring weather one day could either be freezing cold the next day or so hot she would have to turn on the air conditioner. Annie knocked, and after a minute or two, Miss Mabel opened the door.

"Hello, Annie." She leaned on her cane and bent down to pet Chester. "Hello, sweet boy."

Chester wagged his tail, and they went inside.

"How are you doing today, Miss Mabel?" Annie asked.

"I'm fine, child. I've got some iced tea, if you'd like some."

"I'll get it. Would you like some too?"

"That'd be good." Miss Mabel took a seat at the kitchen table. Annie brought over two glasses of tea and set out the salads. The back door was open, letting in the light breeze. Normally, Chester would run out and sniff around the fenced yard, enjoying being off leash, but food was on the table, and Miss Mabel was a soft touch.

"Is this one of them Shoe's salads?" Miss Mabel asked, grinning. "You know how I like them."

"Me too," Annie said.

They sat at the table and ate their salads while Chester sat patiently by Miss Mabel's side. He was periodically rewarded with a sliver of turkey.

Annie took a drink of her tea before she asked, "Do you know Mr. Nichols?"

Miss Mabel considered for a moment. "George Nichols?"

Annie realized she had no idea what Mr. Nichols's first name was. "I'm not sure. He's elderly and lives on the other side of the creek from Farr Reach Farm."

Miss Mabel nodded. "That's George Nichols. I reckon I do know him. He dated my sister Ethel in high school all through their senior year. We thought they was going to get married, but that summer, George just showed up one day and told Ethel he was sorry, but he was going into the army. Broke Ethel's heart."

"Just out of the blue?" Annie asked. "Poor Ethel."

"As far as I know, he'd never mentioned it before." Miss Mabel slipped another little piece of turkey to Chester, who politely took it.

"When was that?" Annie asked.

Miss Mabel cocked her head and pursed her lips. "Let me think. Ethel graduated in forty-three, so I reckon it was June or July of that year."

"Wouldn't he have been drafted, anyway?"

"No, child. Back then, boys didn't get drafted until they was twenty-one. George would have only been seventeen or maybe eighteen."

"I take it your sister didn't wait for him," Annie said.

"No. About eight months after he left, she met Terrance. A year later, they got married. He got a job on a road crew in Fairfax, and they moved out there. The army trained George as a mechanic, so when he came back from the war, he opened that garage and sold gas and fixed cars. I believe his youngest daughter, Opal, runs it now. He and his crazy wife named all their girls after jewelry—Pearl, Ruby, and Opal. Ruby died, though, when she was still little. Sad to lose a child like that."

Annie nodded. "That *is* sad."

Miss Mabel peered over the top of her eyeglasses. "Why you asking about old George Nichols, anyway?"

"I was over at Farr Reach the other day and met him briefly."

"What were you doing over there?"

"I've been dating Preston Farr," Annie answered, feeling herself blush. There was no point in denying it to Miss Mabel. She would ferret out the truth, anyway.

Miss Mabel's jaw dropped, and she sat back in her chair. "When did you break up with Ford?"

Annie sighed. "He left to go back overseas a while ago. He made it pretty clear he wasn't interested in settling down, and I haven't heard from him since."

Miss Mabel leaned over and squeezed Annie's hand with her gnarled fingers. "I'm so sorry, child."

"Don't be. I'm fine. Preston is nice. We're having a good time."

Miss Mabel frowned. "You sure he's nice?"

"What? Why?"

Miss Mabel shook her head. "Them Farrs. My mama was their cook for a while. She always said the Farrs didn't know slavery ended, and Emory Farr thought he owned everything he could see. She got another job just as quick as she could."

"When was that?" Annie asked.

"She was young," Miss Mabel said. "She and Daddy weren't married yet."

"So that was probably Preston's grandfather or maybe even his great-grandfather," Annie said.

Miss Mabel gave her a stern look. "That's true, but you know them apples don't fall far from the tree."

Annie chuckled. "He's nice. I promise."

"Well, at least he's not one of the Emorys."

"What?" Annie asked, smiling.

But Miss Mabel was serious. "The Farrs named all the first sons Emory, and every one of them mean. That's just as crazy as George naming all his girls after jewelry. Course, I guess that makes sense, since they're related."

"Who's related?" Annie asked, confused.

"You didn't notice?"

"Notice what?"

"George Nichols so high yellow he's practically white."

Annie wasn't sure how to respond. "Oh," she said. "Um..."

Miss Mabel raised her eyebrows and shook her head. "The Farrs used to own the Nicholses. Well, actually, they weren't Nicholses then. I think they was Cookes, but that land George lives on used to be part of the Farr plantation."

"But how does that make them—"

"Annie." Miss Mabel shook her head. "The Cookes got that land because they was really Farrs."

"Oh," Annie said awkwardly, even more uncomfortable than she'd been before. "So, one of the Cooke women—"

"Had Emory Farr's children." Miss Mabel pursed her lips in disapproval. "Rumor was that the Cooke woman and Emory Farr's wife were half sisters. Shameful. Just shameful. You be careful with that boy. He's got evil in his people."

Figuring since she'd gone this far, she might as well continue, Annie asked, "Do you know anything about the church that's between the two properties?"

Miss Mabel shook her head. "No church over there I ever heard of. Who told you there was a church?"

"Reverend Mary asked Preston if they could bring the county archeologist over to look at the property because there was supposed to be a community of enslaved people there. And they had a church." She continued, "It's there. Preston and I went and found it."

"That makes sense," Miss Mabel said. "Lot of slaves on that farm, when it used to be a whole lot bigger."

Annie nodded. "Preston said a lot of it has been sold off over the years."

"I'm surprised they got any land left, the way developers do around here."

"True. But he's trying to keep it intact. He doesn't want it turned into yet another luxury housing community."

Miss Mabel made a noncommittal noise and continued eating her salad.

Chapter 17
Friday Evening

After lunch, Annie took Chester for a long walk and mulled over what Miss Mabel had said about the Farrs and the Nicholses. She wondered if Preston knew he might be related to Mr. Nichols. It seemed like something he would have mentioned when they were looking for the church, but maybe not. Perhaps Preston didn't know or didn't want to know.

When she got back to her apartment, she finished the background checks she'd started earlier and wrote the reports, which were really just five-page forms to fill out. By four o'clock, her work was complete.

Annie considered her options for the rest of the day and decided to call Preston's uncle. He didn't pick up, which she'd expected, since he wouldn't know her number. She left a message explaining who she was and asking if he would mind talking about the farm with her. The farm in general seemed like a safer topic than mentioning the church and the bones over the phone.

She ended the call and texted Celia. *What are you doing?*

Making soap.

The hell? Annie typed.

The phone rang in her hand. Celia was calling.

Annie answered it. "Seriously?" she asked without preamble.

"Yes. I ordered half a pig. It came with a lot of fat, so I rendered it into lard yesterday. But it's more lard than I'll use in a year, so I decided to make soap."

"With lard?" Annie asked. She wasn't exactly sure how soap was made, but she wasn't aware that it involved lard.

"Yes. And lye."

"Isn't lye caustic?"

"Yes, but not when you turn it into soap," Celia answered in her patient voice.

"Isn't drain cleaner made of lye?"

"Yes, but there's a chemical reaction between the lye and the lard, and you get this really nice soap."

"If you say so," Annie said. Her soap came from the grocery store.

"I'll give you a bar. It'll change your life."

"Okay." Celia often suggested that something homemade could change her life. "Why don't I pick up a pizza and a six-pack, and you can explain it to me?"

Celia laughed. "Deal. Is this a just-us dinner, or should we invite the menfolk?"

"Can it just be us? I think I need a reality check."

"Sure. I'll see what I can do. Come on over."

"I'll be there in an hour," Annie said.

She hung up and ordered the pizza online.

"You be good," she told Chester.

Annie briefly contemplated walking the three blocks to the microbrewery on South King to have her empty growler refilled then thought better of it and grabbed the keys to her Jeep from the table by the door. Celia had terribly pedestrian taste in beer, and a growler of microbrew would be wasted on her. She detoured by Safeway for a six-pack of Miller Lite before pulling into the spot reserved for carry-out orders in the crowded Fire Works Pizza parking lot.

Half an hour later, Annie headed down Celia's long gravel drive. Her friend was standing on the porch next to an old teak table, stirring something in a Crock-Pot. She was wearing a T-shirt and cutoff jeans and had a big oven mitt on the hand she was stirring

with. Daisy and Duke, Celia's two Doberman pinschers, came tearing around the corner of the house. They stopped short at the car and
seemed disappointed when Chester wasn't with her.

Annie laughed. "Sorry, guys." She grabbed the beer and the pizza
box and joined Celia on the long white porch of her modest farmhouse. The dogs followed her and flopped down.

"Hey," Celia said.

"How goes it?"

"It's almost ready to pour into the mold," Celia said. The scent of
lavender hung heavily in the air.

Annie opened a beer and took a sip. "How long will that take?
Should I put the pizza in the oven to stay warm?"

"Nope. It won't be long now. How's it going with Preston? I expect a certain amount of gossip when you start dating someone, and
it's been woefully lacking."

Chuckling, Annie said, "Sorry." She explained everything that
had been happening at the farm.

Celia stared at her openmouthed. "The hell?"

"I don't even know how to feel. My head is spinning." Annie
opened another beer for Celia and set it on the table a respectable
distance from the chemical reaction. "Preston is obviously pretty
freaked out about the possibility that his brother hired someone to
hurt him, but then, who wouldn't be?"

Celia shook her head in disbelief. "Do you really think he did
that?"

Annie shrugged. "It seems likely, given the evidence, but I don't
know the guy. The most I've seen him is on a video conference call,
and he didn't read as sinister then."

Celia pursed her lips but didn't say anything.

"What?"

"Nothing. So, what about the bones in the church?"

"I'm pretty sure they've been there for decades. I can't see how they'd be connected to what happened to Preston. Weird, though, for sure. And I thought Mr. Nichols's response was really strange too."

"Everything about this is really strange." Celia turned off the Crock-Pot. "Let me just grab some plates." She pulled off the oven mitt, went inside, and came back out a moment later carrying two handmade plates and two cloth napkins. They sat at the other end of the table from the soap-making paraphernalia, and Annie opened the pizza box.

"Mmm, mushrooms, onions, and jalapenos. You know me so well."

"I aim to please." Annie held up her beer bottle. "Cheers."

Celia clinked her bottle against Annie's. "Cheers."

They ate in comfortable silence for a minute. Annie soaked in the view of the rolling countryside. The evening was quiet, and a gentle breeze occasionally stirred the leaves on the trees. "Beautiful day," she said.

"It is, although the pollen is already brutal. Everything is turning yellow."

Annie nodded. Her black Prius had turned a sickly shade of green because of the thick layer of pollen all over it. Her Jeep might be a little beat-up, but at least the tan color didn't show the pollen.

"I asked Daddy if he'd ever heard about a church near Farr Reach Farm," Celia said. "He said that when he and some others first set up the Black History Committee for the Thomas Balch Library, he interviewed some of the oldest residents in the county about what they remembered. An elderly woman he talked to mentioned there being a church on the Farr property somewhere, but she couldn't re-member exactly where it was—just that it was near the creek. But the creek runs through the whole property. Not many black churches from that era are left in the county, so finding it was really important.

Dad approached Lilly Farr on behalf of the committee to ask about searching for it, but she declined."

"Really?" Annie asked. "I wonder why."

"Because white folks like to leave the past in the past, especially if the past makes them look bad," Celia said dryly.

"You think Preston's grandmother knew about the bones?"

Celia shrugged. "Who knows? But she knew about the slaves, and a lot of old landed families are very uncomfortable with that aspect of their history."

"Preston's not like that."

"I didn't say he was."

"We went back there to look for the church," Annie said, hating how defensive she sounded.

"I know."

Annie sighed. "I want to know who she was."

"I thought the crime lab was looking into that."

"They are, but that'll take months. Meanwhile, Gunnar has enough on his plate without dealing with a decades-old murder. Which isn't to say he'll let it drop, but while he's waiting on the lab, he's going to be handling other cases, including the vandalism and assault on Preston."

Celia shook her head. "Don't."

"I have to," Annie said. Although that wasn't strictly true, it felt true. Because she'd found the bones, it felt like her responsibility to give that woman back her name.

"No, you don't. I thought you wanted out of dangerous cases."

Annie scoffed at her. "Dangerous? That woman has been dead for ages. The most danger I'm in is from getting a paper cut at the records office."

Celia frowned at her. "Really? I thought you said Mr. Nichols showed up with a shotgun."

"Which he didn't even point at us," Annie said. It seemed prudent not to mention that she'd freaked out a bit when he'd shown up with the gun.

"Right, but maybe he knows who that woman is. Maybe he even killed her," Celia said.

"Or he didn't even know the bones were in there and was just mad that we were on his land," Annie countered. "Who knows? He's a really old man, Celia. I think I can handle him." Besides, if she poked around and it looked like Mr. Nichols or anyone else had anything to do with those bones, she would hand over whatever she found to Gunnar and let him deal with it.

"What if this is somehow connected to the brother?" Celia asked. "What if she's Preston's brother's old girlfriend or something?"

Annie shook her head. "How, if she's been there for seventy years?"

"You know that for certain? Fifties parties used to be a thing in the eighties. I know because my mom went to some. There are pictures in her school albums and yearbooks."

Annie hadn't known about parties like that. "Well..." She wondered again what Ernie Henley had been planning to burn and why. If Emory Farr was trying to cover up a murder, that put him in a whole new category of felon.

"I'm just saying," Celia continued. "If Preston's brother is willing to pay someone to vandalize the farm and assault him, nothing is stopping him from doing the same to you. Especially if he's a murderer. How much older than Preston is his brother?"

"I'm not exactly sure, but a lot... like, at least ten years." Annie sat back in her chair. "That's all the more reason I need to find out who that woman is."

Celia tapped her fingers on the table in obvious irritation. "No. It's the reason why you need to keep your nose out of it. Besides, since when can you afford to work for free? Are you even allowed to? I thought there were rules against that."

"There are, but they don't apply to looking at historic records. Anyone is allowed to do that. You could do that."

"Maybe I should." Celia got up and took their empty plates into the kitchen.

"No," Annie said, raising her voice to be heard inside. "I'll handle it. I'm just going to do a little research. It'll likely amount to nothing."

"You don't believe that," Celia said, huffing as she came back out.

"I don't know what I believe yet. But Preston is a good guy. He doesn't deserve to have this hanging over him for months while the bones work their way through the crime lab queue."

Celia shook her head again. "I don't like it."

"Well, I don't like it either. That's why I'm going to look into it."

Celia let out an exasperated sigh. "Are you sure he's worth all this? You hardly know him."

Annie sighed and closed the lid on the pizza box. "I don't know. It's been such a crazy few days, and it's made it seem... I'm not sure. Like more time has passed than actually has."

Celia raised her eyebrows. "How do you mean?"

"With Preston," Annie explained. "He came over last night, distraught over this mess with his brother, and..." She shook her head. "I don't know. It's like, all of a sudden, I'm his person, but I don't really know him. Does that make sense?"

"I'm telling you... if it's going too fast, put on the brakes."

"I'm not sure I want to. But Miss Mabel said something today that kind of freaked me out, and now I don't know what to think."

"Miss Mabel is handing out relationship advice? Why does that not surprise me?"

"Not exactly. I took her some lunch, and we got to talking. I mentioned that I was dating Preston, and she said I should be careful because there was"—Annie made air quotes—"'evil in his people.'"

Celia grimaced. "That's legit creepy. Did she say why?"

Annie sighed. "Her mother worked for them and wasn't treated well, but she also said the Farrs used to own Mr. Nichols's family, and the Nicholses have that land because they're related to the Farrs."

"Oh. Like in a Jefferson-Hemings way? What did Preston say about it?" Celia asked before sipping her beer.

"I haven't talked to him about it yet. I just talked to Miss Mabel today."

"So, what's the problem?"

"I'm not exactly sure how to raise the subject with him or even if I should. It's not like he's responsible for the actions of his entire family. Besides, he's under a lot of stress right now."

Celia shrugged. "So don't bring it up."

"But what if it's connected?"

"What if *what's* connected?"

"The family history with the bones in the church," Annie explained.

"I'm not sure what that would have to do with his family owning slaves. I thought you said the woman was dressed like she was from the fifties. Did you mean the 1850s?"

Annie smiled. "No. Definitely the 1950s." She sighed. "I don't even know where I'm going with this."

"Look," Celia said, "clearly, you like the guy—possibly more than you intended to—but you can still pump the brakes. And probably the easiest way to do that is not to look into those bones. Let the police deal with it."

Annie shook her head. "That'll take months."

"Who cares? If you pursue this, it's just going to draw you closer to him. Is that what you want?"

"I don't know. I'm not even sure that's true. If I pursue this, it could just as easily blow us apart."

"There you go, then. Let it be."

"Only one problem," Annie said.

Celia frowned at her. "Which is?"

"I don't want to."

"Annie." Celia sighed in frustration.

"Seriously, I want to know who she is. She's been locked up in that church for what looks like decades. What's a blond woman doing nailed into an old slave church? Did she die there, or was she taken there after she was killed? And why there? Was there a reason, or was it just the closest place to stash her? Boarding it up and nailing the doors took time. Who would have done that, and why not bury her instead? It's really weird, like the church was her mausoleum."

"How do you know she was blond?" Celia asked.

"There was still some hair near the skull."

"Gross."

"Not really. It's far easier to look at bones than the recently deceased or an actively decaying body. By comparison, bones are much less gross."

"If you say so," Celia said. "It all sounds pretty horrible to me." She opened the lid of the slow cooker and stirred the thick contents. "I think this is ready to pour into the mold." She put the oven mitts back on and scraped the contents into a plastic-lined shoebox. "Perfect." She smoothed the top of the hot soap with a spatula. "I'll cut it into bars after it cools."

Annie thought that looked like a lot of work for something she could buy at the store for a dollar.

Celia looked at her. "What if you're wrong about the date, and she's only been there ten or fifteen years?"

"I certainly could be. I'm not an expert, and I'm only going by the clothes."

Celia gave her a pointed look. "What if she really was a girl-friend?"

"Well, she wouldn't have been Preston's. If she were, he would never have taken me over there."

"True. But you already know his brother is shady. I don't think you should get mixed up in this."

"I think it's more likely that Mr. Nichols is involved somehow."

"Why?"

"Because he showed up, and because the church is close to his property."

"And because he's black," Celia added with a frown.

"No," Annie said, shaking her head. "Come on. But he was a young man in the fifties. Maybe it was his girlfriend."

"You think a black man in Loudoun had a white girlfriend in the fifties? Girl, if that was the case, the body you found in that church would've been his."

"You have a point there. Do you know any of the Nicholses?"

"No," Celia said, clearly irritated. "We don't all know each other."

"Hey, I didn't mean it like that. You know a lot of people... all kinds of people. Why are you so prickly about this?"

Celia sighed. "I don't know. I know you're not like that. I didn't..." She shook her head. "It's just that all of this is upsetting, and I think you should stay out of it."

"I'm sorry. I didn't come over here to upset you." Annie valued Celia's opinion and was used to discussing everything with her, but she should have known she would be upset at the idea of Annie in-vestigating a murder, even if it was a decades-old one.

"I wish you would just leave this alone," Celia said. "The last time you stuck your nose into a murder case, you got shot."

Annie sighed. "First off, I didn't stick my nose in. I was hired to do investigative work by the lawyer of a potential suspect, which is a completely legitimate job for a private investigator."

"A legitimate job that got you shot," Celia said pointedly.

"Right, but that was also an active murder investigation with a living murderer. The likelihood that anyone still alive killed that woman in the church is pretty slim—unless it was Mr. Nichols, but he's in the hospital, and who knows if he'll even come out."

"All the more reason you shouldn't be involved."

"The guy is in his nineties. Nothing nefarious happened to him. He probably had a heart attack or a stroke or something. Nothing related to those bones, if that's what you're getting at. I'll be fine. If so much as a whiff of danger comes up, I promise I will hand the whole thing over to Gunnar and go on my merry way. I assure you that as much as you don't want me to get shot, I don't want that even more."

Celia sighed and let it go. As had happened many times in their long friendship, they changed the subject and moved on to more pleasant topics. Annie opened two more beers and listened as Celia explained the difference between cold-processed and hot-processed soap.

"After I rendered the lard," Celia said, "I made crackling. Want some?"

"You know I do."

Annie left after helping Celia feed the horses and her two alpacas. Celia gave her a quart bag of fresh crackling, and Annie spent the drive home vacillating on whether she should share any with Preston or hoard it all for herself.

AS SHE APPROACHED LEESBURG, Annie realized she needed gas, so she pulled into Nichols Garage. The place was convenient, and she was curious. She'd stopped there for gas many times, but she'd never met Mr. Nichols or the daughter who ran the place.

While she was filling up, she noticed the lights were still on in the office. She finished at the pump then walked into the service center. It smelled faintly of oil, like all car-repair places, but was otherwise clean and tidy. A young man was typing on a computer behind a high desk fronted by candy bars and crackers. Disappointed that he appeared to be the only employee around, Annie got a bottle of water from the drink cooler and went to the register.

He looked up as she approached. "Will this be all?"

"Yeah," Annie said. "What time is your manager usually in?"

"Was there a problem?" the young man asked with concern.

Annie wondered if he was new or possibly on probation for screwing up. "No, I just heard her dad was in the hospital and wanted to see how he was doing."

"Oh. She's here. Let me tell her." He picked up the phone and pressed a button. "Someone to see you, Opal." He listened for a moment then told Annie, "You can go on back."

Annie went through the door behind him into a small office dominated by a large gray metal desk that was cluttered but in an organized fashion. The older woman sitting at the desk bore a strong resemblance to her father. She had the same light complexion, high cheekbones, and white hair. "Can I help you?"

"Hi," Annie said. "I'm Annie Fitch. I met your father yesterday afternoon then heard later he was in the hospital."

The woman stood, her eyebrows knitting in confusion. She held out her hand. "Opal Nichols."

Annie shook it. "How's your dad doing?"

"Not great. He's still unconscious and not breathing on his own." Opal was tall and solidly built. Annie didn't doubt for a second that she ran a business with mostly male employees without any difficulty at all.

"I'm so sorry to hear that." If Mr. Nichols didn't recover soon, his family was about to face agonizing decisions.

"Thank you," Opal said somberly. "I'm sorry, but how exactly did you meet my father?"

"I'm friends with Preston Farr. We were on your father's side of the creek yesterday, looking for an old church that we were told was over there."

"So, you went to the house?" Opal asked, frowning.

"No, he came to us. Well, his dog found us first."

"He came to you? At the church?" Opal asked, looking puzzled. "Daddy can't walk that far."

"I think he drove his lawn mower most of the way," Annie explained.

"Why would he do that?"

"I'm not sure. He had a shotgun with him. Not that he pointed it or anything. He just had it."

"Oh, he probably thought it was deer," Opal said. "One got tangled up in the barbed wire from an old fence back there. The dog found it, and Daddy put it out of its misery. But that was years ago." She shook her head. "He should have just called me or my son if he thought something was tangled up back there. What was he thinking?"

"I don't know," Annie said, smiling. "I wonder that about my own father sometimes."

Opal looked at her closely. "Who told you he was in the hospital?"

"I'm friends with Gunnar Jansson, the detective who talked to you yesterday."

"Oh. Something about some bones."

"Right. Do you have any idea whose bones those might be?"

Opal frowned again. "Like I told your friend, those bones are nothing to do with us. That's not even our property, and we never went back there."

"Except to kill deer," Annie said.

"Right." Opal's lips drew to a thin line. "You want to know about anything on that land, ask the Farrs. It's their property."

"Unfortunately," Annie said, "Preston doesn't know anything about that part of the property. He and his siblings were told that the land belonged to your father and that they weren't to go over there."

"That's not true," Opal said. "We don't own it."

"He knows that now," Annie said. "Do you have any idea why it was fenced?"

"Ages ago, when the Farrs had cattle, they used to keep a bull back there. Daddy fed it for them."

"Oh," Annie said. A moment of awkward silence followed. "Well, I hope your father recovers soon."

"Me too," Opal said, the sadness returning to her face.

"Have a good night."

"You too."

Opal walked Annie out, and Annie could feel her staring at her as she returned to her car.

BACK HOME, ANNIE FED Chester and took him for a walk. Her mind whirled with thoughts about what Opal had said about the bull. It seemed callous to put a bull on property once occupied by slaves, especially since it included a church and what looked to be a graveyard. *Did whichever Farr that put that bull back there do it because he was indifferent to the sacrilege, or because he wanted to ensure no one went back there and tried to go into the church? If it was the latter, why did he trust Mr. Nichols to feed the bull? If it was the former, why would Mr. Nichols have agreed to feed it? Surely, Mr. Nichols's family must have some ties to that church and those graves—however distant. How could he not have been offended by the presence of the bull on sacred ground, unless he knew what was in that church?* Annie desperately wanted to talk to Mr. Nichols, but that was impossible for the moment and possibly forever. The likelihood that a man his age would come out of a coma couldn't be very high. She found herself really hoping Preston's uncle would call her back. She had so many questions and so few answers.

Instead of hearing from his uncle, a few minutes later, Preston texted her. *Almost ready for strawberry picking to start. Want to come for dinner tomorrow before chaos ensues?*

Annie thought about that and considered Celia's comment about pumping the brakes. Maybe she should try to slow things down. She stared at her phone for several moments before texting back, *Sounds good.* Dinner with Preston seemed a lot better than eating alone. She could brake later.

When she walked up to her patio with Chester, her phone pinged again.

Five-thirty too early?

Annie replied, *No. I can do that.*

Great. Sorry I keep farmer's hours. He added a winking emoji.

Doesn't bother me, she typed and added a smiley face.

Good. See you tomorrow.

Annie sent a thumbs-up.

She didn't see a way around talking about his family's history, if she had any hope of figuring out who the body in the church was, and she wasn't sure how he would receive her questions. On the other hand, he'd been open with Reverend Mary, so there wasn't any reason for him to balk at answering Annie's questions.

That night, she dreamed about Ford.

Chapter 18
Saturday

The next day, after spending too many boring hours on background checks that didn't reveal anything more nefarious than maxed-out credit cards, Annie was grateful to have dinner plans.

She took Chester out for a quick potty break before she left for the farm. Since she wanted an excuse not to spend the night, she didn't take him with her. Celia might have had a point about putting on the brakes. Not spending the night with Preston was one way of doing that.

Clouds had moved in while she was working, and the temperature had dropped. As she walked to her car, big raindrops started falling hard. Visibility was bad on the way to the farm, but by the time she got there, the weather had eased up into a light but steady rain. Preston was sitting on the porch, drinking a beer.

"Hey," she said as she got out of the car.

"Hey." He grinned. "You want a beer?"

"Yes." Annie stepped onto the porch.

"I was just watching the rain." Preston gave her a quick kiss. "You mind if we sit out here while the roast finishes? We've got a few minutes."

"Sounds good to me," she said and took a seat on one of the old wicker chairs while he went to fetch the beer.

Most of Preston's furniture looked like it had been at the house for a long time, and Annie assumed he'd inherited the furnishings with the house. His bedroom looked decidedly masculine and modern, but the rest of the house appeared to have been decorated by an elderly woman decades ago. Or maybe, she thought, amused by her own sense of humor, that was just his style.

He came back out onto the porch and handed her a Port City Optimal Wit. "I got you some of that wheat beer you like."

"Thanks," Annie said. "Cheers."

They clinked their bottles together, and Preston took a seat next to her.

"These chairs need new cushions," he commented. "These aren't very comfortable." He looked at Annie. "I don't suppose you sew."

She snorted. "Not even a little bit. Can't you crochet something?"

He laughed "Now, there's a thought."

They sipped their beers and watched the rain, then he reached over and took her free hand. She liked the way his calloused hand felt in hers.

"What's for dinner?" Annie asked, trying to change her focus.

"Pork loin roast, mashed potatoes, and salad. Oh, and pecan pie from Mom's Apple Pie for dessert."

Her stomach rumbled. All she'd had for lunch was a banana. "That sounds fantastic."

"It should be," he said. "I'm not a great cook, but I can do a few meals well."

"Nice. I'm a fairly basic cook myself. If I want something amazing, I invite myself to Celia's house for dinner."

"She's a good cook?" Preston asked, raising his eyebrows.

"She's good at everything. I've never seen her take up anything she couldn't do."

"That's cool," he said, turning her hand over in his.

"Celia is very cool. Always has been."

"How long have you two known each other?" Preston asked as he stroked her fingers.

"Since college. We were roommates."

He nodded. "So, a long time, then."

"Yes." The subtle pressure of his fingers felt nice, but she reminded herself that she would not be staying the night.

"Ted seems pretty smitten," Preston said.

"That doesn't surprise me. How long have you known him?"

"Since high school. He's probably my oldest friend."

Annie thought about her oldest friend on the other side of world and wondered what he was doing while she sat on Preston's porch and drank beer. The thought left her with an ache in her heart.

Preston's phone buzzed. She took the opportunity to pull her hand back.

"Ah," he said. "Time to check the roast."

She followed him inside. He poked the roast with an instant-read thermometer and pronounced it done. "I just need to prep the salad and finish the potatoes while the meat rests."

"I can do the salad, if you want."

"Are you sure? It's pretty complicated," he teased as he tossed her a bagged salad.

She chuckled. "I'll soldier through somehow."

He handed her a carton of cherry tomatoes. "I'm trusting you."

While she put the salad together, Preston mashed the potatoes. The sounds of a car pulling up filtered in from outside.

"That must be Alejandro. Crap, I hope the rain didn't screw up something for tomorrow." He walked to the back door. "Ruby?"

His sister came into the house. She'd clearly been crying. "I just dropped Emory off at the airport. I cannot believe—" She realized Annie was standing in the kitchen and looked at Preston. "Oh, I'm sorry. Did something happen? Has there been more vandalism?"

"No, everything is fine. Annie is just... Well, after she installed the security system... I, uh, asked her out."

"Oh." Ruby glanced from one to the other as she wiped tears from her cheek. "I didn't realize. I should have called. Sorry. I can go."

Preston glanced at Annie. Clearly, he didn't want to say what he was about to say. "Stay. There's plenty to eat, and I wanted you two to get to know each other, anyway."

Annie tried to ignore the anxiety that tightened her gut. Preston was clearly way ahead of her in their relationship.

"I don't know," Ruby said. "It's been such a trying day."

"Annie knows what Emory did," Preston said. "She took me to the hospital."

"Oh." Ruby was clearly embarrassed by what their older brother had done.

"Stay," Preston said again, resting a hand on her shoulder.

Ruby sighed. "If you're sure. Thank you. I don't think I'm up for the drive back to Alexandria at the moment, anyway."

"Sit down," Preston said. "I'll get you a glass of wine, and we'll eat."

Ruby took a seat at the big round table. She sat very straight and kept glancing at Annie as she brought the food over to the table and sat down. Preston set an extra place for Ruby and brought her a glass of wine along with two extra glasses for him and Annie and set the bottle on the table. An awkward silence followed. Annie poured herself a glass of wine and watched the siblings, who seemed to be pretending they were having a normal meal. Preston was intently slicing the roast as if it were surgery instead of dinner.

Ruby drank her wine and stared off into space.

"What made you decide to take Emory to the airport?" Preston finally asked. "I figured you'd let him cab it."

Ruby sighed and set down her glass. "I wanted an explanation."

"Did you get one?"

Ruby frowned. "He cried a lot. Told me all about the mess he's in with code violations at the site he's developing, and the lawsuits. He blames it all on the contractors, but who knows? It's not like Emory is above cutting corners, if he thinks he can get away with it."

"You don't know that," Preston said.

Ruby rolled her eyes. "You've always been so blind about him. Just because he took you fishing and went to your ball games doesn't make him a saint. He's an Emory like all the other Emorys—well, except Uncle Emory. He's all right."

"Emory is a family name," Preston explained to Annie. "All the firstborn males are named Emory."

Annie didn't mention she already knew that from talking with Miss Mabel.

"And they're mostly monsters," Ruby said and took a sip of wine.

Annie raised her eyebrows at Preston.

"She's exaggerating," he said.

"No, I'm not," Ruby insisted. "With the exception of Uncle Emory, they were all assholes."

"You don't know that," Preston said.

"I know more than you do. At least I bother with the family history."

"I know enough. Besides, I'm a little more concerned about keeping what we have instead of worrying about stuff that happened a hundred years ago."

Annie tried to remain inconspicuous while the siblings argued, but she couldn't help feeling like it wasn't the first time they'd discussed the topic. She looked at the wooden salad bowl. She was pretty sure her grandmother used to have one just like it. The potatoes were in a bowl that matched the plates. The china pattern had small blue flowers in the center with a dark blue band along the rim. She assumed that Preston had inherited his grandmother's dishes along with everything else in the house.

Ruby let out a soft snort and finished her wine. "Our brother is an asshole. You might not have seen it before, but surely you can see it now."

"Well..." Preston said reluctantly.

"Please," Ruby said. "What does he have to do before you see him for who he is? Kill you?"

"Don't be ridiculous," Preston said. "I'm not saying what he did was right."

"Well, I told him in no uncertain terms that we will not be selling over two hundred years of family history because he's put himself in a pickle. He got himself into this mess. He can pay to get himself out of it."

"I agree with that," Preston said.

"Good," Ruby said firmly. "About time you showed some backbone." She swallowed the last of her wine and poured another full glass.

"Hey! I have plenty of backbone." He glanced at Annie, his cheeks going red.

Ruby rolled her eyes again, and Preston scowled at her.

"Speaking of bones," he said, clearly irritated. "We found some."

Annie almost choked on her wine at the segue. She set her glass down carefully and watched, fascinated.

"What bones?" Ruby asked. She seemed to realize she'd pushed him with the backbone comment and wanted to back off a bit.

"We went over on the other side of the bend in the creek—"

"Why?" Ruby asked.

"Because it's ours, but I've never been over there. Anyway, there's an old church up the bank, and we found a skeleton inside."

"I've never heard of any church," Ruby said, as if that definitively meant there wasn't one.

"Me either, but it's there."

"When did you do this?" Ruby asked.

"Couple days ago."

"Are you sure it wasn't just some animal?" Ruby asked.

"It was definitely human," Preston said. "A woman, based on what was left of her clothes."

"Why didn't you say something?" Ruby asked.

"Seriously? You wanted to hear that in the middle of everything else?" Preston asked.

Ruby considered. "I see your point. Who was it?"

"We don't know. The cops sent the bones to a lab."

"That's crazy." Ruby took another long drink of wine.

"Do you recall anyone going missing or hearing about anyone who disappeared?" Annie asked.

"You mean other than Mom?" Ruby asked with a soft snort.

The hair on the back of Annie's neck stood up, and she looked wide-eyed at Preston.

He frowned at his sister.

"Relax," Ruby said to Annie. "She didn't really disappear." Ruby gestured with her wine glass. "She had an affair with a congressman that went embarrassingly public, so she left. Now she lives in an apartment in Boca Raton."

Preston made a subtle disapproving grunt. Ruby rolled her eyes but let the subject drop. The three of them ate in silence until it started to feel awkward.

When Annie couldn't stand it anymore, she said, "I did find out about the barbed wire. Mr. Nichols's daughter said Emory Farr used to keep a bull back there, and her dad would feed it for him."

"Which Emory?" Ruby asked.

"I don't know," Annie said, looking at Preston.

He shrugged. "Probably Granddaddy."

"But not your father?" Annie asked.

"Our father wasn't an Emory," Ruby clarified. "It used to be that the Emorys always inherited the land, but Granddaddy left the farm to Nannie instead." She raised her eyebrows. "Huge scandal. Uncle Emory moved to DC, and Daddy stayed on the farm to help Nannie, so she was planning to leave the land to him, since he was her son and cared about the farm, but he died before she did, so it went to us instead."

Confused, Annie asked, "Emory wasn't her son?"

"No. Emory was Grandaddy's first wife's son," Ruby clarified.

Annie wanted to ask more about the change in inheritance and the first wife, but Preston cleared his throat. "Who wants dessert? I've got pecan pie and vanilla ice cream."

"Ooh, my favorite," Ruby said. She'd barely touched her dinner.

"That sounds good," Annie agreed.

"Anyone want coffee?"

Ruby shook her head.

"I don't think so," Annie said and helped Preston clear the plates. When they were in the kitchen alone, he said, "I'm sorry."

"Don't be. It's fine."

She helped him put together the desserts, and they returned to the table. Preston set Ruby's bowl of pie and ice cream in front of her before sitting down with his own. Another awkward silence descended as they ate.

Again, Annie couldn't stand it. "So, you live in Alexandria?"

"Yes," Ruby said.

They chatted for a little while about life in Alexandria and living in Old Town versus outside of it.

Ruby looked Annie over with a critical eye. "Are you from around here?"

"My grandparents were. I grew up in Arlington, but I spent my summers here."

"Ah."

"I guess you grew up here," Annie said.

"Not in this house. We lived in the foreman's cottage, where Alejandro and his family live now. Nannie lived here in this big house all by her lonesome, even though Daddy ran the farm, and the five of us were rather cramped in that little house."

"It wasn't that bad," Preston muttered.

Ruby snorted. "Yes, it was. That house only has one bathroom. At least I had my own room. The boys had to share."

"Which wasn't that bad," Preston insisted.

"Not for him, maybe," Ruby said to Annie. "Emory hated it, but then, what teenager wouldn't hate sharing a room with a little kid."

"There's a big age difference, then?"

"Four years between Emory and me. Nine years between me and Preston."

Preston shifted the conversation to stories of growing up on the farm. They sat at the table long after they'd finished dessert. After a while, Preston yawned, then Ruby did too.

"I think I'm going to stay. I'm too tired to drive home. I'm going to go call Ari." She got up and went upstairs.

"I should go," Annie said.

Preston watched his sister walk upstairs. "I wish you wouldn't."

"I need to get back and let Chester out," Annie said, standing.

"Why didn't you bring him?"

"He's still recovering. It's easier to leave him at home, where I don't have to worry about him getting into anything."

Preston nodded. "I understand." He walked her out to her car. "I'm sorry about tonight. I didn't expect her to just show up like that."

"It wasn't so bad," Annie said. "I enjoyed hearing about your family. It's rare for one group of people to go so far back on the same property. It's cool that your family managed to hang on to it for all these years."

"Thanks. I think so too." He took her in his arms and kissed her.

She liked the way he kissed and the way he held her. He was solid, and it was easy to feel safe in his arms. Plus, there was no mistaking that he wanted her there, which was a comfort after the uncertainty that defined her relationship with Ford.

When they separated, he pressed his forehead against hers. "Are you sure you can't stay?"

She smiled and gave him another quick kiss. "Positive."

He opened the car door for her. "I'll talk to you tomorrow."

"Sure," she said. "Good luck with opening day."

"Thanks. It's sure to be chaos. If I survive, I'll text you."

"I look forward to it. If I don't get a text, should I send reinforcements?"

"Absolutely!"

Annie chuckled and started the car. "Good night."

"Night," he said. He waved as she drove away, which made her ridiculously happy. She looked at the clock on her dashboard and realized it was only ten. She asked her phone to text Celia to ask if she was awake.

A moment later, Celia called. "What's up?"

"Weird question," Annie said.

"Excellent. I love weird questions."

Annie chuckled. "Do you have one of those online genealogy accounts?"

"I don't, but I have access to my dad's."

"Do you think I could come over tomorrow and look up some stuff?"

"Will you help me feed the horses?"

"Yes."

"Great. Come at eight," Celia said cheerily.

"I'll be there."

Chapter 19

Sunday

Seven thirty was earlier than Annie was generally out and about, so she got up at six to make sure she was fully alert and caffeinated before she drove out to Celia's. It was a beautiful Virginia spring morning. The forsythia, redbuds, and cherry trees were in full bloom. She took Dry Mill Road and East Colonial Highway, which wound through Clarke's Gap and the small town of Hamilton and took her through parts of the county between Leesburg and Purcellville, where Celia lived, that were still largely undeveloped. Taking the long way around rewarded her with gently rolling hills of green for most of the drive.

When she pulled in front of Celia's house just before eight, Celia was already up and in the barn. She wore dusty riding pants and a long-sleeved T-shirt and was scooping food into various white plastic buckets.

"Hey," Annie said as she entered the barn.

"Good morning. I'm just about done here. Can you take the hay out to everyone?"

"Sure."

Annie hefted several string bags of hay and tossed them into a wheelbarrow. She grabbed the handles and leaned in, starting for the closest of several paddocks that dotted the twenty-acre farm. Celia followed her with buckets of grain that were custom mixed for each horse. Annie marveled that she could keep all the meals straight. Though Annie liked horses well enough, she had never desired to own one. They were too expensive and too much work for an animal that couldn't even snuggle with you on the sofa at night.

When they were done with all the horses, they fed the alpacas. Annie rubbed the soft, curly head of one.

"That's Gertie," Celia said. "Isn't she sweet? Both girls are, really, but I think Gertie is a bit sweeter than Hetty. Hetty gets a little food aggressive."

"They're cute. I think I like them better than the horses."

"I wouldn't go that far. Besides, I'm being paid to board the horses. These girls are just a drain on my economy," Celia said with an affectionate smile toward the alpacas. "Come on. Let's go get some coffee."

"I thought you'd never ask. I haven't had nearly enough this morning."

A few minutes later, fortified with caffeine, Annie and Celia sat at Celia's big oak kitchen table with her laptop and started looking up the Farr family on Ancestry.com. Annie had hoped that because the family had been in the same place for so long and had produced so many offspring, someone along the way had recorded the family history online. She was not disappointed.

"Thank you, mystery cousin," Annie said as she pulled up a tree that showed a series of Emory Farrs in Loudoun. The tree's generator was an anonymous account holder, and none of the living relatives were visible, but all the dead Farrs were thoroughly cataloged.

"What are you looking for?" Celia asked.

"I'm not exactly sure. Names and dates, I guess. I'd like to know who was on that property in the 1950s, assuming I'm guessing right on the clothes."

"And if you're not?"

"Then this is a big waste of time," Annie said, smiling apologetically.

Celia snorted. "At least you're honest."

Annie took a flip notebook out of her backpack and began writing down the names of the most recently deceased. "I can look up some of these names in other databases and try to get living relatives so that I'll have some other options of people to contact."

"This seems like an awful lot of work for something that's probably a wild goose chase."

"I don't think it is," Annie replied.

"You seriously think you can figure out what happened to someone sixty or seventy years ago? What happened to 'the first hours are the most critical in any investigation'?"

Annie chuckled. "I hate it when you quote me back to me. You know that, right?"

Celia just looked at her.

"Yes, those first hours in an investigation *are* critical. On the other hand, cold cases do occasionally get solved, and this could be one of them—provided I can find one person who knows who she might be."

"What if no one knows? What if she just went in there to take shelter from a storm or something and died?"

Annie shook her head. "No. If the church hadn't been boarded up around her, I'd say maybe. But even then, it would be unlikely. There's no road back there. Someone just passing through and taking shelter would be in a church near a thoroughfare. I've been thinking about it. One or possibly both of those families almost has to be involved."

"Why?"

"Because the church is between their two properties with no road to access it, and it was clearly built for the farm workers, probably as a way to entice them to stay on the land after the Civil War. Then there's the bull."

"What bull?"

"A bunch of barbed wire from an old fence goes around the church. That's what Chester got tangled in. Opal Nichols told me that Emory Farr used to keep a bull back there, and her father used to feed it for him."

"He fenced around a church for a bull?" Celia asked incredulously.

"I know. You'd think as a member of an old Southern family, Farr would respect consecrated ground, if nothing else, but even if he didn't, why would Mr. Nichols consent to feeding the bull for him? Unless he didn't want people back there either. After all, Mr. Nichols likely has relatives buried in the cemetery that bull was tromping on, and he may even have attended that church at some point."

"Oh, come on, Annie," Celia said, looking incredulous. "You're telling me you think they conspired to kill some girl? Seriously? A black man and a white man in the 1950s killed some girl together?"

Annie cleared her throat. "Granted, that seems far-fetched, but they *are* family, according to Miss Mabel."

"Just because they share some DNA doesn't mean they're one big happy family," Celia said, shaking her head.

"Of course not, but blood is thicker than water, and there might be a good reason for them to cover up her death."

"So, how do you prove any of that?"

"Well, that's trickier. Right now, I have no idea who she is, but"—Annie held up her notebook—"I'm hoping to track the children of these people, and maybe one of them remembers someone going missing back then. From that, I can get a rough time frame to look at newspapers and even police records from the era."

"Wow," Celia said. "Again, that sounds like a ton of work for what might amount to nothing."

"I know. It's needle-in-a-haystack stuff."

Celia shrugged. "Well, since I don't seem to be able to talk you out of it, come help me turn out the horses, then let's go for a walk."

"That sounds good, as long as we stay away from abandoned buildings. I've got enough on my plate."

"Not a problem. We'll walk the fences. We won't find anything more nefarious than the occasional rotted board."

"Deal," Annie said. Celia's property was beautiful, and a day in the sunshine sounded like just what she needed.

THAT AFTERNOON, ANNIE returned home tired but feeling mentally refreshed. Hanging out with Celia was always fun and relaxing. Chester greeted her at the door more like his usual self than he'd been the last couple of days, so she took him for a short walk then set about cleaning her apartment, which had been neglected of late. She was reading when Preston called at eight o'clock.

"You survived," she said when she picked up.

"Just barely. I've been up since four o'clock this morning and pretty much spent all day narrowly avoiding disasters."

"Sounds grim."

"Actually, it was the easiest opening day we've had since I took over."

Annie laughed.

"I know. This is a ridiculous way to live. I don't know why I like it so much."

"Did Ruby stay and help?"

"No, by the time I got back to the house this morning, she'd gone, but she left a note apologizing for staying last night when I was clearly on a date. She hoped you weren't too put off by her."

"Oh, please. I'm fine. Wait until you meet my family, and my great aunt Ginny harangues you about any and all DC sports teams, and my Aunt Peggy asks inappropriate questions about our relationship, while my father quietly drinks in the corner. Honestly, my brother is the only one who knows how to act around people."

Preston chuckled. "Challenge accepted! But it will probably have to wait awhile. I'm swamped when the farm is open."

"No worries. I'm happy to put the suffering off for as long as possible."

"Weekends are the worst, so maybe during the week next month, we can get together with them."

"Sure," Annie said, suddenly uncertain as to why she'd brought it up. She wasn't really ready for Preston to meet her family, so making an actual plan for him to meet them seemed premature. "We'll sort out something when things calm down for you."

"Great. I don't want to be lame, but I've got another long day tomorrow. I'm going to eat a sandwich and go to bed."

"I understand. I'm glad things went well today."

"Me too," he said, yawning.

"Real quick, before you go. I haven't heard back from your uncle yet. Is it okay if I contact your aunt?"

"She's not going to know anything," Preston said.

"She might."

"No, seriously, my mother and her sister were never close, at least not that I knew about. Anyway, she's from Richmond. She's not going to know anything about the farm."

"Wait, I didn't mean her. I meant your father's sister."

"My father didn't have a sister."

"Oh, um..."

"Who told you my father had a sister?" Preston asked.

"No one. I just saw it on Ancestry-dot-com."

"You looked us up online?" His voice had hardened.

"I was curious about the family tree. Sorry. I thought I might find some names of people who might remember the farm in the fifties."

"Oh. Um, well, it was probably just a mistake. People put up the wrong information online all the time."

"That's probably it, then. I'm sorry. I didn't mean to pry."

"It's okay," Preston said, his voice softening. "I know you're just trying to figure out whose bones those are."

"I know that's weird, but I hate that she's been unknown in that church for so long. It seems wrong not to try to give her back her name."

"I understand, and I think that's good. She deserves to be put to rest." He yawned again.

"Go to bed. We'll talk tomorrow."

"All right. Good night."

Annie wished him sweet dreams and ended the call. She looked at her phone for a moment and clicked on Celia's contact.

Celia answered on the first ring. "Hey."

"I'm sorry to be calling so late, but I need you to check something for me."

"Sure."

"Do you have your laptop?"

"Yeah, hold on a sec." Annie heard her mute the television, then Celia came back on the line. "What do you need?"

"Can you go back into your dad's Ancestry account and look up Preston's aunt Doris Farr?"

The sounds of keys clicking came through the phone. "Here she is. What do you need?"

"Can you look to see if there's a birth certificate attached to her name or anything else that might prove that she's the right Doris Farr?"

"Yeah. I've got a birth certificate and a census form from 1930 and another from 1940."

"Does she have the same parents listed as her brothers? In other words, is she in the right place?"

"Let me check." Silence followed for a minute or two. "It looks like she is. The birth certificate shows that she was born in Leesburg, except it looks like she had a different mother from Preston's father."

"That tracks," Annie said. "His grandfather was married twice."

"Oh, yeah," Celia said. "It looks like the first wife died in early 1939, a couple of weeks after his uncle was born in '38."

"When was the sister born?"

"In 1928."

"Is there a death certificate for her?" Annie asked.

"No, and there isn't a little leaf on her name, showing possible matches to other records either."

"Huh, that's not good."

"Why?" Celia asked.

"Because I just talked to Preston, and he says his father didn't have a sister."

"Maybe they were estranged."

"If that's true, she could still be alive. If so, she might remember that period at the farm really well, assuming she still has all her faculties."

"Maybe, or she could have died abroad, or she might have died here, but there was a name change or a typo that prevented Ancestry's algorithms from associating her name with the death certificate. Given the time period, she could have been part of the war effort—you know, WASPs, WAVES, or WAACs—and died as a result of that."

"True," Annie said. "Well, maybe his uncle will call me back. I'm trying to decide whether I should try calling him again or if that's too pushy."

"Could you get Preston to do it?" Celia asked.

"He's crazy busy right now. The farm just opened for berry picking."

When Annie ended the call, she took Chester out then went to bed. She spent a long time staring at the night sky through the skylight in her bedroom ceiling. Chester lay curled next to her, softly snoring. She'd been letting him sleep in the bed a lot lately. Whether it was to comfort him or her wasn't entirely clear. Either way, they were both happy with the arrangement. His wounds were healing nicely, so the stitches could come out soon. She was ready for him not to look like Franken-dog anymore. Even though she was tired, her mind raced with thoughts about the bones and the two families, but also about Preston and Ford and what she wanted and what she could have.

A text alert interrupted her musings.

Preston had sent, *Getting ready to turn in for the night. Wish you were here.* He'd added a winking emoji.

Don't you need your beauty sleep?

Are you saying I wouldn't get any sleep if you were here? he replied.

Not much.

I'm tough. I say bring it.

Annie laughed and looked at Chester. "Want to go for a ride?"

The little terrier perked up his ears.

"Come on," she said and grabbed her keys and his leash.

Chapter 20
Monday

The next morning, Annie awoke in Preston's bed. Chester was still asleep at her feet, but Preston was gone. He'd left a note on his pillow.

I have to feed the petting zoo animals. Will be back by 7:30. Coffee ready in the kitchen.

Preston

PS: Will attempt to return without head wound. No promises, though. Better get dressed just in case.

Annie chuckled. She looked at her phone to find it was just after seven. She had to go into DC later to confront a delinquent client about payment. Annie hated dealing with clients who didn't pay.

She went downstairs to get a cup of coffee then took a quick shower. While she was looking for a frying pan to make eggs, her phone rang. It was Preston's uncle.

"Fitch Investigations," she answered.

"Hello, Miss Fitch. Um, I believe you called me."

"Mr. Farr, hello. Thank you for getting back to me."

"I'm sorry it took so long. My niece is always fussing at me to check my phone, but I forget to plug it in sometimes, then I have to charge it before I can see if anyone called."

"I understand," Annie said. "Technology is supposed to make everything better, but sometimes it feels like it just makes things more complicated."

"Exactly," Emory Farr agreed. "What can I do for you, dear? You said you had questions about the history of the farm?"

"Yes. Preston tells me you live in DC. I'm going to be in the city later today. Do you think it would be possible for me to meet with you? I'm happy to go wherever is most convenient for you."

"Oh." A long pause followed. "Do you think you could just come here, to my apartment? Would that be okay?"

"Of course," Annie said.

He gave her an address near Dupont Circle, and they arranged to meet at noon.

ANNIE WAS BREAKING eggs into a bowl with Chester at her feet when Preston walked in through the back door.

"Hey." He gave her a quick kiss. "You're looking all bright-eyed and bushy-tailed this morning."

"Are you talking to me or Chester?" Annie asked with an arched eyebrow.

"Both?" He smiled.

"I thought I'd scramble some eggs and make toast."

"That sounds great. I haven't eaten yet." After pouring himself a cup of coffee, he leaned against the counter while Annie made breakfast. "What have you got on your agenda today?"

"I'm going into DC to deal with a client, then I'm going by your uncle's apartment to talk to him."

"Oh." Preston put down his coffee. "I didn't realize he'd called you back."

"He didn't until a few minutes ago." She dropped a couple of slices of bread into the toaster and returned to the eggs.

"What are you going to say to him?" Preston asked with a slightly accusatory tone.

Annie looked at him, trying to gauge why he was asking. "I just want to find out about his childhood on the farm and whether he remembers anyone going missing in Leesburg back then. It was pretty small at that time, only around two thousand people. I would think that if a woman disappeared, it would've been talked about by pretty much everyone. He might remember it." She turned off the burner and got out a couple of plates.

"Yeah," Preston said, frowning. "I guess."

Annie plated the eggs. "What's wrong? I thought you wanted to know who those bones belonged to."

"I do," he said. "I'm just wondering if this is a giant can of worms that I'm going to regret opening."

"How so?" The toast popped up, and she put a piece on each plate and handed him his.

Preston took a seat at the table and reached for the butter. "This is a place people bring their children. That gets dicey if it's associated with something like a murder, even if did happen decades ago."

Annie smiled at him sympathetically. "I don't think old bones are going to make people not want to come to the farm."

"You don't know that. Look, I love this land. But some of its history makes me really uncomfortable, and I can't help thinking that if it all gets laid bare, maybe the families won't come, then I'm going to lose it."

Annie understood his concerns, but she was resolute. "I get that," she said, buttering her toast. "I do. But this is Virginia. I'm fairly certain most people know there were slaves here, and if they thought about this property for two seconds, they would know that slaves provided most, if not all, of the labor until after the Civil War. People still go to Oatlands, Mount Vernon, Sully Plantation, and Gunston Hall, and they all had slaves."

Preston slowly blew out a breath. "You're probably right. The only difference is that Oatlands and the rest are all public sites now.

They're not still in the hands of the same family that did all those terrible things."

Annie slid closer to him. "You're not terrible, and you aren't responsible for the past. But ignoring those bones would be wrong. Besides, the police are already involved. All I'm trying to do is get you answers faster, but everything I'm doing now would be done by the police as soon as they got those lab reports."

"What if it's a Pandora's box?"

"How could it be? It already happened. If you give the county archeologist access to the site and let her decide the significance of what's there, then you can decide what you want to do about it. Personally, I think this county could use more historic sites that show enslaved and post-enslavement communities."

"You've given this a lot of thought," Preston said, raising his eyebrows.

"Celia's father is a founding member of the Black History Committee at Thomas Balch Library. Celia and I have had more than a few conversations about race."

"Celia's black?" Preston asked, his forehead wrinkling in confusion. "I thought she was Hispanic."

"No. Her dad is really light-skinned, like Mr. Nichols, and her mom is Jewish."

"Oh."

"Look, I'm not trying to pretend to be an expert on race relations in Loudoun. Believe me, I'm not."

Preston nodded, tearing off a piece of toast. He was clearly upset.

"What I am is an investigator. So let me try to figure out who that poor woman was." She squeezed his forearm. "Besides, if your uncle doesn't remember anything from back then, you're prematurely upset, because he's pretty much my only lead."

He sighed and gave her a resigned smile. "Yeah, okay."

She leaned over and kissed him. "I'll call you if I find out any-thing."

"Right," he said, finishing the last of his eggs. "I've got to replace a blown belt on the ATV, so if I don't answer, it's because I'm fighting with that."

She smiled at him. "Good luck. I'll clean up here, then I'm going to head out."

BY ELEVEN O'CLOCK, Annie was on her way into DC. Traffic was thick but not as bad as it would have been earlier. Her delin-quent client was a computer programmer with her own development company that specialized in mobile apps. She had listed an address off Seventeenth Street in Foggy Bottom as her place of business. An-nie found a parking garage, gritted her teeth at the cost, and made the short walk to a generic four-story concrete building. She found the app company listed on a big board in the foyer and took an eleva-tor up to the fourth floor. It amused her that a Muzak version of the *Rocky* theme was playing.

The office had a glass door and an open floor plan with comput-ers everywhere. Her client was standing in the middle of the room, talking to a guy around Annie's age. He had a beard and wore a red knit cap, a white button-down, and a gray kilt.

The client looked up and visibly paled when Annie walked in. She strode over to Annie and said in a hushed but firm voice, "You can't be here. I don't have time for this right now."

"That's unfortunate," Annie said. "I can see you're busy, but so am I. You have an outstanding balance, and I have bills to pay." Annie kept her voice just loud enough that the people near them could hear her.

"Okay, okay. Just come into my office." A door in the back led to a cramped room occupied by a desk with a computer and two monitors on it. The woman closed the door and said, "You can't come to my place of business, demanding money in front of my employees."

"Actually, I can," Annie said calmly. "See how I'm here doing it? The next time you hear from me, it will be because I filed the paperwork to take you to small-claims court."

The woman's eyes widened. "You didn't bring back my son."

"Nor did I promise to. I found him, and I brought proof of it. I gave him the letter you asked me to give him, and I had him sign for it. I kept up my end of the bargain. He's a grown man, and I'm not a kidnapper. I'm sorry he wouldn't come back with me, but I told you that was a possibility when you hired me. Now, either pay me, or meet me in front of a judge. Your choice."

The woman's jaw clenched. "PayPal work for you?"

"Yes," Annie said. "Same address as before."

The woman went behind her desk and touched a key that brought the monitors to life. She typed for a moment, then Annie's phone chimed. She had a notification from PayPal that she had money.

"Thank you." Annie reached for the doorknob, but the woman sobbed behind her, so she sighed and turned around.

"I don't think he's ever coming home. He's going to die, if he keeps going like this."

Annie couldn't disagree. "I'm sorry."

"Did he say anything? Offer any kind of explanation? What have I done that's so awful that he won't come home?"

"Possibly nothing. He's on his own path. Hopefully, eventually, it will lead him home. If it's any consolation, he didn't seem angry with you, just resolute. I hope it works out. I really do."

The woman was still crying when she left. Annie felt bad for her—not bad enough to let her slide on payment but bad nonetheless. Her baby boy had grown up to become a drug addict. That couldn't be easy for any parent, but she'd done all she could. Maybe the guy would get himself clean and have a better life, but she didn't hold out high hopes.

On her way to see Preston's uncle, Annie drove north toward Dupont Circle. Mr. Farr had said he lived just a couple of blocks from the Cosmos Club. His building was easy to find, but parking was not. Worried she was going to be late, she hurried as fast as she could down the sidewalk to his building. A couple of minutes past noon, she walked down a dark hallway with maroon carpeting, which had probably once been plush but was past its prime. She found Mr. Farr's apartment and knocked on the door. She was about to knock again when the door slowly opened. A thin, stoop-shouldered man looked at her.

"Mr. Farr?" Annie asked.

"Yes."

Annie stuck out her hand. "I'm Annie Fitch. We talked on the phone."

"Yes, yes," he said, shaking her hand warmly. "Come in. Come in."

"Thank you," Annie said and followed him into his small apartment.

"I was just about to have some iced tea. Would you like some?" he asked.

"That sounds great."

"I like mine sweet with a little mint. Does that work for you?"

"Sure," Annie said and watched as he disappeared through the doorway into a galley-style kitchen. The apartment had a 1920s vibe about it. One wall was a Moroccan-style ornate metal screen that separated the living room from what looked like a tidy bedroom. The rest of the apartment was one great room, with the kitchen and what she assumed must be the bathroom down a short hallway. The walls were white, but the furnishings and accents were dark wood and rich jewel tones. The place was neat but lived-in. A lot of what looked like original art decorated the walls, and some carved figures were on the bookcases, among the books.

Mr. Farr came out of the kitchen with two glasses of iced tea and handed her one. "Have a seat."

Annie sat on a dark-blue velvet settee, and Mr. Farr sat across from her in a matching wingback chair and put his feet up on a wicker footstool with a red cushion on top. "I'm sorry to be so casual," he said, "but I've been having some issues with gout this week."

"Oh, don't feel the need to be formal on my account, Mr. Farr. I appreciate your willingness to meet with me."

"Please, call me Garland."

"Garland?" Annie asked. "I thought Preston said your name was Emory."

"Only the family calls me Emory. I've always preferred my middle name. Emory was my father."

"Ah. Well, Garland, I appreciate you taking the time to talk to me."

He smiled at her and sipped his tea. "So, what did you want to talk about?"

"Well..." She cleared her throat. "I've been dating Preston for a little while—"

"Oh, that's good. Preston always struck me as a nice boy. It was so sad what happened with his wife."

"Yes," Annie said, smiling awkwardly. "Uh, I was at the house the other day when a local reverend stopped by to talk about the property between the farm and Mr. Nichols's land."

Garland set his glass down on an ornately carved end table.

"She was interested in a possible settlement of enslaved people in that area and understood that there used to be a church there, possibly dating to just after the Civil War."

"I see," Garland said. "Is Preston thinking of letting her back there?"

"Well, not the reverend but the county archeologist. It was Preston's understanding that the land belonged to Mr. Nichols. However, the reverend had already talked to him, and Mr. Nichols said it was Preston's."

Garland closed his eyes. "It belongs to all three children, actually, but Preston runs the farm."

"Of course," Annie said, the hair on the back of her neck rising. Garland clearly knew the land in question belonged to the Farrs. "The reverend brought county maps showing the plot, and they corresponded with family maps that Ruby found."

"Right," Garland said quietly. He stood abruptly. "I know it's early, but my feet are bothering me, and I think this tea could use a splash of rum. Would you care for some?"

"No, thank you," Annie said, even more concerned. "I have to drive."

He nodded and shuffled over to a fancy glass-and-brass bar cart in the corner of the room. Annie waited for him to resume his seat before continuing. "The thing is, we went over there."

Garland wasn't looking at her and instead stared at a distant corner of the room. He gripped his glass tightly as he drank and didn't put his feet up again.

"We found the church, but it was all boarded up." As Annie talked, Garland's face sank into a sad frown. "We probably should have waited for the archeologist, but Preston had never been on that part of the property, and we were curious, so we opened the door. It took quite a bit of effort because it was nailed shut."

Garland nodded.

Annie hesitated. His hands were trembling, causing the ice in the glass to clink against the sides, and his eyes had gone watery, but she was in it and didn't want to stop. She kept expecting him to say something, but he didn't.

"When we went inside, bones were laid out on one of the pews," Annie said quietly.

Garland started to cry. At first, just a few tears slipped, but then he sobbed. Annie looked around the room, saw a box of tissues, and went to put it on the end table next to him. It was hard to watch as he wept into his hands. He cried like a child, open and agonized.

After a minute, he pulled himself together, wiped his eyes with a tissue, blew his nose, and finished his drink. He stood and poured himself more rum, not bothering to add any more tea.

"I take it you know who the bones belong to?" Annie asked as gently as she could.

He nodded. "I think you found my sister."

Annie's jaw dropped. "What makes you say that?"

Garland sighed. "My father..." He closed his eyes and started again. "My father and everyone else said she probably ran off with a soldier, but she wouldn't have done that." He shook his head and whispered, "I knew she didn't do that."

Annie sat for a moment in stunned silence. That was not at all what she'd expected to hear. Preston was going to lose his mind if those bones turned out to be his long-lost aunt. Garland wiped his eyes and sniffled, clearly trying to pull himself together.

She blew out a long, slow breath. "Okay," she said slowly. "You know the police will want to confirm the ID. How would you feel about giving them a DNA sample?"

He nodded. "I could do that. I'd like to do it soon. Today if possible."

"Um... let me make a call."

"All right, I'd like to get it over with."

"Sure. I understand." She pulled out her phone, stepped into the hallway outside the apartment, and dialed Gunnar, who picked up on the first ring. "Hey, Gunn, it's me. I have some news about those bones."

"Really? Because I was going to call you later. I got the preliminary report. Female, between the ages of sixteen and eighteen, Caucasian. We don't have a date of death, but the lab found a label in the skirt from a shop in town that was only open from 1941 until 1947."

"That tracks with what I've found," Annie said and gave him a brief recap of what Garland had told her.

"Oh, man," Gunnar said.

"What's wrong?"

"Another set of bones was mixed in with hers. Fetal bones, fairly developed. Most of them were missing, but there were enough for them to know the pregnancy was between five and six months along. Did her brother mention her being pregnant?"

"No. Did the ME have any sense of how she died?"

"No," Gunnar said. "They didn't find any damage to the bones, with the exception of some animal predation. As you know, all the soft tissue was gone, so there's nothing to test. It would be great if we could get a DNA match."

"Garland is willing to do a swab for ID, but he'd like to do it today."

"Can you bring him in?"

"We're in DC, but I can ask him whether he's willing to drive back with me or if he wants to drive himself."

"Then we can do the test as soon as he gets here," Gunnar said.

"Any word on Mr. Nichols?"

"I talked to his daughter this morning. It's not looking good."

"Right. I'm sorry to hear that. Let me talk to Mr. Farr, and I'll text you if I'm bringing him in."

"Okay," Gunnar said.

She hung up and tapped lightly on the door before going back inside to tell Garland they could go for the swab and to ask if he wanted her to drive him. She decided not to mention the fetal bones. Gunnar would want to ask about those.

Garland nodded. "I'm happy to go with you. I don't drive anymore. Can you bring me back here after?"

"Absolutely. But I feel like I should tell Preston we're coming. I'm sure he'll want to see you."

Garland didn't look too sure about that. "I'll just get some shoes on."

Annie texted Preston, but he didn't respond. He was working, so all she could do was hope he saw it soon. Then she texted Gunnar to let him know they were on their way.

A FEW MINUTES LATER, they were in Annie's Prius. Since it wasn't rush hour, traffic wasn't as bad as it could be, but it was never really good in DC. Annie didn't like driving in the city, so she was grateful that Garland was quiet. She needed to concentrate. He stayed quiet the whole way, spending most of the drive looking out the window. Just as they merged onto the toll road, Annie's cell phone rang. Rather than let the car speaker pick it up, she answered on the handset.

"Hey," she said.

"You're bringing my uncle to Leesburg?"

"Yes, we're in the car now."

"Am I on speaker?" Preston asked, clearly irritated.

"No," Annie said.

"What the hell, Annie?"

"I know," she said sympathetically. "A lot has happened. I'll ask if he wants to come to the house after."

"After what?"

"He's doing a DNA swab."

"What? Why?"

"Look, I can't get into this right now because I'm driving. I'll see you in a little while."

"Wait a minute!" Preston shouted.

"I've got to go," Annie said and ended the call. That wasn't fair to Preston, but she didn't want to talk in front of his uncle.

Garland looked at her as she put the phone in one of the cupholders. "He's upset?"

"Just surprised. He'll be fine." She really hoped that was true.

Garland let out a soft snort. "I don't think he likes me. Preston was very close to Charlene, and she definitely didn't like me."

Annie thought about Preston living in the family home with all of his grandmother's things. Then she glanced at the old man next to her and thought about the bones lying in that church and wondered if maybe Miss Mabel was right about the Farrs.

Chapter 21
Monday Afternoon, Leesburg

Gunnar was ready for them when Annie and Garland arrived at the police station. Annie introduced them. She assumed that Garland would want to talk to Gunnar alone, but he asked her to come with him when Gunnar suggested they go to the conference room to talk.

"I'm sorry," Garland said. "That's probably asking too much. I just don't want to do this alone."

"I don't mind. Or if you prefer, I could call Preston, or Ruby if you have her number."

The old man shook his head. "It would take Ruby too long to get here, and I don't want to bother Preston. I know he's very busy this time of year."

Annie nodded. "Then I'm happy to stay."

"Thank you."

They followed Gunnar back to the conference room, which Annie thought was a better choice than an interview room. After all, Garland wasn't a suspect, and the interview rooms made everyone feel guilty of something.

Gunnar got everyone a Coke then sat down across from Garland. Annie sat at the end of the table between them.

Gunnar cleared his throat. "Annie tells me that you think the bones we found in the church on the Farr property might belong to your sister."

"Yes, sir," Garland said.

"Why do you think that?"

"Because Doris was more like a mother to me than a sister. She was ten years old when I was born, and our mother died shortly after. I say this because I want you to understand that we were very close, but one summer weekend, when I was seven, I went to stay with my cousins for a birthday party, and when I got home, she was gone—clothes, purse, everything. No warning, no explanation, just gone. My father and everyone else said she probably ran off with a soldier, but that was ridiculous. She would never have done that without telling me."

"Did your sister have a boyfriend?"

"No."

"You seem pretty sure about that, given that you were just a kid," Gunnar said.

"She didn't have time for a boyfriend. She ran the house, did all the cooking and cleaning and the weekly shopping, went to school, and kept up her grades. There was no boyfriend."

"Maybe she snuck out to meet someone at night," Gunnar suggested.

Garland shook his head. "We lived on a farm. I know it's right in town now, but back then, it was isolated."

"Maybe she drove to meet someone," Annie suggested.

"Doris didn't drive. My father didn't think girls needed to learn to drive, and no one was going to argue with him about it."

"Your father was an angry man?" Gunnar asked.

"Notoriously so. At that time, he was a heavy drinker and unpredictable when drunk."

"I see." Gunnar made a note. "Do you think he had something to do with her disappearance? Was he violent with her?"

"I never saw him actually hit her, but he would go into these rages, screaming and ranting, and Doris would grab me, and we would run to the church on the other side of the creek. We'd wait there until Doris thought it was safe to go home. She'd check and make sure he'd passed out, then we'd go back inside." Garland crumpled with the telling, seeming older and frailer.

"Was this a regular occurrence?" Gunnar asked.

"Once a month or so. It's hard to have a sense of time when you're that young."

"I understand. Was anything different around the time of her disappearance? Something that makes you think your father was involved?"

"He stopped drinking," Garland said softly.

Gunnar looked at Annie. She shrugged.

"I don't understand," Gunnar said.

"After Doris disappeared, my father never took another drink, and he was different somehow. Less..." He shook his head. "Just less."

"Less violent?"

"No. In some ways, he was more violent, at least toward me, but he was diminished. If that makes sense."

"Okay," Gunnar said, glancing again at Annie, who was just as confused as he was. "And you're sure there was no boyfriend?"

"Yes. She couldn't have conducted some clandestine affair. It just wasn't possible."

"What about with someone nearby?" Annie asked.

"There wasn't anyone," Garland insisted. "I told you. We were isolated."

"What about a farmhand or George Nichols? Couldn't she have snuck over to see him?" Annie asked.

Garland shook his head slowly. "No. The farmhands weren't what you're thinking. During the war, there were women and old men working the fields and the orchard. And George was... no. Miss Mayme always seemed to know when we were at the church, and she would send George with tea or lemonade and something to eat, usually cornbread, but there was nothing between him and Doris."

"Miss Mayme?" Gunnar asked, making another note.

"Mayme Nichols, George's mother. She was always very kind to us. Very kind."

Gunnar nodded. "The thing is, there were fetal bones found in with the other bones. If the woman in that church is your sister, she was pregnant when she died."

Garland's jaw dropped, and he shook his head again. "No. She couldn't have been. She would have told me."

"You were pretty little," Annie said gently. "That's probably not something she would have shared with you."

"Maybe it's not her," Garland said quietly, his eyes shifting away from them. "Maybe it's someone else and she really did run away."

Gunnar took the swab out of the DNA kit. "There's one way to find out."

Garland paused, seeming reluctant, but then opened his mouth, and Gunnar swabbed his cheek.

"How long do you think it will take to get the results?" Garland's eyes had gone watery again.

"Now that we have something to compare the sample with, it will go a lot faster," Gunnar said. "It could be as little as a couple of weeks but more likely a month or two—depending on how backed up the lab is right now."

"Oh. I was hoping it would be faster."

"Yeah, I wish it were," Gunnar said.

He walked them out, and Annie started dreading taking Garland to the farm. She didn't know how Preston was going to react to everything, and cutting him off on the phone earlier probably hadn't helped his mood.

As they got back into Annie's car, Garland continued to wipe his eyes.

"Garland," she said gently. "I told Preston I'd ask you if you wanted to go to the farm when we were done. How do you feel about that?"

He stared across the parking lot toward an apartment building where some kids were playing catch. "I guess we can do that," he said finally. "I haven't been back there since Charlene died. It might be good to see the old place. Cathartic, maybe."

"Okay." While she felt for Garland, as they drove toward the farm, she was more concerned about Preston's reaction. When they pulled in front of the garage, the doors were up, and Preston came out, wiping his hands on a rag. He stopped and watched as they got out of the car.

Garland got out slowly and stood for a minute, just looking around.

"Hey, Uncle Emory. Annie," Preston said in a flat tone that didn't sound like he was happy to see either one of them.

"The place looks good," Garland said.

Annie looked at the long rows of blooming apple trees and agreed with him.

"Thanks," Preston said, cutting his eyes at Annie. "How are you doing, Uncle Emory?"

"Honestly, I've had better days," the old man answered and walked slowly toward the house, looking around as he went. He seemed smaller there—older and more stoop-shouldered. The afternoon had aged him.

Preston turned to Annie. "What the hell? You were supposed to just ask him questions about life on the farm. What are you doing taking him to the cops?" He pushed his cap back on his head, exposing a corner of the bandage. "Tell me he didn't kill that woman," he whispered anxiously.

Annie frowned at him. "Why would you think that? He was on-ly a child then. Would you calm down? Let's go inside and talk. He's got a lot to say, and not all of it is going to be easy to hear."

"Oh, of course not," Preston said with irritation. "Nothing ever is around here."

He stormed off toward the house, and Annie reluctantly fol-lowed. She'd started the whole thing when she began poking around. Girlfriend-wise, she was over the line, and she couldn't help wonder-ing if she and Preston would still be together when the investigation was done. When she went into the farmhouse, Preston was in the kitchen, pouring three glasses of iced tea.

"Where's Garland?" Annie asked.

"He's in the bathroom. Why did you call him Garland?" Preston handed her a glass of tea and took the other two into the living room.

"He asked me to. He doesn't like the name Emory. He says only the family calls him that."

"Yeah, I get that. I wouldn't want to be saddled with that name either. It's like a curse."

"Indeed, it is," Garland said as he came into the living room.

Preston handed him a glass of iced tea, and they all sat down.

"Ruby is on her way. I called her when you hung up on me," he said pointedly to Annie.

"Sorry about that."

He sighed. "Right. Well—"

The front door opened, and Ruby entered, looking far less con-trolled than the last time she'd come through that door. Preston stood. She began yelling at him before she was fully inside the house. "What is wrong with you? I told you to shut this down."

"You don't tell me anything, Ruby. How is it that this family keeps forgetting I'm a grown man?"

"Because you don't act like one!" she shouted back at him. "And why is she still here?" She pointed at Annie. "Who the fuck are you to stick your nose in our family business?"

"Hey!" Preston shouted back at her.

Annie stood and held up her hands, palms out. "You know what, I understand why you think that. Honestly, I was just trying to put a name to those bones. That's all. I didn't anticipate this going how it went."

"Of course you couldn't anticipate that," Ruby shouted then turned to Preston. "Which is why I told you to rein her in."

"Excuse me!" Annie said. "Look, like it or not, there's a dead woman on your property, so whether it was me or the police, nothing about this was just going to magically go away."

That seemed to defuse Ruby somewhat, and she stood there, looking from one to the other. "So, what are we saying here? Are we saying Grandad killed her?"

Annie said, "Not necessarily" at the same time that Garland said, "Yes."

She, Preston, and Ruby all looked at him.

"What?" Ruby asked.

"This has gone on too long," Garland said. "Way too long. It ends now."

Ruby sat next to Garland on the sofa and took his hand. "They shouldn't have dragged you out here."

"No," Garland insisted, squeezing her hand. "I wasn't dragged. I asked to come. You all need to hear this."

Ruby jerked her head around and glared at Annie. "She doesn't."

Garland shook his head. "She knows a lot of it already. If Preston wants her to stay, I don't mind."

They all looked at Preston, who rubbed his head.

"Well, I'd like her to stay." He looked at Annie. "If you don't mind."

"I'm fine with that." Although she couldn't help wondering if Preston had only suggested it because he knew it would irritate Ruby.

Ruby frowned at them but didn't say anything.

Annie and Preston took seats in the two wingback chairs.

When Garland didn't continue, Annie said to Ruby, "I went to see your uncle today to ask if he knew of anyone who'd gone missing around here in the 1940s or '50s."

If looks could kill, the look Ruby gave Preston would have felled a lesser man. She put her arm protectively around her uncle.

Garland patted her knee. "I'm all right, Ruby." He took a deep breath and began to talk. "I don't know if Charlene ever talked about your grandfather. He died long before any of you were born, so maybe she didn't mention him."

Ruby and Preston looked at each other.

Preston cleared his throat. "She only ever mentioned him to me in relation to the farm, like information on the trees or the equipment. Insights he had about grafting. That sort of thing."

"I only remember her saying something to me once when we were in the attic and I saw his portrait up there."

Garland let out a soft snort. "She had that down off the wall the minute the last guest left after the funeral."

So, she didn't like him either, Annie thought.

"I asked her why it was up there," Ruby continued, "and all she said was that it was where it belonged and to leave it be."

"Do you think Nannie knew about the bones?" Preston asked, and Annie could tell it hurt him to ask.

Garland shook his head. "No. To my knowledge, Daddy never even told her he had a daughter. At least when I lived here, she never went over to that side of the creek and never had any doings with the Nicholses. I think she found the situation with them unseemly."

Ruby gave Preston a pointed look. He frowned and looked away.

"I don't understand why we were never told we even had an aunt." Ruby clearly had a close relationship with her uncle and was hurt that he'd never mentioned it.

Garland shook his head. "That's my fault. My father and I never spoke of her after that first time when I came home and he told me she'd run off. I asked again the next day at breakfast, but he backhanded me off my chair, and I knew never to mention her again. But I was a child then. I should've talked about her later, after he'd died. I should've broken into that church and found her. I should've told all of you about her. I don't think your father ever knew he had a half sister."

Preston rubbed his eyes and squeezed the bridge of his nose, like he had a headache. "But I don't understand why you think those bones are your sister's. Did you see him kill her?"

"No," Garland said. He explained the same events that he'd told Gunnar.

When he was done, Preston looked at Annie then back at Garland. "I'm not trying to give you a hard time, Uncle Emory, but you were seven when all this happened. All kinds of things were probably going on that you didn't know about."

Garland shook his head. "You were a loved child," he said quietly. "You had the privilege of a childhood unimpacted by fear. That was not my experience. I had to be on high alert all the time. And I was particularly sensitive to both my father's mood and to Doris's. I had to be. And I'm telling you something happened, and I think it started before that weekend."

"What do you mean?" Annie asked.

"I've been thinking about it, and I think it all started earlier that year, when I got the measles. Daddy had never had them, so he sent me to stay with his sister, because her family had all had them already. Doris had already had them, too, so she stayed home to go to school." He wiped his eyes. "I don't know what happened while I was gone, but Doris wasn't the same when I got home. I was little, but I could tell something had changed. When I asked if she was okay, she just said everything was fine. Not even a year later, she was gone, and I was told she ran off with a soldier."

"But what about the rest of the family or her friends? Surely someone had to ask," Ruby said.

"Doris didn't have close friends. She never brought anyone to the house. Neither of us did. We couldn't because there was no telling which Emory you'd get that day. It wasn't worth the risk to have friends over. Besides, she'd graduated from high school, and it was late summer. No one was around to notice she was gone. Then, that September, the war ended, and that was all people thought about."

"What about family? Aunts? Cousins?" Preston asked. "They had to notice."

Garland shook his head. "He told them she ran off. They knew what he was like. I don't think anyone was surprised that she would leave like that."

Ruby sighed and looked at her uncle with a great deal of sympathy. "I have to say, I would probably have run off. Maybe it was the heat of the moment—a last-straw kind of thing—and she didn't have time to tell you."

Garland wiped away fresh tears. "She would've sent a letter."

"Maybe she did," Annie suggested. "And your father intercepted it."

"Maybe," Garland said. "Initially, I believed him. I was hurt, but I knew things were bad, so I thought any day, she would contact me and tell me what happened. But then I found the handle from her purse. We used to burn trash, and one day, I was dumping stuff and found it, as plain as day on the edge of the ash heap. Then I knew he was lying."

"Did you ask your father about it?" Annie asked, but she knew the answer.

Garland just looked at her. "I never asked my father anything. I spent the whole time I lived in that house just trying to be invisible. He might have stopped drinking, but that didn't stop the cruelty. I wasn't the heir he was hoping for. One day, he went after me about something I hadn't done right." He let out a soft snort. "Funny... I can't even remember what it was now. But I ran to the church, only I couldn't get in. It was boarded up. I was sitting on the steps, crying, when George came by. He'd been out hunting. I remember he had his rifle and three rabbits with him. I guess he was on his way home. He didn't say anything to me, just went on his way, but a little while later, Miss Mayme showed up. She had sweet tea and cornbread." He wiped his eyes again. "I asked her why the church was boarded up, and she said I shouldn't worry about it, and if things got hard at home, I could just go on to her house." He sighed. "That same week, my father took me to a livestock auction, and he bought a bull. He put a barbed-wire fence around the church and put the bull in it. I never went back to that building. At the end of my junior year of high school, my father married Charlene. Nine months later, John came along. From the time Doris disappeared to the day I left for college, I spent most of the time I wasn't in school or asleep sitting in Miss Mayme's kitchen. George had joined the army, and I think she liked having the company. At least, I hope she did, because she probably saved my life."

"Did you ever ask her about the church again?" Ruby asked.

"Once," Garland said, "right before I left for college. I told Miss Mayme I was thinking about going into the church again. The bull had died by that time, and it ate at me that Doris might be in there. Miss Mayme told me not to. She said there wasn't any point, because the church was part of my past, and I needed to concern myself with the future, so I didn't do it. My father died a couple months later and left everything to Charlene, denying me the only thing ever guaranteed to an Emory Farr."

Annie had been on the fence about whether or not those bones belonged to his sister, but in light of the new information, she thought Garland was right. Those were very likely Doris's bones.

"I can't believe no one's ever said anything to us, even after all this time," Ruby said.

Garland squeezed her hand. "It was scandalous back then that she ran off with some boy. I'm sure our cousins were instructed never to mention it. By the time your generation came along, she'd faded into obscurity."

"But she never came back," Preston said. "Surely, his brothers and sisters said something to him about that."

"If they ever said anything to him, I didn't know about it." Garland shook his head. "But remember, Emory was the oldest and hostile. I doubt any of his siblings confronted him about her whereabouts. No one ever confronted him about anything."

Ruby had her eyes closed and was rubbing her forehead. "I don't understand. How did she die, then? Are you saying you think he killed her?"

Garland let out a shaky sigh. "I wasn't there, but I've always felt like that must've been what happened."

"But Miss Mayme told you not to go into the church," Preston said. "Why would she cover for your father?"

"I don't know. I mean, aside from the obvious."

"What obvious?" Preston asked, his brow wrinkled with confusion.

"Oh, Preston, come on," Ruby said, clearly exasperated. "I've told you a million times we're related to the Nicholses." She rolled her eyes.

"Maybe, from way back, but they're hardly going to cover up a murder for that," Preston argued.

Ruby scoffed. "Way back? Two old ladies' lifetimes ago. That's it. That's hardly ancient history."

Garland nodded. "Miss Mayme was acutely aware that we were family. Her grandmother, Bessie, was sent by our great-great-grandmother Ida's parents, the Cookes, to help out because Ida was pregnant but having a difficult time. We still have Ida's diary, and she noted when Bessie arrived how much Bessie looked like her and speculated that they might be half sisters. She talked a lot about that in the diary. Then Ida gave birth to our great-grandfather Emory but died in the process. Bessie stayed to help raise the baby and never returned home. She had a son, Frank, three years later, and she and her son were freed in the will when Emory died. Those two were the only slaves he ever freed, and for the first time in the history of the property, a piece of land was carved off for them in the will. So there's really no doubt about the connection. Besides, Aunt Mildred and Miss Mayme looked so much alike that they could have been sisters. It's not like Miss Mayme and Daddy were close, but they never had anything bad to say about each other either, and they were known to help each other out on more than one occasion."

Preston sat back in his chair. "Helping each other out is one thing, but covering up a murder is something else. If Dennis or Gillian killed one of their kids, I wouldn't cover for them, and we *are* close." He grimaced, clearly appalled at the idea.

Garland shook his head. "I don't know."

"Maybe it was because she was pregnant," Annie said.

Preston and Ruby looked at her. Garland stared at the floor.

Annie explained about the fetal bones.

"Oh my god," Ruby whispered and covered her mouth with her hand.

Garland shook his head, tears starting to fall again. "If my father found out, he would have been furious."

Preston looked grimly at Annie. "So, you think he killed her because he found out she was pregnant."

"Maybe," Annie said. "People have killed for less, and if George was the father, that would explain the pact between your grandfather and Miss Mayme. But the truth is, we might never know for sure. Soft-tissue trauma doesn't show up on bones, but neither does something like a miscarriage."

Ruby frowned. "He would hardly have covered up her death from a miscarriage."

"I don't know about that. It was a different time."

Garland nodded. "He wouldn't have wanted anyone to know she was pregnant out of wedlock. The thing is, I never knew her to have a boyfriend."

"Girls know how to hide that sort of thing," Ruby said. "I never brought a boyfriend home until I met Ari. How about DNA? That can tell us who the father is."

"It depends on how degraded the fetal bones are, but I wouldn't count on it. Fetal bones are notoriously hard to get DNA from."

"When will we know for sure?" Preston asked.

"It depends on the lab, but Gunnar thought a few weeks to a couple of months," Annie said.

Garland sat with the occasional tear still slipping down his cheek. Ruby had her face in her hands. Preston sat leaning forward, staring down at his hands. Annie sat quietly and felt bad for everyone involved. She wondered if Garland still wanted her to take him home, and if so, when he might want to do that, but she didn't want to ask. Annie was still trying to decide what to do when Ruby stood.

"I'm going home. I need to... I don't know... sit with this, I guess." She shook her head. "Do you want a ride?" she asked her uncle.

Garland nodded and got up slowly. Preston got to his feet, and so did Annie.

Ruby looked at them. "I don't know what to think."

"Me either," Preston said, shoving his hands into his pockets.

"Understandable," Annie said.

Preston glanced at her then looked away.

"I'll call you later," Ruby said. "We're going to go."

Annie and Preston walked Ruby and Garland to the door and watched as they got in Ruby's Mercedes and drove away. Preston quietly closed the door and went back into the living room. He stood in the center of the room, just staring at the wall.

"Preston," Annie said quietly.

He shook his head. "What the fuck? I had an aunt I never knew about, and my grandfather murdered her. What the actual fuck, Annie?"

"I'm sorry."

"When you... I mean... Did you suspect this?"

"No! Of course not. Who could have predicted this?"

"But you were so curious. You insisted on talking to my uncle. If you didn't suspect, then why—"

"Because I'm an investigator. I used to be a cop. It's what I do."

He shook his head again. "Well, you have really screwed me here, Annie."

"How is this my fault? For that matter, how exactly are you screwed?"

"Ruby was right. I should have shut this down. I should never have let you talk to Uncle Emory."

"He prefers Garland, and asking me not to get involved wouldn't have shut anything down. It would only have delayed it. As soon as Gunnar got the lab results back, he would have done everything I did, and the same thing would've happened."

"You don't know that," Preston said, scowling.

"Yes, I do. I'm sorry it turned out like this, but you seem to have lost sight of the fact that your aunt was murdered and, yes, probably by your grandfather, but he walked free for the rest of his life, while his daughter lay decaying in that church. Are you saying you're okay with that?"

Preston rubbed a hand down his face. "Of course not."

"Good, because that secret has clearly weighed heavily on your uncle all this time, and now that the truth is out, maybe he can get some closure. I don't know about you, but I believe in the truth. I think secrets are destructive. They destroy lives. I know this was shocking to hear. And I know you're worried about how news of this might impact the farm, but a small measure of justice was done today, and I don't regret that. I'm never going to regret that."

He didn't say anything. He just stood with his head down.

She waited for a minute then blew out a slow breath. "Should I go?"

"Yeah," he said tightly.

"Fine."

Annie left with a heavy heart. She considered calling Celia on the drive home but decided she didn't have the energy to get into the whole story again. Instead, she took Chester for a long walk.

Preston's family handled a crisis very differently from hers. If her family had found out that they had a possibly murderous relative, they would still be talking about it. Her father would mix drinks, and they would hash the whole thing out over cocktails then continue over dinner. Her family felt that whatever was happening to one member was perfectly acceptable conversation for everyone else. She'd found that especially irritating when it came to the complexities of her relationship with Ford, but seeing Preston's family close down had her reconsidering. Her father and aunts meddled because they cared. Preston's family walled themselves off under stress, and that seemed sad to her. If it had been Ford instead of Preston, he would have wanted her to stay. He would have sought the comfort of at least a hug and probably more, but Preston clearly blamed her and pulled away, which seemed like a relationship-ending move. She couldn't help wondering, given the family history, whether that was such a bad thing.

Chapter 22
Monday Night

Exhausted both mentally and physically, Annie took a shower and got into bed. She picked up *The Hemingses of Monticello: An American Family* but immediately put it back down. That story seemed a little too close to the events of the day to read before bed. She considered her options then got up, put on a robe, and went to get *The Infernal City* from where she'd left it on the coffee table. She was headed back to bed when a knock came at the door. Chester barked and came tearing into the living room. Tightening the sash of her robe around her, she looked out of the peephole in her front door to see Preston standing there, looking forlorn. She shushed Chester and opened the door.

"I'm an asshole," Preston said without preamble.

She let out a soft snort and stepped back from the door. "Come in." She hadn't expected him to show up and was a little surprised at how happy it made her that he had.

"The most important thing is that we found my aunt and brought some closure to Uncle Em—Garland," he continued while Chester sniffed his shoes. "The farm will be fine. If people stop coming, it won't be because of a murder seventy years ago. You were right. I'm an asshole."

"Just to be clear, I never called you an asshole. I get that you're worried about the farm. But I think you're right—no one is going to stop coming because of something that happened so long ago."

"I'm sorry." He cocked his head at her. "And now I've gotten you out of bed."

"I wasn't sleeping."

"I should go and let you get some rest."

"Or you could stay."

"I don't think I can talk about this anymore today, Annie."

"That's not what I had in mind."

He smiled at her. "Can I shower first?"

"Be my guest."

ANNIE HAD HER HEAD on Preston's chest and was enjoying post-coital bliss when he turned to face her. Despite what he'd said earlier, he clearly did want to talk. "I'm sorry I didn't handle everything that happened today very well."

Annie patted his chest. "That's okay. Days like today don't come with instructions."

"Ruby called after she got home. She told Ari what happened, and he had some really good questions, and now I don't know what to do. Part of me wants to tell the county archeologist to look and see what's there, and part of me thinks that's just asking for more trouble. I mean, I can't help wondering what else might be over there."

"I'm not following," she said.

"Family lore has it that the Emorys were all bad men. Ari suggested that there might be more people in that cemetery than just the people that are supposed to be buried there."

"Ah," Annie said, understanding. "You figure if he killed his own daughter, he might have killed someone else."

"Maybe," Preston said. "Maybe they were all killers. My own brother paid someone to attack me. All I need is for the media to get ahold of some nightmare story of the 'killer farmer,' and I can kiss the land goodbye."

Annie bit back the desire to tell him he could still press charges against his brother and said instead, "You realize that is the absolute worst-case scenario, right?"

"I'm a farmer. We live in worst-case scenarios."

Given what the last few days had been like, she could certainly understand that. "Then let's go through it reasonably. First, we don't know that your grandfather killed his daughter." He started to protest, but she held up her palm to stop him. "I know it looks that way, but looks can be deceiving. We do know she died somehow, and based on the staining on the pew and the floor below it, it looks like she died there instead of being moved into the church from somewhere else."

"Okay," he said glumly. "Then they boarded up the church and never mentioned it again."

"Yes," Annie said. "But who boarded up the church?"

Preston shook his head. "I don't know."

"It's tempting to think the Nicholses had to be involved somehow. The church was so close to their property, and they knew the children took refuge there."

"Yeah, I've thought of that too. But it was our land, and honestly, I'm not sure how likely it would've been back then for a black family to risk going against our family by turning Emory in for killing his daughter. They might've just turned a blind eye for self-preservation."

"True," Annie agreed. "But it wouldn't have just been going against your family, would it? It would have been going against their own family, which seems even less likely. Then, of course, there's the matter of who the father was. Maybe it was Mr. Nichols, or maybe it really was some passing soldier. We don't know and likely never will."

"If it was a passing soldier, are you saying he killed her and boarded her up in the church?"

Annie shook her head. "No. That doesn't make sense. A passing soldier might've gotten her pregnant, but either your grandfather or Mr. Nichols or his mother had to know where she was. Otherwise, she would've been found ages ago, and Mayme Nichols wouldn't have told your uncle Garland not to open up the church."

"Exactly. I think it's pretty clear Miss Mayme knew Doris was in there."

"Yes, which is what makes me think George Nichols must be the father. Otherwise, why would Miss Mayme consent to cover up a murder?"

"But..." Preston rubbed his head. "George knew he and Doris were cousins, and she probably did too."

"Second cousins. So not that close. Besides, forbidden love and all that."

"I don't know. That would have been so risky back then."

"Right, but teens aren't always as risk averse as they should be," Annie pointed out.

Preston blew out a long breath. "What a mess."

"I know." Annie shook her head sadly. "I think this might be as far as it goes, though. I don't see how we'll ever get to the truth of the matter, since all involved are dead or, in Mr. Nichols's case, in a coma."

Preston sighed. "So, you think this is it, then?"

"I do. Once the identity is verified, they'll release the bones to the family, and you can bury her."

He nodded. "Uncle Emory told Ruby he wanted Doris to be buried in the family cemetery, and of course, she should be buried there."

"Seems fitting."

He let out a big sigh. "Ruby thinks I should tell the county archeologist she's welcome to look at the site and excavate or do whatever she wants. She thinks it will exorcise some family demons."

Annie smiled. "And what do you think?"

"I think demons are horseshit."

She laughed.

"On the other hand, she might be right, and you made a good point the other day about the contributions of the slaves to building this county and that we need more recognition of that, so at the moment, I'm leaning toward letting the archeologist go over there."

Cupping his cheek, she kissed him softly on the lips. "Good."

Chapter 23
Monday, May 13

A few days later, just before noon, Annie parked her Prius in front of Preston's garage. With the sun shining and a slight breeze blowing, it was a perfect spring day. Preston was already on the porch, drinking a glass of iced tea. Another glass sat next to him. As she approached, she could see his jeans were dusty, but it looked like he'd put on a clean shirt for their lunch date. She'd brought sandwiches from Puccio's and stepped up on the porch and handed him one. "Soho for you, Manhattan for me."

"Thank you," he said, opening the sandwich. "You're a lifesaver. If I had to eat one more peanut-butter-and-jelly sandwich this week, I was seriously going to spiral into a deep depression."

"Well, I wouldn't want that," Annie said, smiling.

"Me either," he said around a mouthful of sub. "I'm too busy."

Annie opened a bag of chips and set it between them before breaking into her own sandwich. They sat eating in companionable silence for a few minutes, appreciating the warmth and quiet of the day.

When Preston was done with his sub, he sat back in his chair. "What have you got going on today?"

"Not much, but I've got a security job tomorrow."

"Hmm, I'm not sure how I feel about you doing security jobs. What if some man tries to pick you up?" he teased.

"Don't be ridiculous. That would never happen. I'm much too professional."

"Uh-huh," he said.

She tossed a napkin at him, and they both laughed.

A red sedan came down the long driveway.

"Oh, come on," Preston said, letting out an exasperated sigh. "Why is there always someone who doesn't read the sign that says we're closed on Mondays?"

"No one reads signs," Annie said.

"Great." Preston stood.

The car pulled in next to Annie's, and Opal Nichols got out. When Annie saw her, she stood too.

Opal had a large manila envelope in her hand and walked toward them with grim determination.

"Hey, Opal," Preston said. "What brings you out on this fine spring day?"

"Daddy died day before yesterday," Opal said somberly.

"Oh. I'm so sorry."

"Me too," Annie said.

"Thank you. The funeral is tomorrow. The viewing is tonight."

"I'll be there," Preston said.

Annie nodded.

"Thank you," Opal said again. "But that's not why I came by. I was looking through Daddy's papers, trying to get things organized before my sister gets here this afternoon, and I found receipts for a safe-deposit box I didn't know about, which is odd, seeing as how I've been managing my father's affairs for fifteen years."

"Okay," Preston said uncertainly.

"So I called the bank, and they said my name was listed as someone who could open it in the event of his death. I just need to bring the death certificate and you."

"Me?" Preston asked.

"Well, not you specifically—it just says a member of the Farr family."

"Why?"

"I thought you'd know."

Preston shook his head. "I have no idea. It's not like your father and I were close."

"Preston," Annie said softly.

He turned to look at her, then the light dawned. "No."

"No what?" Opal asked.

"I think you'd better sit down."

Annie cleared the lunch debris, and Opal took a seat. Preston told her about the bones and what his uncle had told him, leaving out any speculation that George might be the father of the baby. He also didn't say his grandfather killed his daughter and left it to Opal to draw her own conclusions.

When he was done, Opal sat back in her chair. "What a mess."

Annie couldn't agree more but kept it to herself.

Opal shook her head. "Do you have time to go over to the bank? I'd like to get this over with as soon as possible. Besides, I'd like a little time to figure out what I'm supposed to say to Pearl when she gets here."

Preston wiped a hand down his face. "Yeah, let me just call Alejandro and let him know." He pulled out his phone and stepped off the porch to make the call.

Opal stood and looked over the orchard. "Pretty out here today."

"Yes," Annie agreed.

Preston came back. "You ready?" he asked Opal.

"Yeah." She stepped off the porch.

"I'll clean up here and head home," Annie said.

"Thanks," Preston replied. "I'll call you later."

ANNIE WENT HOME AND took stock of the equipment she'd ordered for a pawnshop in Sterling. After making sure she had everything she needed and that it was all working, she took Chester for a walk and tried not to think about what Opal and Preston were going to find in the safe-deposit box, but her curiosity was killing her. Despite her best efforts, her mind kept listing possibilities: photographs, diaries, or love letters. Unfortunately, she and Chester finished their walk, and she'd still had no word. Since she couldn't do anything to speed up the process, she decided to go over her accounts. She'd just gotten the rent payment from the people who rented out her grandparents' house, and she needed to move some money around and check her accounting software.

The sun was starting to set, and she was thinking about making dinner when a knock came at the door. She looked through the peephole to see Preston standing there. She let him in.

"I'm sorry I didn't call first. I just..." He shook his head. "You're not even going to believe... Jesus, what a day."

"Come sit down. Can I get you a drink? You look like you could use one."

"Do you have any scotch?" he asked, taking a seat on the sofa.

"Yep. Rocks?"

"No."

Annie took a bottle of Cutty Sark from under the kitchen counter and poured two fingers into a highball glass. Chester had joined Preston on the sofa, and Preston was rubbing the little dog's head.

"Here you go."

Preston took a long drink, and Annie sat down, waiting as patiently as she could for him to start talking. It seemed to take forever for him to set down the glass.

He leaned back and closed his eyes. "I don't even know what to think."

"What was in the box?" Annie asked, unable to be patient anymore.

"A letter and a big envelope. The letter said to only open the envelope if anyone went into the old slave church and questioned what they found there, although it didn't say what that would be. The letter also suggested that the best thing to do if both Mayme and Emory were dead would be to burn down the church."

"Which Emory?"

Preston snorted and shook his head. "She didn't specify."

"She?"

"Mayme wrote the letter, and the big envelope was addressed to her and postage stamped August 24, 1945. There was no return address."

"Who sent it?" Annie asked.

"It turns out she did," Preston said and squeezed the bridge of his nose. "Do you have any aspirin? I've got a killer headache."

"Sure."

She went to get a bottle from the bathroom medicine cabinet. When she returned, Preston took two pills and swallowed them with a mouthful of scotch. Annie sat back down.

Preston continued his story. "Opal and I debated the merits of opening the envelope or taking it to the police as it was, but we decided we wanted to see what it said before we did that."

"I can understand that. What did it say?"

Clearly exhausted, he blew out a breath. "It was Mayme's version of the events of August 18, 1945." He shook his head. "Basically, she says that George was coming home from seeing his girlfriend and heard screams coming from the church, and when he went to investigate, he found Doris giving birth and bleeding bad."

"Oh, shit."

"He ran to get his mama, but by the time they got back, Doris and the baby were already dead. Apparently, she sent George home and went across the creek to tell Emory. Oh god..." Preston rubbed his head. "When she got there, Emory had been drinking but wasn't drunk. He was obviously upset about Doris and followed Mayme back to the church. He didn't know she was pregnant. He was grief-stricken, and I guess he accused George of being the father."

"Well, we knew that was a possibility," Annie said.

"Mayme disagrees. First off, she pointed out that George had a girlfriend already."

"That tracks with what Miss Mabel told me. George dated her sister in high school."

"But then Mayme also said that George was aware that he and Doris were cousins and wouldn't have messed with her like that."

"That also tracks with what we know."

"Right, but then she said that six months before, Doris had come to the church alone and in a bad way." He closed his eyes and shook his head.

Annie took his hand. "It's okay."

Preston looked at her. "It's really not. Doris told her that her brother had measles and had been sent to stay with his cousins, which we know was exactly what happened. Miss Mayme didn't come right out and say Emory raped Doris, but that's clearly what she thinks happened."

Annie grimaced. "That's horrible."

"Yeah."

"I don't understand, though. Why was she boarded up in the church?"

"Apparently, that was Miss Mayme's idea. She basically offered to help Emory to turn the church into a kind of mausoleum for Doris and to support the story that she ran off if Emory promised to leave George out of it."

"Why would she do that?"

"Because Emory's best friend was the county sheriff. Leesburg didn't have a police department back then. Mayme said she knew they could railroad George right into jail—or worse, lynch him—if she didn't think of something quick, so they boarded up the church, burned Doris's things, and kept the secret in the family."

"Wow," Annie said. "That's... Wow."

"I know. It's so much worse than I imagined."

"Yeah, that's not where I thought this was going. Did she say anything else?"

"She said when they were done that night, they said a prayer, and she told Emory he had to stop drinking because whiskey made him the devil."

"Too right."

"Apparently, it worked. Uncle Em—Garland said his father did stop drinking. Of course, it sounds like he was still kind of the devil, so I'm not sure how much good it did."

Annie grimaced but didn't say anything.

"I know it's crazy, because she got so many things we already knew right, but..."

"But what?"

"I don't know. I've been thinking about this all day. I just wish she'd actually said whether Emory raped Doris. I mean, she's vague about it, and it just leaves me with..."

"Doubt?"

"Yeah. Not that something happened—I don't doubt that her father might've beaten her. But to rape her... It's just too much."

Annie sighed and squeezed his hand. "Maybe she didn't say because she wasn't sure. We only have Mayme's account, and she makes it clear that her primary concern was George's safety, which, given the climate back then, was more than reasonable. So while there's no reason to doubt it, there's also no reason to take it completely at face value either. We don't know whether Mayme was assuming Emory raped Doris, or Doris told her he did. Then there's George."

"You think George raped her?"

"No, that's not what I'm saying. But they were two young people living quite close to each other. She was isolated and without friends, according to your uncle. Who knows how close she and George were?"

"Mayme said George knew they were cousins and that he had a steady girlfriend."

"Yes, and Miss Mabel confirmed that, but she also said George up and joined the army suddenly and broke her sister's heart. Maybe he did have a relationship with Doris but knew it couldn't go anywhere, so he also had a girlfriend. Or maybe it wasn't really a relationship so much as one ill-advised moment between friends. Either way, it's unlikely he would have shared that with his mother. There's also the possibility she had a boyfriend no one knew about. Garland was pretty young. It's not like she would have confided in him, so who knows? Just because she didn't drive to meet anyone doesn't mean someone couldn't have driven to the edge of property and met her in the orchard at night or somewhere else. It's a big farm with a lot of places to hide. My point is that unless they can get DNA from the fetal bones, we won't ever really know."

"Do you really believe any of that, or are you just trying to make me feel better?" Preston asked, leaning over and resting his head on her shoulder.

Annie put her arms around him. "As Gunnar always says, it's not about what you believe. It's about what you can prove, and we can't prove much without DNA."

Preston sat up and looked at her. "But what do you believe? Seriously."

Annie gave him a sympathetic smile. She hesitated to answer. On the other hand, lying seemed like a bad plan, if they were going to move forward with their relationship. "I think if the people who knew him, like his wife and son, said he was a monster, then he was probably a monster."

Preston sighed. "Yeah, that's what I think too." He eyed her. "So, you were just saying all that other stuff to try to make me feel better."

She hugged him again, and he put his head back on her shoulder.

"As much as I want to stay right here," he said, his voice muffled against her neck, "I need to go get changed for the viewing."

"Do you want me to go with you?"

"Ruby and Uncle Garland are meeting me at the funeral home. It's about time we start integrating family events, don't you think?"

Annie nodded. "I think so."

He kissed her and stood up. "I'll call you later."

"Sounds good."

Epilogue

Annie loaded the dishwasher with dinner dishes while Preston dozed on the sofa on Sunday night. Theoretically, she'd come over to have dinner and watch a movie, but Preston had fallen asleep twenty minutes into the film, and she'd seen it before.

A knock came at the door. Chester, who was dozing next to Preston, barked, and Annie went to open it while Preston stirred awake.

Gunnar stood at the door, looking sweaty and somewhat the worse for wear. *Vikings do not belong in Virginia summers,* Annie thought.

He frowned momentarily when he saw her but quickly recovered. "Hi."

"Hey. Come in."

"Thanks," Gunnar said as he followed her into the living room.

Preston was getting to his feet. He ran a hand down his face to wake up.

"I got the results back from the lab," Gunnar said. "They confirmed it was your aunt."

"No surprises there, then," Preston said.

"No."

"They already released the bones," Annie told Gunnar. "The funeral is tomorrow evening after the farm closes."

"Were they able to get anything from the baby bones?" Preston asked grimly.

"The lab said the fetal bones were too degraded to extract DNA, so there's no way to determine paternity."

"That's okay," Preston said. "It's not like it matters at this point."

Gunnar cleared his throat. "Right. That's all, really. I just wanted to tell you in person, so I stopped on my way home."

"Thanks." Preston shook Gunnar's hand. "I appreciate it."

"I'll walk you out," Annie said and followed the big man to his car. "Thanks for coming out and telling us."

"It's more respectful than a phone call when a death is involved," Gunnar said. He looked over her head at the house. "Are you living here now?"

"No. We kind of trade off."

"Ah. So, I guess you're pretty happy, then."

"So far, so good," Annie said.

He nodded. "Well, good night, then."

"Good night," Annie said and watched his car head down the long driveway back to the road.

THE DAY OF DORIS'S funeral, Annie arrived at the farm in the late afternoon and parked in front of the garage next to Ruby's Mercedes. The day was overcast, turning the blistering summer heat to merely oppressive. The drive to the farm wasn't long enough for the air conditioner in the car to cool it off, so the back of the black linen-blend dress Annie was wearing was already damp. Ruby and Ari were talking to Preston on the porch, where both ceiling fans were running full speed. Like Annie, they were all wearing black.

As Annie approached, Ruby said, "He swears the guy was going to torch one of the outbuildings and that he didn't know anything about the church, like that makes it better. I am so done with him. I don't know how Rita can stand it. I just wish she and the kids would come down here."

Ari rested his hand on her shoulder to soothe her. "Maybe they will."

"Well, at least he's not coming. I'm not ready to see him yet," Preston said as he finally caught sight of Annie. "Hey." He came down the steps to kiss her cheek.

"Sorry I didn't get here sooner. I was on a client call. Is everyone else here?"

"No. Uncle Garland is inside. We're waiting on the pastor and a few more people, then we'll walk up to the graveyard."

As he said that, a white Ford Expedition drove down the driveway. Opal and a woman who had to be her sister got out. Ruby went inside to get her uncle while Preston and Ari went to greet the new arrivals. Annie followed.

"Thank you so much for coming," Preston said as he shook hands with both women.

"It only seemed right," Opal said.

Preston introduced Annie to Pearl, Opal's sister.

"It'll be good to finally put all this to rest," Pearl said.

"I think so too," Preston replied.

They all stood for a moment in awkward silence. Annie knew how uncomfortable Preston was with the events surrounding the death of his aunt. She couldn't imagine it was any easier for Pearl and Opal.

A silver Buick Regal came down the driveway.

"Oh, good. That's the pastor," Preston said.

Ruby and Garland came out of the house, and the small gathering walked through the orchard and up the slope to the family cemetery. The bones had been cremated and put in a small pewter urn that Garland brought out of the house and carried with him to the gravesite. They'd debated about what to do with her remains, but ultimately, Garland thought she deserved a headstone among the rest of the family. He'd ordered one like Preston's grandmother's stone, in laser-cut black granite, which stood in stark relief next to the worn, softer stones of bygone eras.

As the pastor spoke generically about the tragedy of a young death and offered a prayer, Annie read the headstones that were still legible, noticing that the site for Doris's grave was on the opposite side of the cemetery from her father's. He lay under a simple gray granite stone that he shared with his first wife, Lilly, who died in 1939, aged just thirty-three. Next to them was his second wife's much fancier stone. Annie wondered who'd made the decision to spring for that. She returned her attention to the funeral when Garland stepped forward.

"My sister, Doris, was the most loving person in my life. She stepped in as my mother when our mother died, and I will be forever grateful for her efforts. Doris was my protector, my teacher, and my champion. Not a day goes by that I haven't missed her. I'm grateful today for you all coming out so that we can finally lay her to rest with her name and with the rest of the family."

Preston took the urn from Garland and knelt to place it gently in the small shallow grave in front of the headstone. A spade was leaning against the back of the stone, and each member of the family, including Opal and Pearl, took a turn adding a shovelful of earth over the urn as Garland stood with tears streaming down his face. Ruby put her arm around him while the pastor said the final funeral prayer. Then the group walked back to the house, where Alejandro's wife had set out food for the family.

No one stayed long. Garland thanked everyone for coming, but Annie could tell he was relieved when Ruby and Ari took him home. She stood on the porch with Preston and watched them drive off.

He finished his glass of iced tea then sighed. "I need to get changed. I've got to finish filling in the grave and put the sod plug back on it."

"You need some help?"

He looked at the way she was dressed and arched an eyebrow.

"I brought a change of clothes."

"In that case, yes. Well, I don't really need help, but I would appreciate the company."

She smiled at him. "I'll go get my bag."

PRESTON DIDN'T SAY anything as they walked back to the cemetery, but he held her hand. In his other hand, he had a water bucket for the grass. She watched as he finished filling in the hole with the spade then covered it with sod and watered it.

He leaned on the spade as if it were a cane and looked around. "I guess that's that."

"You okay?" Annie asked.

"Yeah. This has just been a lot, you know?"

"I do." She looked around at the graves. "You have a really big family."

He nodded. "One of these days, I'd like to add to it."

Annie smiled awkwardly. She was in no way ready to have the kind of conversation about the future that Preston's comment could lead to. She really liked him, but the last few months had been pretty intense, so she wasn't ready to make big plans based on what they'd gone through thus far as a couple. To deflect the comment, she said, "Doesn't it creep you out that one day, you'll be in here?"

He shrugged. "Not really. Everybody ends up somewhere."

"That's true."

He took her hand again. As they walked through the orchard, the air heavy with the sweet smell of fruiting trees, Annie couldn't help thinking about where she had ended up and how different it was from what she'd expected. For so many years, she'd thought that she and Ford would eventually end up together, but having Preston's warm, calloused hand in hers had her rethinking that vision of the future, which was both heartening and sad. She sighed.

"You okay?" Preston asked.

"Yeah. Like you said, this has all just been a lot."

He nudged her with his shoulder. "Should be smooth sailing now, though."

"Oh yeah. Everything else in life, piece of cake."

They both laughed as they walked back to the house.

~finis~

Acknowledgements

I would like to thank the following people:

Michele DeFrance, who for years read almost every word I wrote minutes after I'd written it. Her unwavering enthusiasm for my writing is so heartening.

Victoria Robinson, master genealogist, who was so helpful and so patient with all my questions.

Marie Brownhill, who answered all my weird legal questions.

Heidi Siebentritt, Loudoun County archeologist, who answered so many questions for me.

Kristin Brown, who is a fountain of information about Loudoun County and a conduit to so many people in Loudoun that I needed to talk to.

Brenda Bauer, for all those long walks, during which I worked out the plot of this book then reworked it virtually every time we went out.

Master Police Officer Doug Shaw of Leesburg Police Department. Everything I got right was because of him, and anything I might have gotten wrong was entirely my fault. His patience with my questions deserves an award.

My father-in-law, Lieutenant Colonel (Ret.) Desmond Flanigan, who answered all my questions about the early days of the GI Bill.

My mother, Sarah Crumpton, who not only is unfailingly supportive but also answered my questions about fashions and everyday life in the 1950s.

Robin Scalone, my elementary school writing partner, who started me on this journey.

Jennifer Stevens, who edits anything I write that is more complicated than a grocery list.

Sara Gardiner, who makes content edits seem like an ego boost.

Susie Driver, whose line edits are clear and concise. She's a good sport, even when we disagree.

Erica Lucke Dean, who is always willing to answer even ridiculous questions.

Lynn McNamee and Red Adept Publishing, who have been so supportive of this series.

I'm blessed with an enormous family and many friends. Thanks to all of you.